Before I Wake

Also by Mary Ellen Johnson

Travels Across Time

Before I Wake

Eternal Beloved

The Knights of England

The Lion and the Leopard

A Knight There Was

Within A Forest Dark

A Child Upon the Throne

Lords Among the Ruins

Flames of Rebellion

Before I Wake

TRAVELS ACROSS TIME

BOOK ONE

MARY ELLEN JOHNSON

This is a work of fiction. Names, characters, places, and incidents either are the product of the author's imagination or are used fictitiously, and any resemblance to actual persons, living or dead, business establishments, events or locales is entirely coincidental.

Book and cover design by eBook Prep
www.ebookprep.com

September 2022
ISBN: 978-1-64457-329-7

ePublishing Works!
644 Shrewsbury Commons Ave
Ste 249
Shrewsbury PA 17361
United States of America

www.epublishingworks.com
Phone: 866-846-5123

Author's Note

I consider *Before I Wake* a memoir of the life I *should* have lived—if I were far more adventuresome and interesting and had actually been transported back to the thirteenth century.

Alas, none of that is true. I have written all the books mentioned, though under the name Mary Ellen Johnson or in the case of *The Landlord's Black-Eyed Daughter*, as Mary Ellen Dennis. (Thanks to a good friend and co-author, Deni Dietz, who did all the heavy lifting on publication.)

The core of the story—my regression back to thirteenth century England and Ranulf Navarre—is essentially true and its essence *has* haunted me since I was a young wife and mother. Beyond that, as my character declares, I have always been more of an observer than a participant in life.

Regarding Tintagel, during the time of *Before I Wake* it had been deeded to Richard of Cornwall and not Ranulf Navarre. The other facts about Tintagel are as true as I can make them from my research. As is the unfolding of Simon de Montfort's rebellion and the Battle of Evesham.

I hope you enjoy my fake memoir!

Mary Ellen Johnson

Part One

1969-1972

I have been here before,
But when or how I cannot tell:
I know the grass beyond the door,
The sweet keen smell,
The sighing sound, the lights around the shore.
You have been mine before,—
How long ago I may not know:
But just when at that swallow's soar
Your neck turn'd so,
Some veil did fall,—I knew it all of yore...
"Sudden Light"

— DANTE GABRIEL ROSSETTI

One

I married Husband Number One, Dwight Latimer, the year after my high school graduation. Since few people officially dated in our small Colorado town, Dwight and I had kinda, sorta "hung out" for several years.

Dwight wasn't really handsome—his ears stuck out and he had a cowlick that reminded me of Alfred E. Neumann—but he was charming with an infectious laugh and engaging personality. A natural salesman, Dwight's goal after graduating college was to become a millionaire selling hearing aids.

"Think about it, Mugwump," he said, using a pet name which had absolutely nothing in common with my actual name, Magdalena Moore, save for the first letter. "The only people interested in hearing aids are those who need them. Built-in client base."

Hearing aid salesman wasn't quite my idea of a proper profession. I came from a blue-collar background; my dad was a plumber, and I was thinking more along the lines of some sort of union apprenticeship.

But, okay, I'm game.

In the late sixties, young men enrolled in college fresh out of high school to evade the draft. Unfortunately, Dwight, who was three years older, had flunked out after one semester and, because of his low draft number, chose to join the Marine Corps. Which meant much of our semi-engagement was long-distance and low-key with phone calls from Camp LeJeune, where he was stationed, and occasional leave home. Until Vietnam escalated and Dwight, plus all the guys in his platoon, knew it was a matter of time before they received their deployment orders.

In the aftermath of the Tet Offensive, fighting had intensified. Five hundred thousand young men and counting, tossed into the maw of America's war machine. The nightly news was a phantasmagoria of thwomping helicopters swarming like angry wasps across the sky; running or crouching or bivouacked soldiers; bombs dropped from screaming Skyhawks; body counts, body bags and row after row of flag-draped coffins disgorged from the belly of cargo planes. Our generation appeared to be bleeding out before our eyes. Plucked from high school football fields and small towns that displayed the Stars and Stripes all year round, not just on the Fourth of July. From family farms in the heartlands planting and harvesting crops many would not live to see. From sprawling metropolises with stacked high-rises and postage stamp lawns and failing public housing projects. Even a few from the wealthiest zip codes when the sons were particularly patriotic or such screw-ups that Daddy's money or disapproval couldn't shield them from the attendant consequences. Vietnam was a miasma hanging over us all.

Life was precious, the clock ticking. It seemed only natural that Dwight and I get married ASAP. Too caught up in being the faithful wife, my husband's *raison d'etre* once he was shipped off, I didn't notice that my fiancé was considerably less excited about being a groom than I was about being a bride.

After a tiny wedding in our tiny Catholic church, Dwight and I drove to California where the Marine Corps Air Station of El Toro was located. On summer weekends, we fled our cramped base housing for Huntington Beach. There we rubbed baby oil on our exposed limbs and alternated between sunbathing and paddling far enough out on the water to ride our Styrofoam boards back to shore.

Huntington Beach teemed with bare-chested young men and bikini-clad women whose wealthy parents purchased their custom-painted VW bugs and vans with surfboards strapped to their roofs; who stayed stoned and attended just enough college so that they, those privileged males, could maintain their draft deferments.

I felt like an outsider—Dwight with his regulation haircut and me with my fears that were universes beyond unwelcome tan lines and whether the Beachboys, Beatles, or the San Francisco sound was "groovier."

"We're grappling with matters of life and death here!" I wanted to scream at all those clueless hard bodies.

I just knew that the moment I let down my guard, the moment Dwight and I truly relaxed, he would receive his orders. I've always held the admittedly insane belief that if I worried in advance about the possibility of death, heartbreak, betrayal, bankruptcy, or a multiplicity of other disasters, I could prevent them. Or, if not, at least blunt their pain when they actually occurred.

Ha!

The first time I saw the Pacific Ocean, I felt so inconsequential, as if I were less than a tear dropped upon its seemingly endless expanse. I liked boundaries. Where I could be cocooned by mountains and other landmarks, anchored to Mother Earth rather than cast adrift.

And yet, staring at the horizon, at the blue blanket that gradually faded into a pale smear of cloud and sky, something stirred within me. I'd not seen anything wider than the South Platte River, yet the Pacific seemed familiar. The blending of sea and sky, the immensity of the vista, even the caress of the ocean breeze evoked the oddest feeling. One I couldn't quite name, as I couldn't understand my reaction. Like when you can almost remember something, but it remains elusive, tucked away in a neglected corner of your brain.

Yet, much, much later I would look back on that day and realize this was the first of countless clues leading to the man I loved.

And hated...

Inevitably, Dwight's orders arrived. During our final beach outing, we rode our Styrofoam boards, after which my husband scooped up a couple of beach towels from our blanket.

"Hey, Mugwump," he said, wrapping a towel around me. "I'm gonna miss you."

Dwight was largely undemonstrative, so I nestled gratefully in his arms, inhaling the wetness of the skin on his neck and collar bone—a curious combination of clammy and warm. Against my lips, his skin tasted of fish and salt from the sea. I closed my eyes to better savor the moment, only to experience the oddest feeling.

I have been here before.

I thought those words, the first line of Dante Gabriel Rossetti's "Sudden Light," a poem that had so profoundly affected me I'd memorized it in its entirety.

I was aware of strong arms around me, of that scent that had triggered a nagging...something. A longing of such fierceness pierced my heart that I gasped against Dwight's skin. A whirlwind of thoughts and images came and went so swiftly I couldn't differentiate one from the other.

I opened my eyes expecting...what? Certainly not this chatter of voices, not the pretentious yachts bobbing on the horizon, not the unfamiliar arms looped possessively around my waist or the freckled, sunburned flesh.

Despite the summer heat, I shivered.

What is wrong?

Could I be pregnant? Are my hormones already so unbalanced I'm going crazy?

While we packed up our gear and readied to leave, I still felt unsteady on my feet.

What if I'm not pregnant? What if this is some kind of portent?

A Creedence Clearwater song drifted across the blankets and umbrellas and baking bodies, crying about a bad moon on the rise. "*Trouble on the way... Voices of rage and ruin... The end is coming soon...*"

Does this mean my husband will die in Vietnam?

As you, dear reader, will soon notice, I pretty much always misread signs and premonitions, as I do the events in my life, both large and small.

Dwight most definitely did not die overseas.

But our marriage did.

ON THE NIGHT before Dwight left, we lay in bed, arms entwined. Both of us cried. My husband would be gone an entire year! At nineteen, that was an eternity. I'd hoped I was pregnant so that should anything happened to Dwight, I could at least carry on the Latimer legacy. I would see Dwight's eyes in those of the son he would never hold and wept with the devastating beauty of it all. A young war widow. How tragically romantic. I imagined myself atop some high promontory, clutching my babe while the wind snapped my old-fashioned gown around my legs. Gazing out to sea, eyes on the horizon, chin jutting, determinedly facing the future without my spouse, who had somehow been transformed into a sea captain who'd gone down with his vessel somewhere around Cape Horn.

As it turned out, I wasn't pregnant.

Point of fact: the imagined scene possessed about as much truth as my marriage.

Two

Nineteen seventy ushered in many changes. I landed a job as receptionist at Willow Wand, a small Colorado Springs publishing house, where I decided to become a famous writer. My best friend and maid of honor, Sherralinda Grant, who had become enamored of all things Eastern, struck out for India, determined to follow the Beatles in their quest for Enlightenment.

"Come with," Sherralinda said, before departing. "We'll be back way before your hubby's tour is over."

"If I'm going to travel, it will be to England," I said, feeling noble and self-sacrificing. I was certain Dwight carried my photograph inside his wallet and a favorite letter near his heart in the modern-day version of a holy relic. The superstitious part of me feared that my daily correspondence, written regardless of how long my day or how little was actually happening in my mundane life, might be the only thing keeping Dwight alive. Otherwise, he could come down with terminal trench foot or step on some punji stick trap that would blow him to smithereens.

"Someday, we'll travel," I said to Sherralinda. "When Dwight is safely home and we're more settled. Hey, we've got a lifetime ahead of us."

True enough.
Just not a lifetime together.

Three

It's kind of a trope to say that when America's young men, who'd been tossing footballs one year and grenades in the jungles of Vietnam the next, returned home, they were all messed up.

Not Dwight. He came back pretty much the same. However, since I didn't really know him all that well before his departure, I was in for some surprises. Such as the fact that my natural-born salesman husband ditched the hearing aid idea and decided he would make a fortune on pet coffins constructed of the finest corrugated cardboard. When that flopped, he moved on to used cars. Then timeshares on yet-to-be-built Colorado condos.

Increasingly, I was haunted by the feeling that I was marking time, accompanied by such a restlessness as if I were always fidgeting, always pacing, always checking myself lest I break into a run though outwardly I appeared calm enough. Increasingly, I distracted myself with writing. Character sketches, plot ideas related to my research on fourteenth-century England, short stories I hid away in my desk drawer, maudlin poems about sticking pins in the pin cushion of my heart and time bending in upon itself and searching for a lost love who refused to show his face.

After moving into a two-bedroom duplex in a sleepy part of Colorado Springs, I assured myself my life was on track.

Another of my delusions, soon to be shattered by a battered cardboard box containing all the letters Dwight had received during his tour. After shoving the box in the back of our bedroom closet, he said, "Don't mess with that, Mugwump. Contents are kinda private."

It only vaguely registered that Dwight shouldn't care whether I might "mess" with correspondence I'd largely written.

I'd already become an expert at seeing only what I chose to see.

When the movie, *The Blob*, which is about a radioactive ooze that resembles jello and eats people, had been released in the 1950s, it was accompanied by a silly theme song.

According to the lyrics, the Blob could creep and leap and glide across the floor while gobbling up entire Pennsylvania towns unfortunate enough to be in its path.

That's how I felt about Dwight's box. It was a live thing, pulsating on the top shelf of our closet, lying in wait until the time I gathered enough courage to investigate its contents. Once loosed it would do its own version of creeping and leaping and gliding, ending how? In the annihilation of our marriage?

I became obsessed.

Sherralinda, who'd returned from India to open a bookstore/coffee shop/New Age hangout called Druids & Dragyns, finally forced me to deal.

"I'm sensing you're unhappy," she said, while we sipped herbal tea and shared an organic brownie. "Your aura is so dimmed. Talk to me, Maggie."

Sherralinda swore she'd developed psychic powers during her travels—she never did meet the Maharishi—but a stranger could tell I wasn't at my best.

While I'd previously avoided more than the most general expressions of discontent, today the truth gushed out of my mouth with all the force of projectile vomiting.

Afterward, Sherralinda folded her hands upon the café table and, as if pronouncing an edict, said, "That box is calling out to you. You must answer that call."

Sherralinda often spoke like that.

On a weekend when Dwight was off hawking timeshares, we retrieved the container and sorted its voluminous contents into neat piles atop our queen-size bed. My correspondence was pretty much a mountain—and like Mount Everest, I discovered, largely unexplored. Nearly half of my letters had never even been opened. (Later, when I confronted Dwight, he told me they were boring. "C'mon, Mugwump. If you can't even write an interesting letter, what makes you think you can write an entire book?)

Dwight did open all of Betsy Yarrow's correspondence.

I couldn't blame him. Nurse Betsy turned out to be quite the gifted spinner of erotica. At least when involving my husband, who'd obviously inspired her.

After we'd finished reading Nurse Betsy's explicit recountings of her and Dwight's trysts during various R&Rs, Sherralinda reached out to clasp my hand. "I'm so sorry."

"Better to know now," I managed. "Before..." Before what? A fat bank account that we would fight over in a divorce settlement? Other affairs? Physical altercations? A child?

Obviously, my life could have used a lot more planning.

Part Two

1975-82

Last night, ah, yesternight, betwixt her lips and mine
There fell thy shadow, Cynara! thy breath was shed
Upon my soul between the kisses and the wine;
And I was desolate and sick of an old passion,
Yea, I was desolate and bowed my head:
I have been faithful to thee, Cynara! in my fashion...
"Non sum qualis eram bonae sub regno Cynarae"

— ERNEST DOWSON

I met Husband Number Two, Zak Ridarelli, outside the cinder block refreshment stand at Colorado Springs' Arcadia Drive-In. Sherralinda was inside buying popcorn, Milk Duds, and Cokes, while I watched Robert Redford racing down a dark alley fleeing CIA villains in *Three Days of the Condor*. Only to have my vision blocked by a huge—and obviously very rude—man who ambled toward me.

"Move, please," I said, eyes on the forty-foot screen. "I can't see through you." Though I'd been divorced for three years, I was still pretty much off men. Especially inconsiderate boors.

"Excuse me, darlin'," the giant rumbled. If a mountain could speak it would possess that voice—rough and rumbling and impossibly deep. My gaze snapped from the cinematic action on screen to Pikes Peak come to life.

And I was done for.

Zak was a union lineman—big and broad and playful and sexy as hell. When Zak entered a room, women stopped talking, nudged each other, and immediately began producing pheromones.

I didn't stand a chance.

What I liked most about Zak, besides the sex, which was fabulous, and his looks—dark hair and eyes and biceps bigger than my head—was his easy-going personality.

Nothing ever seemed to rile Zak. "I'm a simple man," he said. "Work hard, play hard, fuck hard. That's about it."

Excellent philosophy.

Remembering the mistakes from my first marriage, however, I would take charge of my destiny. We must agree, at least, on the most important goal in my life.

"I want kids. Sooner rather than later."

Zak had a teen daughter from an earlier marriage, so I knew he was capable.

Zak shrugged. "I like kids."

All I needed to know.

At that time, Zak's employer was building power lines in Breckenridge, which was nearly two hours from our house in Woodland Park. Which meant Zak only came home on weekends.

While I was busy with my job at Willow Wand Publishing—I'd been promoted to editor—and had begun writing my first historical novel, *The Lion and the Leopard*, Zak was seldom far from my thoughts. I hated being separated from him. When he drove away on weekdays, a part of me went with him. Bereft was a word I sometimes used, if only in my thoughts. My need for Zak Ridarelli bordered on scary. I found something distasteful about being so emotionally dependent on a man.

Don't love too much. Don't need too much.

Each Friday night, Zak burst through our front door, tossed his duffel bag of tools in the corner, and cried, "Welcome me home, darlin'." After which he scooped me in his arms, carried me into our bedroom, and tossed me on the bed.

I, Magdalena Moore, was in heaven.

Five

"I was a saloon keeper in Dodge City," said Sherralinda, who was currently exploring past life regressions. "I saw the entire gunfight at the O.K. Corral from the front door of my saloon."

"Okayyy." I reached for the flowered teapot she had placed on our tiny wooden table and poured us each a cup of Druids & Dragyn's signature spiced tea. I refrained from reminding her that the gunfight at O.K. Corral had taken place in Tombstone rather than Dodge City.

Currently, we were alone in Sherralinda's cozy bakery. Tibetan monks chanted "Om" in the background, though Sherralinda played an eclectic mix of just about everything.

"Viola—she's the hypnotist—says I'm a very old soul." Sherralinda had already shared her life as a camp follower in Napoleon's army. "I died at Waterloo. Blown to bits by a cannonball. Unpleasant!" She stared into the middle distance, as if contemplating that particular demise. "Last week we regressed me way back. To a Neanderthal, I think. I was awfully hairy and had a limited vocabulary."

"Sounds like some of the men you've dated."

She laughed. "It does, doesn't it?"

A bell jangled, announcing the entrance of a young woman pushing a stroller. I was immediately captivated by the baby inside. While the mother placed her order, I cooed to the rosy-cheeked toddler, who kicked her chubby legs and smiled, revealing several pearly nubs.

"*Hush, little baby, don't say a word...*" I sing-songed, before falling silent. How many times had I imagined rocking my child to sleep while singing that particular lullaby or reciting nursery rhymes? Would our baby have Zak's dark eyes or my grey ones? His black hair or my caramel brown?

Why can't I get pregnant? We've been married three plus years. No birth control, plenty of sex, and Zak's already fathered a daughter. So, what's the problem?

Ashamed of my sudden stab of jealousy, I angled my chair away from the toddler. Such a simple thing. Sperm meets egg. Sperm fertilizes egg. Nine months later, *Voila!* Baby!

At least that's how it had worked billions of times for the human species.

I'm only twenty-eight. We have plenty of time.

After the mother and baby left, Sherralinda returned to her chair and previous train of thought.

"I've decided. You *must* do a past life regression. I'm going to book you with Viola."

The Crosby, Stills, Nash and Young song, "Déjà Vu," was playing, appropriate for our current conversation.

Do I believe in reincarnation?

Not that a person could come back as a praying mantis, but beyond that, yeah, the concept made sense.

The chorus of "Déjà Vu" declaimed that CSN&Y—all of us—have been here before.

Here before... Here before...

"All right," I said. "Make me an appointment."

I am standing in front of a huge wooden door held together with four black iron bands. Actually, two doors, like the doors to a cathedral, though these lead to a bailey, then deeper into the heart of our castle to the keep, which is my destination. I look down to see my tiny slippered feet planted upon the planks that comprise part of the drawbridge.

I look up to see, above and around the doors, whitewashed stones which, depending on the manner in which the afternoon sun strikes them, reveal the faintest tint of rose. The colors remind me of cherry blossoms, though this year's petals have long since littered the ground in the small orchard beyond our enceinte. I wonder, because I am afraid to ponder what awaits me inside the keep, whether Maman will allow me to pick cherries at harvest, or will she say I am too old?

Somewhere in the background, like the buzzing of a fly, I hear a voice, Viola's voice, guiding me.

Unnecessary. I am fully here, a slightly built girl standing on a drawbridge, gathering the courage to meet my future.

Though I am this girl, I am also observing her/me from above. Currently viewing myself from the back. I have light brown hair that falls in a silky cascade to my waist. My gown is blue.

The doors swing open, as if I am expected. I don't see anyone, not even in the bailey, which is curiously deserted, though I suspect my perception is faulty. I am so nervous I have tunnel vision.

I step into the great hall, which is filled with lords and ladies, all attired in intense colors—blues, yellows, oranges, reds, green the color of the summer grass in England's fields. Because I am in England, of course I am. Two long linen-draped tables flank me on either side. In front of me, a raised dais.

A pair of large carved chairs in the center. My parents. Even as I walk forward, observer me gasps, "They're so beautiful!" My father, brown-haired and bearded with sharp features, my mother, her perfectly oval face accentuated by an ivory wimple.

Observer me is surprised by my parents' beauty, since that is not how our ancestors are usually portrayed. Still, I am here, and this is what I see. Breathtaking parents—and a plain girl so frightened my legs tremble beneath my gown. A plain girl whose name is...

It is on the tip of my tongue, teasing my consciousness, though I can't quite pull it forward. What is my name?

The conversation in the great hall dips; I sense all eyes upon me. I, who prefer to hover unnoticed in quiet corners, am the unwelcome center of attention.

I approach the dais. I am so very small. I feel as if I am the size of a doll, though that can't be so. I just feel so hesitant and uncertain, which makes me long to bury my face against Maman's surcoat or hide in the buttery among dusty casks of wine. Today is the most important day in my life and I am too young! Years are a muddled thing, but I calculate I am around twelve. My mother's smile is kind, and I sense she is silently urging me forward, to remember my training, to behave as the lady I soon will be. My father looks solemn, a bit relieved since negotiations have been tedious. I am vaguely aware of pages behind them, carrying platters and jugs.

My heart begins a sudden racing, faster and faster until I fear it could force its way from my chest.

I know **he** *is sitting beside my father, at his right hand. We have not even met, officially. Maman confided that he has seen me, but I've not been allowed that return courtesy. All I know is that he is very old, fifteen years older, and I am afraid of him. Certainly afraid to risk a glance at him, even out the corner of my eyes.*

My father is speaking, not so much to me, I don't think, but to the assembly.

After he finishes, I gather the pitiful rags of my courage and dare a glance at my fiancé.

My first glimpse of the man who has haunted me through the centuries, the man I'd never even sensed until this moment. Like a flash of lightning, his name blazes upon my consciousness: Ranulf Navarre

My breath catches. My initial quavering glance hardens into an endless stare. I am not so young that I cannot feel attraction, if not desire. Ranulf Navarre is the most mesmerizing man I have ever seen.

Black hair nearly brushing his neckline, big even sitting down, his shoulders wider than my father's, and my father is more physically impressive than...the comparison eludes me. Our king? Our prince? I am too captivated by my fiancé, too undone by his presence, to think clearly. Ranulf Navarre, in turn, scrutinizes me through eyes so big and brown—the color of my pony's or the roe deer I've seen in the Royal Forest. But nothing soft or gentle resides in those depths—not now, when he is weighing and measuring me, considering my worth as his future bride. And certainly not later, when he torments me into madness.

This I instinctively know, even when I cannot possibly know such things.

I cannot look away. As our gazes hold, Ranulf's irises darken until they appear black. Or have I confused that with the shifting shadows in the great hall? I cannot tell; I cannot think. Ranulf Navarre's surcoat is the color of blood —or more perhaps the color of red wine when raised to the light. It perfectly sets off the darkness of his hair and eyes and complexion.

Even among the jeweled colors of those around him, my soon-to-be-husband glows more brightly than all the rest combined. I've never seen the like.

My legs shake so violently I must forcefully lock my knees in order to remain standing. The rest of the room fades; there is no one here, anywhere, save for the two of us...

Like a fly buzzing, I hear Viola. Her voice is soothing but carries a commanding edge. "Move forward. To another event that is important to you."

I think I remember my name. It's a simple one. Mary? Eve? Alice? Jane... Janey. That sounds right.

Yes.

Now I am a grown woman, though I still feel small as a youngling.

Once again, observer me notes that she/I remain a colorless creature. The

kind of person who is so forgettable that a moment after you meet me or we hold a conversation, my face, my demeanor, my very existence vanishes from your memory. Everything about me—from my hair to my gown to my slippers—is the color of dust. What a contrast to the living flame that is my husband.

But where is Ranulf? He is not at my side.

I am standing on a parapet, gazing in the direction of the rocky path where I will first glimpse the procession. I am waiting, waiting for the return of my husband. Devastated. And so angry. I love and hate Ranulf Navarre in equal measure. I feel both emotions so strongly my very soul vibrates with the battle between them. I hate him because he is so big and strong and has a way of twisting everything so no matter the infidelities, the cruelties, the barrenness, it is always my fault. And I accept that, this insipid Janey does, if only on the outside. Inside, I am such a cauldron of contradictory emotions, so maddened by the resultant chaos that I do not know how my physical body—my muscles and cells and bones and the blood coursing through my veins—has not exploded. Because the love, the ache for Ranulf Navarre, the pain surely encompasses the universe....

More buzzing, so irritating that I imagine waving my hand in front of my face to brush it away. I am so deep into this scene.

I've wandered into an endless forest, so black and dense I'll never be able to find my way out. How could I? There is no way out. Not for me.

Agitation rises like vomit. Panic. I am waiting, not for the return of my husband, but for the return of my husband's body. Ranulf is dead, dead because he dared revolt against the king, he and that Frenchman and all the men that Frenchman and his sons led to their doom. I warned him, didn't I? But what did I warn him of? What did I say? My head hurts with remembering. Or am I trying not to remember?

In the distance, I glimpse torchlights. Approaching in a slow, solemn funeral cortege. A scream escapes my throat.

I am thrashing upon the couch. Not on the parapet. On a soft upholstered couch, my head upon a feather pillow.

Once again, Viola, her voice more insistent, cuts through the memory. "Move on, to when you are leaving this life."

I relax, sink back into the comfortable surroundings. Now I am both observer and Janey. I see her/me laid out as if asleep, but I am hovering high above the ground. Not floating exactly. More like the magician's trick where his assistant appears to be levitating. My body—so insignificant—a mere husk of a human being.

"What did you learn from this life?" asks Viola.

I answer without hesitation, with a firmness I never expressed when alive.

"I will never let a man control me again. Ever."

Seven

Following my regression, I walked around in a daze, unable to concentrate on anything other than the images dredged up during that fateful session. Wisps of dreams trailed me everywhere, teeming with knights in battle armor; a shadowed face, long hair caught by the wind, creating a dark halo around his head; torch lights, held aloft by robed figures, snaking down a hill; darkness laying like a blanket across an elaborate tomb. Unable to make sense of any of the images or scenes, I passed them off as arising from my research for *The Lion and the Leopard.*

Zak was building transmission lines, this time near Vail. For the first time, I was glad he was gone. I could not bear for him to see me unravelling, like a spool of cable wire reaching its end. When I thought of my husband, my memory held an image of him—the length of his hair, the exact shade of his eyes, the curve of his nose—that did not match the man who shared my bed each weekend. My initial reaction, no longer than a heartbeat, was that Zak Ridarelli was a stranger, a mistake, while my real husband was somewhere in hiding. I tried to act normal, but everything felt off-kilter; *he* felt off-kilter and when I looked into his eyes I wanted to weep.

*Not my husband. Not **you**!*

I imagined erasing Zak's face and body and re-drawing it so it would match the man in my regression, Ranulf Navarre. Other times I wanted to beat my head against a wall in order to pulverize the image of Ranulf, the being of him from my brain. Tear him out from the roots of my mind like some sort of diseased plant.

Is this madness?

I sketched endless drawings of my long-ago husband's face and form. In high school, I'd won awards for my watercolors and charcoal sketches, but the reconstructions left me frustrated. They were never right. Ranulf Navarre remained elusive, hidden from me, and it was driving me insane.

Lovemaking with Zak, always transcendent, was suddenly unsatisfactory. I kept having flashes of my knight, my husband—his face above me, his caresses on my body. Come and gone so quickly, like the glimmering of trout in a stream. I felt like a coin being flipped in a coin toss—this way, that way. Now I'm here, now I'm there.

"Hey, darlin', something wrong?" Zak asked, wrapped in post-coital embrace.

"Of course not." I forced myself to stretch up and kiss him on the lips. But I worried he sensed that I was pulling away. Would he think I'd grown cold? Look elsewhere to "fuck hard"? Over the years, I'd received phone calls from women asking for him, but he'd always had an explanation—old girlfriends or hookups of linemen buddies or someone he'd met in a bar, perfectly innocent, who'd morphed into a stalker. I was very much aware of the way women threw themselves at Zak, but I believed his protestations of fidelity.

Because I wanted to.

Because I couldn't face the alternative.

My first husband's betrayal had hurt.

But Zak? Zak Ridarelli would wreck me.

Eight

I found out the nature of Zak's betrayal following a phone call from Zak's ex. Susan left a message on our answering machine concerning his daughter.

"Lexie will be graduating next month, and she wants you at her graduation for reasons I'll never fathom, you lying, cheating son of a bitch." said his ex. "And since you made sure Lexie is the only kid you'll ever have, the least you can do is show up for her graduation."

Click.

I stared at the answering machine as if it might spit out more information, as if it might explain the phrase "Since you made sure Lexie is the only kid you'll ever have..."

What does that mean?

It couldn't mean... What could it mean? Could Zak have had a vasectomy?

Zak was working overtime and wouldn't be home for a couple of weeks, giving me plenty of time to prove my suspicions wrong. Easy enough. For such a seemingly carefree guy, Zak kept meticulous records.

"I'd rather suck a dick than cross the IRS," he'd said when moving his file cabinet into my study. Now I searched through tax returns with attached receipts dating back two decades, various insurance policies, the usual credit card and utility bills, warranties to appliances or vehicles that had been defunct long before I entered the scene.

Medical records.

Near the back of that particular file, I found it. The papers outlining the vasectomy he'd had performed following his daughter's birth.

Numb.

Incapable of processing the magnitude of Zak's lie.

Replaying the very short pre-wedding conversation we'd had on the subject, I realized my husband hadn't exactly lied. "I like kids," Zak had said, simply failing to add, "And I'm incapable of producing said sperm in order to have more."

I closed my eyes.

Exhausted.

Strike two.

Another wrong choice.

Twenty-nine years old. Two husbands. No kids.

Zak hurt. He'd burrowed deep into my soul, all the way to the core. His betrayal gutted me. Whatever he'd awakened in me, I had no choice but to smother it to death. I couldn't stay with a man who'd lied so cavalierly about something so important. Who'd allowed me to chatter on about children, who said nothing when my period was late, and I expressed hope I might be pregnant.

Some things are beyond forgiveness.

This is what happens when you love. I remembered Janey's declaration upon her death: "I will never let a man control me again."

THE END TURNED out to be easier than I'd anticipated. The minute Zak walked through the front door, he knew something was wrong. But he pretended. We both did.

After our usual quick tumble, a shower and eats, we generally spent the rest of the evening making love. As we did this night. I allowed it because it would be the last time. I would savor it. Pull the memory out during the desolate future that yawned before me because surely, after Zak Ridarelli no other man would interest me.

Zak was more forceful than usual, more eager to assert his dominance, to remind me—as if I could forget—what an incomparable species of male he was.

Our last time, I vowed I would not hold back; I would respond to his caresses even more enthusiastically than usual. Zak matched my urgency with one of his own. Losing myself in the moment, I quit thinking. I was a leaf borne upon a stream of pleasure.

Tomorrow'll be soon enough to return to earth. For now, I'm happy to fly...

Zak was on top of me, careful as always to brace himself so that he didn't crush me with his full weight. Mouth against my ear and his breath hot against my skin, he whispered, "Beg for it, baby. Tell me how much you need me to fuck you."

I felt myself stiffen. *Baby?* He never called me that. And while he enjoyed risqué talk, he generally commanded me with actions, not words.

"You want me. Tell me how much. Tell me how you ache for my—"

"Have you been reading my romance novels?" I twisted away, denying him access to my ear. Our bodies were slick with sweat, and I was still high off his lovemaking. Digging my fingernails into the muscles on his back, I said, "Shut up and get back to work."

Zak chuckled. He kissed down the side of my neck, then once more up to nip my earlobe. What was with the ears?

"Do you like this, baby?" He shifted enough that he could enter me with one expert thrust.

I grunted. Yes, but no. My body was responding but my mind was not so sure. MY erogenous zones were definitely in danger of shutting down. What was going on here? Did Zak Ridarelli expect me to surrender control to him, to debase myself so much—

"Tell me you have to have me. That you'll do anything to please me."

When had Zak turned into some cheesy porn star? Oblivious to his caresses, my mind raced.

Have you even been working overtime, or have you found yourself a new plaything?

Something stirred, something buried so deep in my consciousness, something so vile I fought back a wave of nausea. *Mockery. Betrayal. Humiliation.* This scenario between us—between me and *someone*—was oddly familiar. Though it could not be, not in this life. But it was an echo of a similarly played event that had ended...

And then Zak said, "Beg for my cock."

I kneed him as much as I could in my awkward position. "Get the hell off of me, you fucking dick!"

Zak rolled off of me. "What the hell, Magdalena? What's chapped your ass?"

I told him; indeed, I did.

By the end of 1980, I was a single woman.

Again.

The Lion and the Leopard is a historical novel about a beautiful English noblewoman in love with two men—her husband and her husband's liege lord. *Lion* is set in the opening years of the fourteenth century, during the disastrous reign of Edward Caernarvon, Edward II, who is deposed by his queen and her lover, only to be murdered, according to most accounts, by having a red-hot poker rammed up his anus.

It was published in 1982, the year of my first visit to England.

ALL THROUGHOUT MY TRIP, I could not shake the feeling of being followed. Initially, I dismissed it as a reaction to my tour guide, who politely, efficiently, relentlessly kept us, her charges, in sight. However, even when striking out alone, when merely one of many visiting such sites as the Tower of London or Westminster Abbey, I found myself surveying those around me for a face I'd seen once too often. Repeatedly, I experienced that prickling between my shoulder blades or the goosebumps rising on my arms that warned of unwelcome scrutiny.

I am over-excited, I rationalized. Traveling to a land that had so long stirred my imagination left my nerves as overwrought as a Victorian maiden's.

When gazing at green and yellow fields edged by hedgerows from our tour bus or the ruins of a castle perched high on a hill or upon entering a cathedral nave, I would think, *I am home. This is where I belong.* Since most of my family came from the British Isles, I attributed such fancies to genetic memory.

I was well into research on what would become my *Knights of England* series, so I sought out new places, as well as those I'd written about in *The Lion and the Leopard*—Dover Castle, Canterbury Cathedral, the tiny village of Fordwich and vast swaths of lands including the Welsh Marches and Yorkshire Dales.

When strolling along York's Shambles—a street with buildings dating back to the thirteenth century—I identified my watcher. In that same lightning flash I'd experienced during my regression, the name came to me: Ranulf Navarre. I winced at the revelation. In the two-plus years since my session with Viola, I'd convinced myself that the experience had been an exercise in wishful thinking. As a novelist, I'd created fictional characters for *The Lion and the Leopard.* Under Viola's expert guidance, I'd simply concocted more of the same.

Still, here, on my tormentor's turf, he took up residence in my mind like an unwanted guest. Breathing in the soft summer air, I wondered, *Did it smell the same when you walked the earth? Was the sky a more vibrant blue? Did you ride past these very hedges? Are those fields of wildflowers similar to those you knew?*

I imagined Ranulf reaching down to pluck several by their stems and inhaling their fragrance before expertly weaving them into a garland. Imagined him ambling along Canterbury's High Street, pausing at King's Bridge to toss the garland into the lazy-running River Stour, after which he joined pilgrims heading for Thomas Becket's tomb.

While refusing to give a thought to that Janey character, with her woebegone personality and timid manner, Ranulf Navarre was fast becoming an obsession.

Not real, I reminded myself. Maybe I was experiencing a remnant of that life we'd lived together. But we hadn't lived a life together or apart or anything else. I would not glimpse his face before he stepped back into the shadows of a minstrel's gallery, or his blood-red surcoat among the shorts, T-shirts and ball caps of the typical male tourist.

In Fordwich, where I had set so much of *The Lion and the Leopard*, I entered the tiny church of St Mary the Virgin and found myself holding my breath, anticipating that I would find Ranulf kneeling before the altar.

Imagine my surprise when I *did* see Ranulf Navarre; I swear I did.

And during what more fitting activity than a joust?

CHILHAM CASTLE—MORE of a manor house built in the Jacobean style—stood watch over the reenactment unfolding beyond its gardens. Verdant field, casually dressed tourists, white tents topped by banners bearing the coats of arms of participating jousters. Unhelmed knights, looking heartstoppingly handsome while circling the lists on their destriers, greeted the cheering crowd with gauntleted salutes. Lions, dogs, boars, griffins, manticores and eagles snarled and leapt from their surcoats, jousting shields, and caparisons. I stood in the front row, pressed against a metal barrier, notebook in hand. I'd intended to jot down notes but was too caught up in the enchantment for such distraction.

The scene was eerily familiar—the fragrance of recently mown lawn, the haze hovering above Chilham's treetops, sunlight dancing like fireflies across the surface of the pond beyond the lists.

I closed my eyes and there it was, oddly, the scent of salt water upon skin. The taste of it upon my lips. But that had been the Pacific Ocean and the man had been Dwight Latimer, who had nothing to do with any of this, who I hadn't thought of in years.

I shivered, shaking away the sensation, forcing myself to concentrate on the scene at hand.

The first pair of knights had already taken their positions on opposite ends of the field—the more distant one in black and yellow, his mount looking like some monstrous bee; the closer, azure trimmed in silver. My attention wandered away from the bee knight to the spectators on that side of the barricade.

I saw him then, standing a bit apart, his back to me. The sight so ordinary and so clear and so impossible. He was obviously another reenactor because he was dressed for the period. My eye must have been drawn to the vermilion of his surcoat, which ended past his knees in the style of the thirteenth century. And his hair, the color of midnight just as I remembered, falling nearly to his shoulders. I recognized it all: his height, the set of broad shoulders, even the way the fabric draped around his hips where it was cinched by a leather girdle, a girdle I knew sometimes held his sword. How many times had I seen him standing just so, his booted feet planted apart looking out...what was he looking at? The image blinked on and off like a hazard light, too quick to register.

Ranulf Navarre. He had followed me here to Chilham Castle.

But that was impossible.

I forgot about the battling knights, lances yet at rest, destriers prancing on either side of the tilt line impatiently awaiting the signal to engage. I willed the man to turn so that I might see his face and know...**know**...his face was not the face of Ranulf Navarre.

As if in obedience to my command, the stranger half turned, enough to reveal his profile. His very familiar profile. Perfectly formed, the strong nose and chin, the fall of the hair, which was not all one length but curved in flattering waves, like some seventies' rockstar. Only he wasn't an inhabitant of the current century; he was the man of my past, the man who'd been lurking in my unconscious, waiting to be called to the fore, to remind me, "I am here. Did you think you could forget?"

I shook my head, as if that could dislodge this madness. Reality was not a man who had been stitched out of juvenile longings. I was experiencing some bizarre trick of the light, of my heart, of a peculiar confluence of circumstances. Here in this pseudo-medieval environment, it was easy to be deluded.

The figure turned full circle to directly face me. The brilliance of his surcoat was broken by the heraldic symbol on his chest, that of a black hawk. Vaguely, I heard someone shout, a trumpet's blare followed by the pounding of hooves as the jousters raced toward each other.

Bracing myself for the inevitable disappointment, I raised my eyes to the knight's face.

You!

Every perfect detail burned into my brain. The man who, during our initial meeting, had weighed and measured my worth as if I were a sack of grain, who'd taunted me for my tears and pleadings to "please, please love me..."

"Ranulf!" My hand went to my heart, as though to regulate its erratic rhythm. It could not be him, yet it was.

Our gazes met and held. The moment seemed to stretch forever, the way they say it does after you die. Face to face with the man I loved, even after all these centuries.

The combatant nearest me passed in a flurry of billowing cloth and straining stallion. Lances cracked. Spectators roared. Ignoring the spectacle, I made my way along the barrier toward Ranulf.

I know it's you. But it can't be you.

Another pass of the jousters, impeding my vision. I pushed against various bodies, toward the spot where I'd last seen what must be the doppelganger version of Ranulf Navarre.

Gone. My gaze swept the crowd. No scarlet surcoat; no flowing black hair. I then retreated to the tents where those milling about were dressed in period costumes. After an unsuccessful search, I headed for the stalls selling food, beverages and trinkets. Peering among the artisans working their crafts, hoping for a glimpse of him.

"Where are you?" I whispered. "How could you do this to me?"

So like him.

Ranulf Navarre had vanished.

As if he'd never been.

1983

"Yet each man kills the thing he loves
By each let this be heard.
Some do it with a bitter look,
Some with a flattering word,
The coward does it with a kiss,
The brave man with a sword!"
"Ballad of Reading Gaol"

— OSCAR WILDE

Ten

I blame the "Incident at Chilham" for my third marriage. To say I was totally undone by the experience would be an understatement. I'd obviously been deranged before that, perhaps the moment I'd set foot in England.

It's really very simple.

If we can't trust our senses, we're untethered to the world around us, aren't we? And I couldn't. What if I'd manufactured *all of it*? While solipsism might make for interesting intellectual discussions, the possibility that the external world might not exist beyond our individual minds terrified me. Because, if it had all been the fault of malfunctioning synapses, I was no more than a balloon bobbing along, drifting aimlessly on a current until... POP! If I'd been caught up in some sort of hallucination, how could I ever distinguish reality from fantasy?

I kept circling back to two facts. First: the regression had taken place in my mind. That was irrefutable. Had the rest of it, as well?

Second: I recognized Ranulf Navarre because he'd *never changed*! But I looked nothing like this Janey character. I was taller, my figure more voluptuous, my hair a darker brown, my face prettier, and I certainly didn't slink about like a beaten cur. There was no way my knight could have been stalking this iteration of the pitiful creature of my regression—because he wouldn't have recognized her. If Ranulf Navarre had actually existed, he couldn't have known Janey had been reborn into Magdalena Moore. I would have meant nothing to him.

Sherralinda disagreed. "He could have recognized your essence, " she said, upon my retelling. "Soul connections cannot be severed."

Unable to shake my distress, I quit reading or watching anything with a supernatural or horror bent. I put aside my second medieval novel, *A Knight There Was,* lest something in the research or writing trigger another delusional episode.

Sometimes when I couldn't sleep, I called Zak, who was now working out of Colorado Springs. Wrapped in his strong arms, I felt so much safer. While Zak and I could never really be together again, he still swore I was his woman. Indeed, he had been faithful to me in his fashion. I was especially grateful that he didn't question me or remark on my agitation or suggest I see a therapist or go on anti-psychotic meds. He simply held me and assured me, "Everything will be all right."

I wanted so very badly to believe him.

Eleven

My short-lived flirtation with Evangelicalism occurred because I needed answers that took me out of myself, not to mention my secret fear I was going crazy. I appreciated the support of my friends and my parents, though Mom and Dad thought anything I did was *wonderful* and "You're going to be more than fine, dear." I was comforted by the personal testimonials recounting the miracles God performed in believers' lives.

"And just remember Matthew 10:30," said our group leader at least once a session. "'The very hairs of your head are all numbered. Do not fear therefore.'"

The stories shared at the meetings Sherralinda and I attended at the Waters of Life megachurch reminded me that my problems weren't too big to be fixed, that others had triumphed over drug addiction, promiscuity, failed marriages, and, yes, even mental illness.

I only need to surrender.

While Sherralinda had begun studying astrology and swore she was perfecting her so far non-existent psychic powers via tarot readings, she enjoyed attending.

"I'm so open minded my last boyfriend said I had holes in my head. I pretended that was a compliment."

Handsome Hustler—I will not dignify the bastard with his given name—looked like Robert Redford, who in the early eighties was one of the hottest actors on the planet. Long blond hair—at least I thought so at the time—the most dazzling blue eyes—at least I thought so at the time—and H.H. wore an earring (clip-on, I later discovered) when earring-wearing men were unusual

~

HANDSOME HUSTLER HAD QUITE the tale to recount to us ladies seated in the Waters of Life Auditorium.

How this particular bad boy found himself serving life in prison before a religious conversion followed by...wait for it...*Miracles!*

H.H. begins his tale. "My best friend and I were out drinking. In those days I did a lot of drinkin', druggin', whore—fornicatin'." He quickly corrects himself. "We were in a bar not too far from here."

Since I was ignorant of any bar unattached to a family-friendly restaurant, I imagined a dark, dangerous place with scarred wood floors—very sticky— crammed with tattooed bikers wearing black leather and bandanas around their shaved heads or really long, greasy hair. Accompanied by their biker molls. ("Chicks," Sherralinda later explains, as if she's an expert on that particular alternative lifestyle.) What horrors would we find in such a place? Topless waitresses? Men in assless chaps? Graffitied bathrooms advertising lurid sexual acts? Drinks without coasters?

From its Harley clogged parking lot, these ne'er-do-wells would dispense what? Drugs or revolvers with filed off serial numbers or counterfeit Gucci handbags?

I am so caught up in my imaginary scenario, I miss much of H.H.'s story, which now nears its climax.

Sherralinda nudges me to pay attention.

Some Sons of Silence dude is hassling H.H's buddy, a dude named Taco, and Taco's girl.

Sherralinda and I, who had exchanged shocked glances at the mention of "Sons of Silence," have eyebrows shooting up to our hairlines at "Taco."

Taco? Is he Hispanic? Does he work at Taco Bell?

Is Handsome Hustler pulling our leg?

H.H. assumes a dreamy expression. Pauses in his narrative. Not a sound from his enraptured audience. I'm still wrestling with the incongruity of "Taco, " though it does sound a bit more menacing than "Happy Meal."

"And then...

"This guy puts his hands on Taco's girl and the next thing we know there's fists flyin' and *Bam!* One of the Sons of Silence is down. His head slams against the metal footrest that goes around the bar."

An auditorium of teased hair, padded shoulders, modestly dressed bodies leans forward, heavily mascaraed eyes boring into the speaker.

"The man's dead." Handsome Hustler snaps his fingers. "Just like that."

H.H. finishes his tale—how he takes the rap for Taco because his girlfriend is pregnant and "I was single." He shrugs. "My life was worthless anyway." And how after being sentenced to life in prison, he falls on his knees and dedicates his life to God.

The result?

"I stand before you today a free man."

Taco's best friend (Burrito?)--I don't dare risk a glance at Sherralinda lest we both start giggling—confesses to the crime. Handsome Hustler is completely exonerated.

After H.H.'s talk ends to thunderous applause, he gestures to the back of the room. "I have copies of *Behind Bars with J.C.* for sale. I'd be honored to autograph a copy for each of you lovely ladies."

When we reach the front of the line, Sherralinda leans forward. "My friend's also a writer."

H.H. flashes me his Robert Redford smile, which is beyond dazzling, and scribbles his phone number in the front page of my newly purchased book.

"Call me!" he whispers.

Unfortunately, I do.

Twelve

What drew me to H.H.? Primarily, the fact that he wanted tons of kids. As the Incident at Chilham faded and I rationalized it away or pretended it didn't happen, my desire for children again took center stage. I was thirty-two years old. Not ancient, but definitely getting up there when it came to first pregnancies.

H.H. was the opposite of Zak, even saying no to premarital sex. I liked the way he was so certain about everything...so practical...so stable. I would be safe with him. Handsome Hustler was the perfect partner to keep me grounded when I went off on flights of fancy where I imagined being stalked by a phantom.

You will not be surprised when I reveal the following: nothing about H.H. turned out to be true. Not his thick, tawny hair—wig—his beautiful blue eyes—contact lenses—or his rap sheet. He *did* have one, though it didn't include murder.

H.H's speaking engagements took place in towns boasting colorful mining histories—Vail, Aspen, Breckenridge, Leadville, Telluride, and Steamboat Springs.

Before each speech, he explored architectural landmarks, snapping roll after roll of film with his Nikon camera. He took a special interest in banks.

"Thinking about some sort of coffee table book, maybe," he explained.

I wasn't sure how many people would be interested in a bunch of photographs of old banks, but H.H. increasingly reminded me I didn't know much about a lot of things, so I kept my mouth shut.

H.H.'s primary focus was branches with ATMs, which were a bit novel at the time. While photographing the exteriors, he'd send me inside to withdraw money.

"Why do you insist on ATMs?" I asked, totally oblivious of the truth: that H.H. was scoping out exits, security, all the usual things clever criminals do before committing their crimes.

"You learn a lot in prison," Handsome Hustler said, before adding, "I like to live on the edge."

I found his cryptic remark simultaneously alarming and thrilling. I was not an edge sort of person. Witness my reaction surrounding the Incident at Chilham. One weird thing happens, and I suffer a nervous breakdown. I preferred being an observer rather than a participant, particularly in my own life.

"What do you mean, live on the edge?" I asked.

H.H. bared his teeth. "You'll see."

Willow Wand Publishing had graciously granted me a leave of absence, which allowed me to accompany H.H.. While I didn't dare yet muck around in the Middle Ages lest I trigger another bizarre happening, I had started writing again, blocking out my gothic romance, *The Landlord's Black-Eyed Daughter*, based on the Alfred Noyes poem, "The Highwayman."

During H.H.'s talks, I sat in the front row, though I'd reduced his once fascinating story to blah, blah, blah. Not only did I notice that details of H.H.'s "testimony" changed over time, but I resented disrupting my career in order to act as his glorified assistant, cashier and part-time chauffeur.

When I expressed my frustration, Handsome Hustler replied, "You're just jealous that my book signings are way more popular than yours."

"I don't do book signings anymore."

"Right," mocked H.H, curling his lip in an unchristian fashion.

"Because at your last one a woman with a chihuahua dressed up as Baby Barky sold ten times as many copies of her books as you did."

That was true. The author, who wrote children's stories with names like *Barky's First Tooth* and *Barky Sings a Song*, took unfair advantage of the fact that Barky was a shameless publicity hound. And apparently some people thought the chihuahua, who looked remarkably like a rat in a diaper and bonnet, was adorable.

But it was cruel of Handsome Hustler to remind me.

UPON RETURNING HOME from a mid-week jaunt to Aspen, we were greeted by several police cruisers. Apparently, on the previous day, Aspen's Colorado Miners Bank had been robbed.

"You were caught on camera," said one of the officers, while clasping H.H. in handcuffs.

If you need yet another example of my naiveté, I was genuinely stunned.

H.H. immediately tried to shift the blame.

"Magdalena was the mastermind. It was her idea to case the interiors while withdrawing money. If you give me a plea deal, I'll turn state's evidence."

That whopper caused me several sleepless nights, though I was comforted by Zak Ridarelli's offer to drop H.H. down a mine shaft. "Nobody'd ever find him. Just say the word, darlin'. It'd be my pleasure."

While Handsome Hustler awaited trial, Sherralinda and I decided to investigate his background. Yeah, way too little too late, but I was belatedly looking for answers. Who was this guy, really? Had he lied about everything? How could I have been so duped?

And betrayed?

Again.

Turns out H.H. *had* served five years at Territorial State Prison for fraud and burglary. He was still on parole, which might explain why he never left Colorado and kept a separate business calendar, which Sherralinda and I subsequently examined. Nowhere had he penciled in *"Apptmt w/ parole officer because I am a convicted fucking felon."*

Divorce number three was finalized before Handsome Hustler went to trial.

The Haunting

1984

Yesterday, upon the stair,
I met a man who wasn't there
He wasn't there again today
I wish, I wish he'd go away...
...Last night I saw upon the stair
A little man who wasn't there
He wasn't there again today
Oh, how I wish he'd go away...
"Atigonish"

— HUGHES MEARNS

Thirteen

I was well into *The Landlord's Black-Eyed Daughter*, where my plucky heroine, Bess, is on the run with her highwayman, Rand Remington. They are being relentlessly pursued by a Bow Street Runner, and while I enjoyed writing about the gothic darkness and foreboding atmosphere of the Yorkshire Dales, it didn't feel quite right.

Medieval England still beckoned. I could not resist incorporating a piece of it into *Landlord*, this time mimicking my long-ago regression, sketching Plucky Bess falling asleep and dreaming of a horrible battle wherein Ranulf Navarre's demise is primarily due to Janey's betrayal. While I'd used the scene as a plot device, mirroring Bess's relationship with her highwayman, the words flew onto the computer screen, almost like automatic writing.

This really happened, I thought, my fingers dancing on the keyboard. *You engineered Ranulf's death*. Even as I completed the scenario, my mind rejected it. Since I had no outside proof that Ranulf Navarre even existed, the rest was fantasy. Better just to move along.

Which was easier said than done.

On the bulletin board above my Kaypro computer, I'd pinned a photo of the tomb of Edward the Black Prince, as well as one of Dover Castle, Union Jack flying high and taut in the wind.

I'd framed a print of *Hellelil and Hildebrand, the Meeting on the Turret Stairs* and hung it on the wall opposite my computer. Sometimes I found myself staring at the doomed lovers until the brilliant blue and orange of their surcoats blurred into one.

Beneath my daily life, beneath my foray into an eighteenth-century highwaymen and his lover, I heard medieval England's siren call, leaving me with a sense of restlessness, of matters left unsettled.

What I did not know is that, while I *was* fleeing something, it wasn't the call of a mythical siren; it wasn't medieval England; it wasn't even Ranulf Navarre.

It was my destiny.

THE CASTING of the runes is an odd thing. We may believe we are running fast and determined in the opposite direction from our fate, only to discover we are running toward it.

Fourteen

All numbers have a mystical meaning, at least according to Sherralinda.

I was thirty-three years old and thrice divorced. Here I was on this third day of the third month, at three o'clock in the afternoon, according to the clock above the door of Tres Magos Antiquarian Book Shop.

About to slam head-on into my past.

"Three Wise Men," Sherralinda said later, after she'd looked up "Tres Magos" in a Latin/English dictionary. "You know what that means, don't you?"

"The owner likes Christmas?"

"No, dummy, it's all about the number three. This year your life will be shaped by three. Quite exciting, actually. Three is all about magic and accessing one's intuition. Wisdom. Understanding. Good fortune, and most importantly, fertility."

I didn't point out that other than an occasional romp with Zak Ridarelli, I would have to conceive immaculately. Or that Sherralinda was engaging in selective reinforcement. Let me count the ways. We were living in the year 1984, not 1983 or 1933 or 1333, for that matter. My PO Box and street address were devoid of threes. I didn't own three cars or three houses. I have two arms, two legs, two eyes... You get the picture.

Anyway, while I didn't accept Sherralinda's explanation for what I uncovered inside the old bookshop, I couldn't dismiss the event itself as coincidence.

Tres Magos Antiquarian Bookstore, located directly across from Acacia Park with its towering trees and old-fashioned bandshell, was a Colorado Springs fixture. Lingering in front of its charmingly arranged display window, I noticed two books—a hand-sized *Medieval London*, and a second with the *Danse Macabre* stamped on its cover.

Naturally, I had to buy both.

The interior of Tres Magos looked exactly the way an antiquarian bookstore should—crammed shelves pushing up to a high ceiling, an office loft in the back corner which was a chaotic mess of papers, books, newspapers and magazines. Overhead, two lazily rotating fans, their blades casting shadows on stacked display tables and worn wing-backed chairs. The room smelled faintly of grass and vanilla, as such places do, and even more faintly of dust carried from all the places that had housed all the books. The proprietor, who gazed down at me from his perch on the rung of one of those sliding ladders, was out of central casting—untidy white hair, bifocals, suspenders, old-fashioned cuffed trousers and collarless shirt. He wore a snooty expression, as if having decided I'd wandered into the wrong establishment.

After explaining that I'd like to purchase the two books in the window and asking what else he carried on medieval England, the man's demeanor softened. He directed me to a well-stocked section. I'd already set aside several more must-have titles before picking up *Simon de Montfort: Father of English Democracy*. Not my time period. I knew little about the mid-thirteenth century other than that a French baron, Simon de Montfort, who had something to do with the founding of Parliament, had rebelled against a feckless king and lost his life in the bargain.

I have no idea why I hesitated over the book. Perhaps because of the rich maroon cover with letters edged in gold. Or its elaborate spine. Or the comfortable way it fit in my hand. Perhaps the bookplate on the front endpaper, which bore a coat of arms and nothing more. The space to indicate its owner was blank.

Silently addressing *Simon de Montfort: Father of English Democracy*, I asked, *Are you an orphan? Were you so unloved your original owner refused to claim you?*

I opened *Simon*. It was obviously old, with faded diagrams and small print. Its pages, which exuded a faint musty smell, were thin, more like onion skin than regular weight, and difficult to turn. I imagined sad, neglected *Simon* tucked away in some university basement or the library of one of its namesakes' distant relatives. After running a finger through the table of contents to see if anything caught my attention, I flipped to the index, seeking familiar names or places or events that might be useful as historical background once I returned to the fourteenth century.

I found *his* name under the heading "Second Baron's War." Quite a short list of lords who'd supported Simon de Montfort during the ensuing civil war. A war that had been quick and brutal and had ended in the rebels' annihilation.

There it was: *Ranulf Navarre, 2nd Baron Navarre.*

"It's you," I whispered, after overcoming the shock. "You *are* real!"

Once home and settled atop my futon, I extracted *Simon* from my book bag with shaking hands. Eventually, I calmed enough to check the index for more references to Ranulf Navarre.

Nothing. Still, hoping for *something*, I decided to read the entire book in one sitting. An interesting story—another great rise and even greater fall. Good and bad kings, weak and powerful opposition, plots and counterplots. As inevitable as the waxing and waning of the moon in that brutal age.

I pictured my nemesis, my lover, my husband standing behind me, his surcoat a flame, the sleeves of his mail gleaming in the lamplight. Peering over my shoulder as I neared the end of the book.

You think to find me in those pages, Janey? How foolish you are. How foolish you've always been.

It was well past midnight by the time I finished *Simon*. My ghost was correct. Ranulf Navarre was not mentioned again.

Still, one important truth had been established. Ranulf Navarre,

2nd Baron Navarre did exist. He'd not been a creation of my febrile mind. After placing the book atop the stack beside my feet, I looked across the room to the print of my doomed lovers on the turret stairs.

Did Ranulf Navarre and I kiss upon a winding stairway? Had Ranulf once loved me before it all turned sour? Did I somehow send him to his doom?

Not me. Not Magdalena Moore. Jane. Janey.

I felt so very tired, too tired to turn off the light and stumble off to bed.

So, I sat in the stillness, hands splayed upon my thighs, staring at something I could no longer see.

If following that March day, you would have told me I would be in England before summer's end, I would have said, "No way." But Sherralinda, who was always looking at interesting ideas for Druids & Dragyns, had decided to attend the annual Fey Faire near Coventry.

"Come with me," she said. "All expenses paid, of course."

How could I refuse?

After a week of re-visiting some of my favorite castles and cathedrals, Sherralinda and I boarded a train to the West Midlands. There we settled in a charming Bed and Breakfast located on the outskirts of Coventry.

Sherralinda planned to offer her "Psychic Pet Communings" free of charge at the Faire. "I'm still practicing," she said, settling back on her bed. "But my animal totems advised me to branch out."

I suspected my friend had switched from humans to pets because, unless she encountered a talking rottweiler or hamster, they couldn't continually tell her, "You're wrong!" "Nope!" "Incorrect!"

From a stack of brochures located on a dresser between our beds, I pulled one out advertising "The Battlefield of Evesham."

Once again, that queer stomach drop, that sense I was being moved around like a piece on a chessboard.

I scanned the brochure and discovered, not at all to my surprise, that Evesham the town and Evesham the battlefield were less than an hour's drive away.

My dreams that night were vivid and violent. Mailed knights and battles and castles and a dark-haired man in a vibrant surcoat astride a black destrier furiously wielding his arming sword. Not like a regular dream, but more like scenes from a movie played at triple speed.

Waking up the next morning in a tangle of sheets and sweat, I knew I had no choice but to follow where I was being led.

Sixteen

Dressed in jeans, a purple tank top, and walking shoes and carrying a bottled water, I struck out for the appropriate bus stop. While I worried that exploring the possible site of Ranulf Navarre's death might trigger another bout of my psychological sickness, I also felt a sense of anticipation.

Besides, I was stronger now. If I could survive three disastrous marriages and the threat of a prison stint, I could handle a self-guided tour of an ancient battlefield. Not once during my current trip had I imagined being stalked. My gyro might be a bit wobbly, but not so much as I'd feared since finding the proof that Ranulf Navarre actually existed.

The battlefield was located right outside Evesham, a charming market town surrounded on three sides by the River Avon—as it had been in 1265. I stopped for a bit of information at the Almonry Heritage Centre, a beautifully restored fourteenth-century building.

"Take High Street to Greenhill," said the elderly tourist guide whose name tag identified her as Dorothy. "Quite a pleasant walk, really." She handed me a map of the battlefield.

According to Dorothy, I would be retracing the same route as Simon de Montfort's rebels before engaging Henry III's troops. "It was raining that morning," she said. "Most unpleasant. Four thousand dead in the space of a few hours. Will you be here this evening for the festivities?"

"Festivities?" I echoed, momentarily confused by the abrupt change of subject.

"Fourth of August, luv. Today is the seven hundred nineteenth anniversary of the battle. Do check out the medieval market on Evesham Church grounds. It's quite interesting."

Anniversary? Warning goosebumps accompanied by a frisson of panic. *Crap!* What were the odds? Out of all the days I might visit, I'd chosen the anniversary of the battle?

Would the craziness of my first trip return? Would I once again imagine myself being stalked by a man who'd been dead for centuries?

Dorothy urged me to visit Simon de Montfort's memorial stone near the bell tower, as well as other related delights.

"You do know what happened to the Earl of Leicester's head after he was killed, don't you, luv?" With her tightly permed white hair, sensible trifocals, and lace collared blouse accessorized with pearls, Dorothy was surely a favorite with her grandkids, spoiling them with homemade "biscuits" and readings of *Winnie-the-Pooh*.

"Montfort's head?" I repeated.

"Yes. The Marcher lord who brought Leicester down was Roger Mortimer. You know the Mortimers, of course."

As if we'd just enjoyed a spot of tea together.

However, I *did* know them. I'd written about another Roger Mortimer, the lover of Queen Isabella, who'd deposed the hapless Edward II in *The Lion and the Leopard*. And, like Simon de Montfort—like so many—Roger Mortimer, 1st Earl of March, had been undone by his own greed and hanged like a common criminal.

"One of medieval England's most important families," I said. "The same names seem to repeat themselves, don't they?"

Dorothy nodded approvingly. "After the first Baron Mortimer hacked off poor Simon's head, he had it sent to his wife. She displayed the head at a celebratory feast. As well as a few other body parts, some say."

"Oh!"

Not knowing how to further respond, I thanked my malevolent granny, gathered the map and various brochures and headed for the door. What possessed me to pause with my hand on the knob and turn back to Dorothy, I can't say.

I cleared my throat. "Have you ever heard of a knight named Ranulf Navarre?"

This was the first time I'd uttered his name to anyone other than Sherralinda. It felt wrong, as if I were outing someone with secrets I'd no right to share.

Dorothy laid down the fountain pen she'd been using to enter something in an old-fashioned ledger and studied me, her expression still kindly. "One of the rebels?"

My throat felt tight. I nodded.

"No, luv. There were so many."

I was not surprised. Nor should I have been disappointed, though I was. "Thanks anyway."

Dorothy adjusted her glasses. "Was he a relative of yours?" Her tone was respectful, as though we were commiserating over the recently departed.

"Yes," I said.

~

EVESHAM'S BATTLEFIELD was a gentle slope of meadow, copses of trees and in the distance, a stone tower. Similar to thousands of other English landscapes, though few could claim Evesham's bloody history.

The afternoon was fair, the sun pleasantly warm upon my bare arms, but had I not known this was a site of monstrous carnage, I would still have been discomfited by the stillness.

If silence were an odor, my nostrils would reek of it.

Not a silence that could be attributed to Mother Nature, however. This was the hush before the descent of the trapdoor, the jerking of the hangman's noose; the thump of the guillotine's blade; the first pump of lethal cocktails into the outstretched arm of the condemned.

Evesham's horrors had been manmade.

When referring to cemeteries of our war dead, it's a cliché to speak of "hallowed ground." Evesham didn't feel like hallowed ground. It felt like ground that had been salted, forever poisoned by the blood of thousands sacrificed because an ambitious earl wanted to rule England while a weak king wanted to keep his crown.

I hesitated at the entrance, uncertain whether I should simply return to Coventry. I knew enough details of August 4, 1265, to worry that my cursed imagination could kick into overdrive.

God knows what it might conjure.

Still, I was here. Once again, I was being unsubtly guided. Nothing to do but soldier on.

I set out on the deserted dirt path. No breeze stirred the grasses or the leaves in the branches of the trees occasionally overhanging the trail.

Is this how you died? I wondered, silently addressing Ranulf Navarre. *Championing a man who couldn't decide whether he wished to be saint or despot?*

I could see Ranulf's eyes, long-lashed and dark, nearly black, scrutinizing me as clearly as if he stood before me. As I remembered them scrutinizing me the day of our betrothal. As I knew they'd scrutinized me as a woman.

No, not me. That Jane character.

While continuing along the gently curving path, I imagined it all: screaming horses. Screaming men. Lightning cracking across a sky so dark it might have been midnight rather than mid-morn. Earth slick with mud and blood, sucking down destriers and foot soldiers so they could not move, could not flee.

Were you here? Did you know you would die? Did you regret your allegiance to Montfort? Did you give even a thought to your poor, hapless wife?

A drop of sweat trickled like a misplaced tear from my temple to my cheek.

"Was he a relative of yours?"

"Yes."

My hiking boots whispered upon the hard-packed earth. An orchard, ripe with fruit, occupied a corner of the battlefield. I fancied I saw movement there, someone walking among the neatly spaced rows. The first sign of human life since I'd entered.

Seemingly out of nowhere, cumulonimbus clouds had appeared from the direction of Evesham's suburbs. Hoping to complete the circuit ahead of the threatening storm, I increased my pace. With each breath, the air thickened until it became a leaden weight in my lungs. Could I be inhaling all the fear and terror, all the hatred of that day? All those crying out with voices I could not hear?

Do you have stories you wish me to tell?

Thousands of corpses had been scattered like macabre pick-up sticks while a bitter rain beat upon them. Reluctant warriors most had been, dying unknown and unmourned save for their loved ones praying, praying, praying for their safe return.

No monuments, no markers, no obelisks, no stained-glass windows for those unfortunates. Instead, historians—and visitors—focused on the few who had orchestrated and implemented the slaughter of Evesham.

For slaughter it had been.

Even by the standards of the day, the Battle of Evesham had been barbaric. Ignoring custom, England's prince, Edward Longshanks, had forbade the ransoming of captured barons, which had added to the carnage. Those rebels who had escaped the battle were ridden down in surrounding wheat fields, drowned in the River Avon, chased through Evesham's streets and put to the sword. Montfort himself had been brought to ground by a pack of assassins dispatched by Longshanks himself. The pack had slashed its way through Montfort's bodyguards, pulled the earl off his horse and hacked him to pieces.

Before meeting his fate, Montfort had cried, "Our bodies are theirs; Our souls are God's."

Simon de Montfort was famous for his piety.

Did God grant you that much, taking yours and the other rebels' souls, leaving human and animal scavengers to desecrate your bodies?

Or had God turned His face away from the Earl of Leicester, as so many of his contemporaries had claimed? Was it those lost souls who kept watch over the battlefield? Was I feeling their pain? Their despair? Their rage when they realized they'd been betrayed by Welsh comrades who'd fled rather than fight, by Simon de Montfort's son who'd dawdled too long over dinner when he should have been marching to meet his father?

You were a fool for following a man stupid enough to think he could cross a king.

Here it seemed natural to directly address my husband, if only in my mind.

Not my husband. Her *husband.*

My hand squeezed my water bottle, causing it to crack like a pistol shot in the quiet. I felt an unreasoning anger, as if Ranulf Navarre had personally wronged me.

Are you buried here?

My gaze roamed the landscape. The monks had lain to rest fallen lords in Evesham's Abbey while digging pits in the nearby cemetery to accommodate common soldiers.

It was then I experienced that familiar prickling between my shoulder blades. As abruptly as if I'd been jerked by invisible reins, I halted. Someone was watching me. Was this where Ranulf Navarre would step out of the field in his scarlet surcoat?

Tamping down a rush of panic, I scanned the area—orchard, forest, meadow, the occasional lone tree standing sentinel.

There.

He stood shadowed in one of those trees. Perhaps thirty feet away. The figure I'd seen earlier? But how had he gotten there without my seeing him?

The stranger was too far away to distinguish facial features, even if they hadn't been hidden by a hoodie and the protective umbrella of branches. A big man, dressed in dark jeans and sweatshirt, his legs planted apart, his arms loose at his sides. Watching me, no mistake about it. Was his stance belligerent? No, I wouldn't describe it thus. More...alert, intent.

I wasn't afraid. More unsettled, I'd say, as most women would be in such a situation.

A wind sprang up, bringing with it the unmistakable scent of rain. Which was probably why the stranger had flipped up his hoodie in anticipation of the storm. The light shifted so that I could see the sleeve of his sweatshirt, which was vermilion rather than black.

Show me your face. Are you clean shaven or bearded? Let me see you!

Even though I couldn't distinguish eyes from nose or mouth or chin, I knew the man returned my stare.

Neither of us moved. My heartbeat sped up, readying for fight or flight.

Clouds boiled overhead; I heard the first growl of thunder. Practical me warned I needed to retreat; foolish me wanted to signal I wasn't intimidated. To stay just as I was, forcing the man to make the first move. To reveal himself. To show his face. To apologize for his rudeness.

Fool! Hadn't I yet learned that bad things can happen, had certainly happened to me?

Ultimately, I was the one who turned away, who backtracked from whence I'd come. Imagining the man's contemptuous sneer. "How weak you are!" What other adjectives? Pathetic? Worthless? Wretched?

You had an endless supply, didn't you?

My grip on reality was fraying. I needed to be gone, to return to people and traffic and the usual noises of civilization. I forced myself not to run and did not risk a glance until I'd neared the entrance.

I wasn't surprised to see that my watcher had become the man in the poem.

The man who wasn't there.

I wish, I wish he'd go away.

Part Four

1991-1995

"...I don't want to go among mad people," Alice remarked.
"Oh, you can't help that," said the Cat: "we're all mad here. I'm mad. You're mad."
"How do you know I'm mad?" said Alice.
"You must be," said the Cat, "or you wouldn't have come here."

— ALICE IN WONDERLAND~ LEWIS CARROLL

Seventeen

Forty years old and cast adrift. My parents had died after a freak tornado flattened their tiny town on Colorado's eastern plains. While Mom and Dad had retreated to their basement, well...I doubt I'll ever be able to go there in my mind. The proceeds from their will left me comfortable enough to quit my publishing job so I spent the next year sprawled out on my couch watching Home Shopping Network and reruns of *Columbo* and *Matlock* on Classic TV. Travel? Grocery store and back. Friends? Only when they showed up at my door and I couldn't avoid them. Writing? Never turned on my computer.

I did spend lots of time crying. Marveling at all the tears. Each day thinking I'd cried myself dry, only to find the reservoir overflowing the next.

Yeah, I know I was depressed, but I refused to dull my grief with medication. This was a normal reaction to my parents' death, to all the losses and all the pain I'd accumulated over my increasingly ridiculous life.

The same refrain ran through my thoughts: *I will emerge stronger on the other side, or I won't emerge at all*

Zak Ridarelli married an acupuncturist and moved to Washington where he worked for Seattle City Light.

Sherralinda bought an organic farm where she lived with Larry the Reporter. Larry had approached my friend with the idea of exposing this crazy New Ager who billed herself as "Psychic to Gentle Woodland Creatures." Instead, he'd fallen in love.

I was happy for both Zak and Sherralinda. I *did* believe in happy endings. For others.

By 1992, I had returned to writing full time. I was up to book five in my *Knights of England* series, which chronicled Edward III and England's golden age—until all that gold turned to dross. I spent an inordinate number of pages elaborating on the "dross" part. Black Death, brutal chevauchées, the Hundred Years War, illnesses, rebellions, dynastic overthrows and lots of angst among my major characters.

Perfect.

Does my state of mind excuse my fourth marriage?

I'd like to think so.

But it doesn't.

Looking back on my multitude of marriages, I've tried to pluck out the common thread drawing me to each spouse. A passion for life? More like narcissism and sociopathy, or in the case of Husband Number Four, mania and psychosis. My longing for a child? At the age of forty-four, conceiving would have qualified as miraculous.

With each man something had been missing, something I sensed on the deepest level, something I kept searching for and could never find.

Which still does not explain Bobo le Blaze.

~

THE WARNING WAS RIGHT THERE in Bobo's first name. Had I paid attention, which as you know, I seldom do.

Rearrange the letters: Bobo=Boob.

Artiste and sculptor of ceramic figures with elongated limbs and distended faces.

Another larger-than-life character. Like a bald teddy bear, big and burly and--I imagined wrongly—the cuddly sort. Everything about him was grandiose. Gestures! Dreams! Exclamatory sentences!

Who came up with the wonderful idea, while living in my house and transforming my garage into a studio, that his ticket to fame and fortune was spirit animals. More particularly one: a gopher. Which he would sculpt and market in all its various forms, including essence of gopher, whatever that meant. Oh, and by the way, being his wife, I was obligated to fund his dream (delusion)!

It got increasingly easier to divorce my mistakes.

2002-2008

"It would be so nice if something made sense for a change."
Alice in Wonderland

— LEWIS CARROLL

Nineteen

Most lives are routine, with adventures sprinkled over them like salt. Some with more flavoring than others. Mine was pretty bland, which suited me just fine. At age fifty-one, I was content. I wrote, hung out with friends, volunteered at the local animal shelter, took the occasional trip overseas.

I booked several European tours everybody mocks, where we're all herded from ruin to ruin by a guide who must be the reincarnation of Saint Patience. Finally, a trip to Ireland and Scotland and then to England, which I approached with equal measures of trepidation and nostalgia. That other life, that other fantasy, those little hiccups in time, felt as if they'd happened to someone else.

And I suppose they had. I didn't bear much more than a passing resemblance physically or mentally to the younger Magdalena Moore.

I did not encounter Ranulf Navarre in Dover or Canterbury or York or Caernarvon. I was not stalked or stared at.

This did happen.

We were staying in Penzance, using it as home base for day trips around the area. I'd specifically booked this part of the tour because it included Tintagel. I was writing about Tintagel in the final book of my series, *Flames of Rebellion*. My shy but studly Lancelot of Glastonbury has a platonic rendezvous with his best friend's wife there. Legend claimed that Tintagel was the birthplace of King Arthur (half of England and Wales claimed something similar). By late fourteenth century, the time of my Lancelot, Tintagel was a ruin, but once it had been an impressive fortress. I was eager to *feel* the environs for myself.

The night before our scheduled day trip, I dreamed of *him*. I'd not done so in years. In fact, I'd decided I'd forgotten how to dream since upon awakening I could only recall endless *nothingness*. Yet there he was, more vivid, more real than ever. Ranulf Navarre, leaning against a parapet, strands of hair snaking about him in a breeze off the sea. I stared at him, at the familiar surcoat, at his mailed sleeves and the coif pushed back from his head, as if he'd just returned from a journey.

"I missed you," dream me said, approaching him. He did not turn his head but continued staring out at the water. Had he not heard me? Was I invisible to him?

Then, as is the way in dreams, I was me but not me. I was *her*.

Ranulf Navarre turned to me. Once again, my soul was consumed by the power of his gaze.

"I've missed you so," dream me repeated, feeling such a sense of relief. "Where have you been? Why have you been hiding from me?"

"There you are, Janey," said Ranulf Navarre, ignoring dream me. The corners of his mouth lifted in a sardonic half-smile. "It's about time."

Not a nightmare. In fact, it was a welcome reunion of sorts. So why, when I awoke, was my heart pounding and my cheeks damp with sweat —or tears?

When our group gathered for breakfast, our tour guide stood and announced, "So very sorry, folks. We are not going to be able to visit Tintagel today. It has been unexpectedly closed for—"

I didn't hear the rest of it. Even that was to be denied me.

"I guess it isn't time, after all," I said, silently addressing Ranulf. I felt the most peculiar sense of relief. And sorrow.

~

ANOTHER SHORT, short accounting of my final husband. Number Five. Then, I promise, I am DONE!

I will recount and dismiss Husband Number Five in a handful of sentences. Renaissance man: historian, brilliant conversationalist, master chef, world traveler, expert handyman. Perfect companion for my old age.

When he proposed, he vowed, "I am the man you've been seeking. I am the one who will make you whole."

"I don't need anyone to make me whole," I'd responded, a bit snappishly. I'd long ago quit believing in soul mates, in the idea that we were all seeking our psychic doppelganger. Yet, I must have been persuaded on some level because I agreed to marry him. Almost immediately after the ceremony, Number Five morphed into a soul sucking vampire, a bottomless well of need. An incubus, draining my life from me. He was not my shadow; he was the entire darkness crushing me.

Once I got free of him, I made a vow.

Not only would I never marry, I would never allow another man into my life.

Ever.

2013

"It is no means an irrational fancy that, in a future existence, we shall look upon what we think our personal existence, as a dream."

— EDGAR ALLAN POE

Twenty

March 2013: I waited in front of Glastonbury Abbey's ruins for Felix Eastoft, the man in possession of a secret. While Felix had sent me a charming letter praising my *Knights of England* series, he'd been especially intrigued by my mention of Ranulf Navarre in *The Landlord's Black-Eyed Daughter*.

"*My family enjoys an unusual connection with the baron, which has long been a source of mystery and speculation,*" he'd written. While Felix now resided in Glastonbury, his family was originally from Tintagel. Over time, following the exchange of numerous emails, he, oh, so politely suggested a visit. *"I am in possession of a few related artifacts I trust you would find compelling. Perhaps the artifacts and my tale will appeal to your sense of mystery—and even provide inspiration for a future novel?"*

Now here I was, after having checked into a local Bed and Breakfast, impatiently awaiting the man I hoped could shed light upon my lifelong obsession.

I recognized Felix Eastoft from photos we'd exchanged. He was tall and thin and slightly stooped, perhaps from his many years as a postman. His face was kindly, his eyes intelligent and he smiled when he recognized me. We hugged like old friends.

After setting out for Felix's home and exchanging the usual pleasantries, I prodded him to reveal the purpose of my visit. I'd traveled all this way, through all these years and was bursting to know...something, to finally, finally have the curtain pulled back for the grand reveal.

"Ranulf Navarre," I said when our conversation reached a pause.

Felix nodded. We were walking along a winding cobblestoned street where the residences were mere feet from traffic. "You do know he was the baron of Tintagel during the time of Simon de Montfort."

My eyebrows lifted. *Tintagel?* "I never read that. I thought that was Richard of Cornwall." Richard of Cornwall had been the second son of the bad king John Lackland. Enamored with all things Arthurian, Cornwall had built a castle there in the "old style," at least the style he fancied would have been Arthur's.

Felix smiled benignly. "Richard of Cornwall had far larger ambitions than Tintagel Castle. Cornwall sided with King Henry against Simon de Montfort. Sometime in the 1240s, we believe, he granted Tintagel to Ranulf Navarre."

Putting flesh on the bones of my obsession. *I'm getting closer to you,* I thought, unable to suppress an excited shiver. Did I dare ask about Ranulf's wife? Did I *care* about his wife? I would wait and see following Felix's revelations.

We reached a semi-detached home with a brightly painted yellow front door. After guiding me through the small living room and kitchen area to the patio, Felix gestured to a small wrought iron table with a chair on either side.

"I'll put the kettle on," he said, before disappearing through the sliding glass doors. After several minutes he reappeared, bearing a tray containing a tea pot covered by a Union Jack cozy, two delicate teacups and saucers and a plate of biscuits.

"My family lived in Tintagel or thereabouts for generations," he said, while serving us. "My wife was happier here in Glastonbury, and my children live just down the road so..." He shrugged. "I do miss Cornwall and visit each fall."

Felix's voice trailed away; his gaze swept the trellises of rose bushes along his fence, the apple trees flanking his property line. I imagined him in summer, bent over his flowers, weeding the vegetables in his raised bed, helping his grandkids pick apples. Such a quiet, ordinary life. Who would have guessed this kind soul held my heart in his hands?

Not my heart. Answers. I forced myself to raise the porcelain cup to my lips, to sip, to savor the bite of black liquid. *Tell me. Show me. I've waited forever for this moment.*

"I cannot trace my ancestors directly to Ranulf Navarre."

I was startled by Felix's declaration. In point of fact, I'd never once speculated that Felix Eastoft might be a descendant. Was that because I'd assumed that my regression, along with my reimagining of the relationship between Ranulf Navarre and his pathetic spouse from my dream scene in *The Landlord's Black-Eyed Daughter*, had been correct? That *Landlord's* Janey had been as barren as Regression Janey? As barren as I was barren?

"Does that matter?" I replaced my cup atop its saucer and refused a biscuit from the offered plate, wishing Felix would get on with it.

"I suppose any familial connection to Lord Navarre is irrelevant, isn't it? We've traced the box itself..." His voice trailed off.

I had no idea what Felix was talking about.

He rose then. "Dear Ms. Moore. You have been more patient than I deserve. Please pardon my manners. I hope you will not be disappointed."

After reloading our repast on a tray, my host disappeared inside. After several minutes, he returned carrying a wooden container, clearly ancient and covered with the remains of what had once been vivid paintings. Its steepled top vaguely resembled the roof of a church.

"Is that a reliquary box?" I knew a bit about them from my research into goldsmithing. Generally, reliquaries were richly carved and fashioned from gold or silver. They generally held some body part belonging to a saint, with the rarest possessing a sliver of the true cross or some other relic that could be directly tied to Jesus Christ.

Felix smiled, clearly pleased at my identification. "This is quite a modest version, isn't it?"

I stared at the box, which was approximately 17x11x12 inches and made of a wood that, where visible, was nearly black in color. I experienced an almost overwhelming urge to reach out and touch the faded illustrations, to caress the steepled lid.

There was once a cross here. Having no idea where that thought came from.

"We usually keep the reliquary in a safe deposit box," Felix was saying. "We've had it authenticated so we know it dates to the 1200s."

My mind raced, unsuccessfully seeking connections. Right century, but what could such a sacred object possibly have to do with Ranulf Navarre, who had only been marginally religious?

Wait. How would I know that?

"You have guessed from whence the reliquary originates, haven't you? Especially since you wrote about its home."

Before I could reply I had no idea, he finished, "The Chapel of St. Julitta. We've traced it there."

I raised my eyes to him in wonder. "At Tintagel?" The tiny chapel, which had been a ruin by the time it played a part in *Flames of Rebellion*, had been named after an obscure martyr. There probably weren't more than a handful of churches in all of England that shared its name.

"The paintings are scenes from St Julitta's life. But its contents are what will most intrigue you."

I realized I was holding my breath, that my heart was hammering against my ribs and my fingers making nervous circles on my jean-clad thighs.

What? Get on with it!

Felix flipped up a clasp and slowly, deliberately raised the lid to retrieve a clear plastic envelope. Not what I was expecting. I braced myself for disappointment.

The envelope was approximately the size of a sheet of stationery. It appeared to encase a thick piece of paper.

Felix placed the envelope face down in front of me and tapped the plastic with a forefinger. "Parchment," he said.

Okay, but it was blank. Two possibilities here. Either Felix Eastoft was exhibiting an irritating flair for the dramatic, or he'd revealed himself to be several pancakes short of a full stack.

"Our family discovered the box and its contents in the seventeenth century during an expansion of our cottage," he said, seemingly oblivious to my rapidly souring humor. "We were not prominent enough to have a priest hole, of course, which had become so common in the larger manor homes. The reliquary was simply hidden away inside a wall and forgotten."

I stared at the envelope, itching to grab it and flip it over, to *finally* see what was on the other side. A deed bearing Ranulf's name? His will? Another blank piece of, oh, I don't know. Invisible ink?

I sensed Felix's eyes on me. Finally, after a sadistically long time, he placed the document face up with a flourish and exclaimed, "Ranulf Navarre!"

I stared at the parchment. Indeed, a face had been drawn on its surface—the colors remarkably preserved despite the ensuing centuries.

That face. *His* face.

"Ranulf," I whispered. With impossibly shaking fingers, I traced the lines and curves of the portrait through its plastic covering. So realistic I could almost believe I touched flesh and blood. Full sensual lips, strands of hair that carelessly framed his face. Dark slash of eyebrows, one raised, as if mocking the observer. His eyes, eyes that had long haunted my dreamtime, staring directly into my own.

I must have gasped out a sob, for Felix asked, "Are you well, Ms. Moore?"

My fingers repeated their exploration, again and again. Across Ranulf's lips, his eyes, the curve of his jaw, the contours of his carelessly arranged hair. I imagined a wind rising off the sea to tug at his locks, imagined him turning away from his post to watch my approach with hooded eyes. Trying to decipher his expression, hoping he might—

"Oh!" I could almost understand the context of the images flooding my brain. Almost.

I gazed down at my seeking fingers, at the image seemingly smirking back at me.

How often, following my regression, had I attempted to sketch Ranulf—only to give up in frustration? The nose had never been quite right, the mouth too wide or narrow, his hairline, the width of his forehead somehow wrong, wrong, wrong.

Yet, the face in front of me was also wrong. Not in its execution, which was perfect.

But that's the problem, isn't it?

Medieval artists had no interest in accurately recreating the world around them, which is why their work can appear amateurish to modern eyes. Whether drawing farm animals or monarchs, they were interested in symbolism and elaborate adornments rather than creating a portrait that resembles a contemporary photograph.

No proper medieval artist would have drawn *this* Ranulf Navarre.

For the first time, I noticed the writing beneath the monochrome. One printed word: RANULF. And beneath that this sentence, written in longhand, *I mourn for my love.*

I felt lightheaded. Spots danced before my eyes. My body slumped; my forehead rested against the glass tabletop. An invisible hand squeezed my throat until I struggled to fill my lungs. Felix's distant voice ordered me to "Place your head between your legs. Breathe! Breathe!" He wrapped my fingers around a glass of juice and ordered me to drink.

More instructions. More liquids. More expressions of alarm.

Gradually, my head cleared.

"It's just such a shock," I managed, raising my eyes to Felix. "None of it makes sense."

Felix continued studying me, his expression a mixture of concern and curiosity. After my "episode" had dissipated and I could truthfully assure him I was fine, I urged him to continue.

"Tell me everything you know. I have to understand."

So, he did. The parchment, or at least the preparation of it, had been traced to the proper time period, though the ink was impossible to date.

When I pointed out that the style of the drawing was all wrong and asked whether it could have been sketched at a later date, he allowed it was "a possibility."

"But since the provenance of both the reliquary and drawing can be traced to the 1600s, that seems an inadequate explanation, doesn't it?"

Once more, I reached out, following each individual letter of Ranulf's name with still trembling fingers. All capitals, nearly two inches tall, with lines re-traced so often they could have been made with a broad tipped sharpie. I imagined the writer repeatedly jabbing the nib of her quill into the parchment. Angry. Frustrated. Perhaps she —because I knew it was a she—was making some sort of statement. Claiming Ranulf as her own? Or crying out with her actions: "Look at me! See me! Love me!"

Tears burned my eyes.

Felix focused on the writing next. While some form of Textura script had been used throughout the Middle Ages, this writing was clearly cursive.

"Nor is it composed in Latin or Middle English or Anglo-Norman French, as would have been the case," he continued. "The words are English, modern English. Imagine that! The style...the formation of the letters... all of it... could have been written yesterday."

Yes. Yes, I know that.

"And therein lies the mystery," continued Felix. "Which no one has been able to solve."

I licked my lips, as if I could actually speak, actually explain something I myself could not understand. When had I learned cursive? Third grade? Whenever, I knew the identity of the person who had drawn the portrait, who had brutalized Ranulf's name and penned that plaintive line.

The handwriting on a thirteenth-century piece of parchment that had long been tucked away inside an obscure reliquary, belonged to Magdalena Moore.

Belonged to me.

I FOUND CLUES, if not answers, the next day on Glastonbury's High Street. The shops were a mix of New Age, ancient religions, and a confusing blending of various mythologies. I lingered in front of one with a window display that included jewelry, crystals, a replica of a Cavalier hat complete with plume, wood carvings of wizardly figures, and a prettily embossed sign promising "READINGS."

Upon entering the shop owner greeted me with a smile. "Welcome!"

Like so many of the women I'd seen in Glastonbury, her long grey hair waved every which way, and her clothing was a mishmash of hippie and Renaissance with a velvet bodice and flowered ankle-length skirt. Rings, necklaces, a choker, two studs in her ears, and a third piercing through which dangled large, hooped earrings completed her ensemble.

While browsing the crowded but artfully arranged interior, I was aware of the shop owner's gaze on me. Hardly surprising since I was her only customer.

I'll have to buy something, I decided, feeling awkward under her scrutiny. *Perhaps a thank you for Felix and his hospitality.*

I wandered around the various displays, pausing to inspect the jewelry, which had a definite Celtic vibe.

"Knights," came a voice. "All around you."

I jumped and whirled to face the owner, who had moved closer to me without my notice. Her eyes, bright and sharp as a hawk's, swept my face, as though seeking something.

"Excuse me?" I said, my mind immediately flying to Ranulf. *It's just a coincidence.* Mentioning knights in Glastonbury was a safe bet, though the intensity of her perusal was disconcerting.

Then I remembered the sign in the window.

The woman was angling for a reading.

"One knight," she said. "Oh, very dark."

The way the woman said it scared me, as if she were an oracle dispensing judgment or dangerous prophecies.

"What do you mean?" I asked, deep-sixing my earlier skepticism.

The shop owner looked over my shoulder causing the hair to rise on the back of my neck. I imagined that if I turned, I would see *him*. As I imagined the whisper of his breath upon my flesh.

"Describe the knight," I demanded. "Tell me what he has to do with me."

The woman's gaze drifted back to my face.

"Have you ever heard of soul retrieval?"

"Pardon?"

"Sometimes a trauma can cause our souls to fragment, to be off in other spaces."

I pictured a baby part of me, wandering off in the darkness. Rather than laughing at such a ludicrous idea, I felt a profound sadness, an urge to collapse on the floor, curl myself in a ball and weep inconsolably.

"When that happens, we can feel lost in our own bodies and not quite engaged in our lives. Sometimes that is where our addictions originate, or depression and suicidal tendencies. Even PTSD. During the soul retrieval process—"

"I don't have time for a...reading," I interrupted, annoyed that she was trying to set me up for some mumbo jumbo performance.

"Ancient," the woman said, scanning my length. "The pain."

The woman spun away and disappeared behind a curtain covering the back entrance of her shop. Upon returning, she opened her palm to reveal a necklace with a pendant consisting of a white stone streaked with pink. The tightly linked chain coiled around it like a snake.

"Crystal, she said. "I've blessed it. Please take it." She extended her hand farther. "My gift to you."

Having no idea how to respond, I stared at it and her. I knew all about the healing power of crystals, that they were supposed to be transmitters to aliens or whatever. It all seemed like nonsense—interesting, but nonsense all the same.

Still, what if the woman indeed possessed a gift? Could she actually tap into other dimensions? There were people who could do that, Sherralinda notwithstanding.

"Did you really see a knight?" I asked, hating my pleading tone. "Did he have dark hair? Dark eyes?" Knowing I was behaving like the stereotypical mark, supplying the "psychic" with information—and not caring. If Glastonbury was as magical as promoters claimed, maybe I'd been guided here for a specific reason.

The shop owner nodded, though I wasn't sure what she was agreeing to, and she didn't further elaborate. Instead, she grabbed my hand, lifted it, placed the necklace into my open palm, and repeated, "Take it. Always wear it. You will find it useful."

Feeling awkward, I obediently slipped the necklace over my head and positioned it beneath my jacket and blouse so that the pendant nestled against my flesh. The shop owner nodded her approval, smiled, and retreated behind the counter.

I hesitated. Now I really, really had to purchase something—a gift for Felix. I decided upon a lovely abstract wooden sculpture that kind of resembled a forearm and clenched fist.

"Would you wrap that for me?" I asked, counting out the proper pound notes and coin for payment.

The shop owner covered the piece with tissue paper and tucked it inside a sturdy striped bag. Upon handing it to me, our fingertips brushed.

"Where from here?" she asked, her gaze once again piercing.

"Tintagel," I managed, searching for any change in the woman's expression.

Did her eyes narrow ever so slightly? The corner of her mouth twitch? "Do you see him?" I wanted to ask. "Is he behind me?" Instead, I headed for the door.

"Do not forget," the woman called after me. "Always wear your crystal. Always."

Ranulf Navarre

1264

I am the wound and the knife!
I am the slap and the cheek!
I am the limbs and the rack,
And the victim and the executioner!
I am the vampire of my own heart.
The Flowers of Evil

— CHARLES BAUDELAIRE

Twenty-One

Once again, I dreamed. Ranulf's face, perhaps made more vivid because of the drawing, invaded my head. Eyes black as the night skies, black as his soul, watching me. My nemesis. Destroyer of my world. Worse, I became trapped in one of those hypnogogic states that seem so disturbingly real. When I seemed to rise from my bed to watch armored knights on horseback, banners flying, racing across a narrow strip of land while the waters crashed below. Though a part of me remained anchored to my hotel room, I clearly saw Ranulf fling himself from his horse and stride toward me. I could not gauge his expression, whether he was excited or determined or angry, and felt myself shrink inside like a frightened child.

After swimming from half-sleep to full awareness, I wondered at my precarious state of mind. Increasingly, I appeared to be mixing up time periods, fact and fiction, re-stitching it all into a waking dream.

What is true and what is not? Sometimes it was hard to keep reality and fantasy in their proper slots.

This much I did know. If I couldn't reach some sort of satisfactory conclusion after today's visit and after querying a few local historians, I was done. I would fly home for the last time. I would lock away a lifetime of longings and delusions as securely as Ranulf's drawing had been locked away in St. Julitta's reliquary box.

I am too old to continue chasing ghosts.

Tintagel was within walking distance of my lodgings at Camelot Castle, a charming hotel romantically steeped in all things Arthurian.

The grounds of Tintagel Castle would open at ten a.m., so, mindful of the hotel receptionist's warning that the wind blows cold off the Celtic Sea, I dressed in wool slacks, a sweater and a windbreaker. After enjoying a full English breakfast, I set out, studiously ignoring the odd tingling I'd experienced off and on since my arrival, as if my limbs had pins and needles from where they'd gone to sleep.

Just another reminder, if I needed one, that since I'd met Felix Eastoft at Glastonbury, nothing felt...normal.

Other than the few cars outside Camelot Castle, the area appeared deserted. Probably too early in the season. My boots crunched on the shale; a feeble sun touched my face.

I'm here. Here! Tintagel!

Tintagel Castle was built half on the mainland and half on a jagged promontory overlooking the Celtic Sea. Time had eroded the isthmus that had once connected the two sections. A footbridge had been erected so that visitors could explore the entire promontory. The area was ruggedly beautiful—treeless and bare, with ground covering clinging like moss to great slabs of slate, scarred by the ruins of Richard of Cornwall's Arthurian obsession.

While today's buildings, those that had not tumbled into the relentlessly encroaching sea, might be little more than rubble, nature's landscape remained inviolate.

I am seeing what you saw, I thought, striding along the pathway. *What you and Lady Jane both saw. Breathing the air you breathed. Feeling the identical sun and the breeze. Hearing the screeching of seagulls, just as you did. The cawing of ravens. The barking of seals.*

As did you both.

I was assaulted by a sudden wave of dizziness and swayed, nearly losing my balance. Bending over, I placed my hands on my knees until the feeling drifted away like smoke in the wind. Cautiously, I straightened, gauging my equilibrium. Normal enough.

I continued walking, shrugging off the dizziness as the aftereffects of lack of sleep.

When did I first notice that something around me had definitely changed? The atmosphere had grown unnaturally still, the way it does before a tsunami. I felt as if I were moving in a bubble, isolated from my surroundings. Even the light was peculiar—the colors different, as though veiled by a mist or diffused through smoky glass.

Quit imagining things. You're fine.

But I wasn't. With each step, I felt more... vague... There was no other way to explain it. Like when you emerge from a fever or a particularly intense dream. Nothing seemed quite normal.

I'd felt this way before. Following my regression, during my first trip to England—as if I were floating between two realities, between the past and present.

Reflexively, I grasped the crystal pendant beneath my sweater.

"Always wear your crystal. Always."

"Knights all around you."

Feeling another wave of dizziness, I closed my eyes.

What is happening?

When I opened my eyes, I grew even more unsettled. The landscape shimmered, like heat haze rising from asphalt. I forced myself to resume walking. One foot in front of the other. Again and again.

The wave of whatever it was passed.

"It's okay," I muttered. "You're okay."

Liar. I hadn't been okay since I'd exited the taxi at Camelot Castle. A sudden tingling, an invisible blanket of sensations, wrapped itself around me.

"One knight. Oh, so dark."

You have been mine before...

RANULF.

Am I dying? Had my heart somehow exploded, causing instantaneous death? I imagined myself sprawled on this lonely trail, eyes staring blindly heavenward while circling, calling seagulls pooped on my corpse.

But the sea gulls had vanished. As had the ravens. And where were my fellow tourists? I'd not seen one person since leaving the hotel.

Like Snow Geese migrating to warmer climes, everyone had disappeared. No wind now, not even the slightest breath of a breeze.

The tingling increased. Different now. Beginning at the tips of my toes, rising up my legs and torso. Higher, higher until a thousand prickles warmed my face. Drifting upward and out the top of my skull.

Or the crown chakra, as Sherralinda would call it.

Sherralinda...all my exes...my friends...will they be sad when they hear the news? "Crazy woman dies chasing a delusion."

Another bout of tingling. No, numbness. Which was definitely one of the symptoms of a heart attack. Or maybe a stroke.

I closed my eyes, bracing myself for the terror that would overcome me now that I knew I was dying. So far, not really. It all felt surreal, as if happening to someone else.

But it's not. It's happening to me.

Gradually, the shimmering disappeared, though something had definitely changed. What? A subtle shift in the surrounding landscape? Yes. I also felt very different, though I couldn't pinpoint exactly how.

Looking down, I spied, not the veined hands of a well-worn woman, but smooth, supple skin. I blinked. The vision remained, though blurry, as if a film covered my corneas. I flexed my fingers. Small, delicate, with smooth knuckles. These were not Magdalena Moore's hands, not now, not ever. Next, I noticed my hiking clothes, which had somehow been replaced by a long-sleeved undergown topped by a brilliant blue surcoat. And my feet, peeking from the hem of my gown, were clad in short leather boots with the thinnest of soles and tied around the ankle.

Am I dreaming? Had I fallen on the path and hit my head—on a wide path made of rock? That was different from the path I'd trodden only moments ago. At least, I think it was moments ago.

Okayyyy. What is going on here?

An internal check on my reactions. Not as freaked out as I should be. I didn't even feel all that surprised. Was this what I'd been expecting, yearning for since my regression?

I resumed walking. My body felt smaller and slighter, as if I were somehow shrinking. My stride was more graceful, without the stiffness and clumsiness inevitable with age.

Interesting.

Even as I heard the first screeching of sea gulls, even as a breeze caressed my face, I raised my hands to my ears. Another non-surprise. My hair was caught in a crespine. On my "real" hair, which was jaw-length, a crespine would have drooped like an over-large pair of earmuffs. Obviously, the hair stuffed on either side of my ears and held together with a net of something or other was far more abundant.

So...

Physically, I'd somehow been transformed into someone else—at least until I could come up with a better explanation. In the meantime, I was still thinking like Magdalena Moore. Pretty much. At least I seemed to be. Wasn't I?

It was then I noticed the transformation in my surroundings.

"This can't be right," I whispered. I was standing in front of Tintagel Castle's gatehouse. Not a ruin but an actual gatehouse, with a raised portcullis and the porter's lodge above. I recognized all this, even though I'd only seen it in reconstructions.

None of this had existed for hundred of years. None of this could be *real.*

If I were on a psychiatrist's couch right now, the doctor would no doubt ask, "How does that make you feel?"

How *did* it make me feel?

I conducted a second inventory. Bewilderment, a bit of fear. But more than both, excitement and anticipation.

If this is a dream within a dream, please God allow me to linger awhile longer.

My thoughts also seemed to be undergoing some sort of transformation. How to explain? I was still processing everything as Magdalena Moore. Sort of. But the Magdalena part was more of an observer, impartially surveying my surroundings.

Impossible as those surroundings might be, none of this seemed impossible.

It seemed familiar.

What part of me is thinking that? What is happening?

Had I suffered some sort of traumatic brain injury? Seizure? Might I have somehow recreated my fictional characters, even brought them to life? Had I entered a different dimension? Like "The Matrix," which I hadn't actually seen and might not be relevant, but some sort of alternate universe?

I have been here before,

But when or how I cannot tell...

Unlike the poem, I did realize, though. At least the "when." Isn't this where my current trip had been leading? My entire life, really?

Passing beneath the portcullis, I heard voices from the upper ward, where retainers and guests were housed, where knights daily practiced their sword play and other martial exercises. While I'd learned that from research, now it was more of a knowing—as I instinctively knew the layout, say, of my Colorado cabin.

The more deeply I ventured inside the gatehouse courtyard, the more sharply my surroundings came into focus. By the time I reached Tintagel's stable, located to my right, my vision was perfect. I knew that the stable had stalls for twelve horses, including a huge black destrier named...

I knew the destrier's name, knew who he belonged to.

How can that be?

Several horses were tied in front of the stables, some with saddles, a couple bearing panniers. All with the dust of travel upon them. But no men or women.

Upon passing, one switched a tail; another, a dainty roan, swiveled its head toward me and nickered.

My mare. I know her name, as well.

The rest had their heads down, seemingly interested in nothing beyond being unsaddled and unpacked, fed and rubbed down.

A thought in the back of my mind: *They, at least, are real.*

Automatically, I veered to a vice located past the stables, leading to the battlements. No need to question how I knew its location. Or why I approached it with such certainty.

I had climbed those stairs many times. As had *he.*

The wind picked up. The curtain wall had been constructed so dangerously close to the sea I could hear its roar. I climbed to the top of the vice. Paused.

This is it.

Now, this very moment.

The moment I had waited for—for how long? Knowing what I would see, I turned my head.

There you are. As I knew you would be.

In the middle of the battlement, looking out at the sea. That wine-red jupon, belted at the waist since he wasn't wearing his sword. Exactly as I remembered. The curve of his long warrior's body as he leaned forward on a crenel, his gaze fixed upon the horizon. The wind whipping his hair about his head, hiding his face.

The way you hid yourself at Evesham. The way you fled me at Chilham.

I paused. My heartbeat hadn't accelerated, as it surely should. This all seemed so right, so familiar, what I'd been anticipating forever. And yet a part of me *was* terrified, wanted to race down those stone stairs and reverse my steps, back to Camelot Castle and to a contemporary early March morning.

Is this our beginning? Our ending? Are we running like hamsters on a wheel, endlessly circling round and round and round...?

I wet my lips, as if to call his name, though nothing escaped my throat. My left hand crept up to the crystal before reminding myself that it would not be there. Not in this century. Yet, there it was, warm and comforting in my grasp.

I would reflect on that anomaly later.

Two conflicting desires warred as I drank in the sight of my ... beloved? I wanted to race to him and throw my arms around him, to kiss him and claim him. And conversely, to creep forward, to approach him slowly, lest my appearance displeased him.

I opted for the second. Hesitantly, my tread stealthy upon the walkway. He could not possibly hear me above the moaning wind, the thundering waves. Yet I saw his shoulders stiffen. Ever so slightly, not so much that most people would notice. But I noticed. As I'd learned to notice everything about him.

He straightened and turned toward me. The wind slashed strands of hair across his face, as though still seeking to shield his identity. Impossible. *I would know you anywhere.*

Here you are. Finally.

Capturing me with those cursed, hypnotic eyes, eyes that had haunted me longer than I could remember.

Now I felt it, all my senses exploding. I couldn't breathe, couldn't think, could only stare at him, this man I'd chased down the centuries.

Ranulf Navarre's mouth turned up in the ghost of a smile.

"Welcome home, Janey," he said.

Twenty-Two

Ranulf took one step toward me, still too far away to touch me or I him. He was much bigger than I'd anticipated. But perhaps that was because I sensed I was physically smaller. Or perhaps because he was one of those who, no matter the circumstances, attracted universal attention. Someone, to use an overworked cliché, larger than life. Exuding such an aura of power, of supreme self-confidence, that I couldn't imagine any human being, or any act of man or God prevailing against such as he.

Force of nature, I thought, for the first time understanding the meaning of that second well-worn phrase. My former calm had been replaced by a jackhammering pulse and lightheadedness, as if all rational thought had been sucked from my skull.

Ranulf! Ranulf! Ranulf! Why did you so long hide from me?

Yet, hadn't I always known, if only in the most distant, darkest part of my heart that I'd refused to call to the fore, that I would end up here?

All this I observed as Magdalena Moore. As though I were watching a movie. But a movie in which I was so transfixed by the storyline that I experienced the identical emotions as the actors on screen.

Yet I was also Lady Jane, with all that entailed.

Our eyes locked; his mouth turned up on one side, as if amused by something—though not enough to favor me with a full smile. I remembered that exact curve; I'd sketched that exact curve, hadn't I?

Rather than speak, I crossed the distance separating us, leaned up on tiptoe—*How very tall you are!*—looped a hand around the back of Ranulf's head, pulled him down and kissed him.

That much I dared, though I knew *she* would not.

Clearly surprised, he stiffened before returning the kiss. Not passionately, as during foreplay, but welcoming enough.

For me, the feel of those lips against mine was like coming home. From war and plague and desolation to the only place I could belong. I would have been content to stay there forever, mouth upon mouth, wrapped in my husband's strong arms, pressed against that body for which I'd ached.

All too soon, Ranulf drew back. Laughing low in his throat, he said, "I trust then your journey was successful." Spoken in the Anglo-Norman French of the period.

I responded in kind, even while mentally translating to English. "Aye, lord husband."

Those eyes flicked down to my stomach and up again. "Let us hope the prayers of the Black Monks worked their magic. I grow weary of —" He shrugged and did not finish.

Immediately, I knew to what he was referring. His wife—pathetic Lady Jane—had once again been petitioning God to cure her barrenness. Bending her knee at some local shrine, dedicated to whatever saint, begging them to please, please intercede with God and allow her to conceive.

How well I, this new Jane, understood what a pointless task that would prove.

I HAVE TWO MAIDS, Lenota and Eve. Lenota is much older and wears a simultaneously disapproving and watchful expression. I know instinctively she has been with me since childhood. Eve, who possesses a sultry voice more suited to a siren than a sweet-faced lass barely out of her teens, had accompanied me to St Michael's Mount, my most recent destination. I know this because Eve, who is short—though she looks me square in the eye, which is a further reminder of my diminished height—fluttered about me upon my entrance to Tintagel's great hall, chattering so that I had difficulty keeping up, particularly when I still had to process everything from Anglo-Norman French to English and back again.

"When did ye change from your traveling clothes, my lady? Why did ye not summon Lenota and me to help?"

"Where have ye been hiding that surcoat? I've not seen it."

"I do love that shade of blue, my lady." No matter how innocent the words, no matter how they were delivered, Eve always sounded as if she were ready for bed sport. Perhaps she was, in an innocent sort of way, for her expressive green eyes repeatedly wandered to the man standing behind my husband. Col, Ranulf's squire. That much I'd also gleaned. Dark-haired and blue-eyed, with a body nearly equal to his lord's, Col was another strapping specimen of manhood. While Ranulf was in a class of his own, his fellow knights were undeniably impressive. They moved with the agility of athletes—lithe and graceful...and deadly. Yeah, I'd marched against Vietnam and agreed with the singer, Edwin Starr's, sentiment about war; what was it good for? *"Absolutely nothing!"* But in this century, everything about these men, from their mail to their swords and surcoats, their long hair and beards, to the ingrained arrogance that came from their positions as protectors of a kingdom, was *hot*.

Perhaps I should have written historical romances after all.

The afternoon passed in a daze. So many impressions, so much to process while groping my way through a world that was, surprisingly, largely familiar. Not only had I reconstructed it in my novels, but I was viewing much of it through Jane of Holywelle's eyes. Yes, Jane of Holywelle appeared to be her/my name.

I was not too overcome, however, to notice that, after my "reunion" with Ranulf, after I'd followed him to the great hall—two steps behind—he had deliberately abandoned me.

Undeterred, as soon as I could detach myself from those clamoring for my attention, I approached him. He was standing near the hearth fire, conversing with the retainers who had accompanied me on pilgrimage. When I slipped next to him, all conversation ceased. Col looked at me with interest, Ranulf with what could be polite indifference but which I sensed was annoyance, the other men with a mixture of respect and alarm.

While I might be Tintagel's lady, we women never intruded upon a man's domain simply to "hang out" lest we damage our reputations.

I was breaking protocol and didn't care.

Though I refrained from placing my hand on Ranulf's arm, our bodies brushed, and I fancied I could feel his heat through layers of clothing. I smiled at each of his men in turn and said the equivalent of "Don't mind me, continue," which was totally inappropriate.

After several moments of awkward silence, Ranulf shifted away so we weren't touching.

"What is it, lady wife?" he asked. Those dark eyes, fringed by lashes so long and thick they appeared false, hypnotized me the way a cobra hypnotizes its victim. His aloofness didn't matter, nor his rudeness.

"I've just missed you so," I blurted, not caring the nature of our audience.

What did matter was that Ranulf slowly, deliberately turned his back to me.

His response was clear enough. Even without words, I got the message.

Twenty-Three

Glorious, glorious.

I've entered a dream. The light around me was softer, the shadows greater, particularly with the smoke drifting up from Tintagel's central open hearth to darken the ceiling beams and dull the wall murals. Costumed—no, ordinarily dressed—men, along with a handful of women, were seated at three long tables topped by white linen coverings and early spring-cut flowers arrayed in jugs. A handful of pages scurried from cupboard to table bearing dishes; Ranulf's household knights, the others who'd accompanied me to St Michael's Mount all tucked into their food with gusto; a lone minstrel drifted among the diners while playing a lilting melody on his recorder.

As great halls went, Tintagel's was small and plain. Ranulf's scarlet banner, centered by a black hawk's head, hung from various poles, and tapestries that appeared more like modern-day drapes adorned the walls, providing a bit of protection against Cornish winters. The light from the fire pit and torches in their wall brackets suffused the scene with a flattering, even romantic glow, as if it were being filmed through a diffuser.

Ranulf and I were seated at the dais, close enough that our arms brushed when we shared our meal from the same trencher. Each time I felt a tingle of excitement, though Ranulf made an elaborate production of ignoring me. Which, in my deluded brain, meant he was as aware of me as I was of him.

I knew that I must comport myself as if I were Jane of Holywelle, behave as she would behave, but I was drinking up centuries of want, of wandering half alive until this moment, when I'd finally, finally found him.

Ranulf was so...not beautiful. He was just everything. Never had I seen the like.

But I had, so very long ago.

This is what you've been searching for. My gaze kept returning to him with a hunger that could not be sated. *This is why you never felt quite right, why you kept trying to recreate this world with a puny mess of words.*

I was so overcome I struggled to breathe.

Although Ranulf seemed to be enjoying our simple repast, I could only choke down a few morsels. The fish, the only meat allowed during Lent, was pleasantly seasoned, though I grimaced following my first sip of wine. Not so much at the quality. I wasn't a wine drinker in any century.

Beckoning to one of the pages, I handed him my goblet. "Please water this down and add honey." Imperiously ordered as befitted the lady of the manor. giving. Something was definitely kicking in—either research or memories.

At my instruction, Ranulf turned away from Col, with whom he'd been conversing, and fixed me with an appraising look. So, he *had* been listening. He need not speak the words for me to understand that he was calculating whether my aversion to wine might be due to a queasy stomach, which might therefore be due to pregnancy. I'd already noticed that, somewhere during my interaction with everyone from the scullery maid to Tom the Steward to ancient Father Abel, who drowsed over his trencher, their gazes slid to my stomach. As if they could see the fruits of my prayers in a handful of days. Was this what had driven Jane of Holywelle to madness? Did all of Tintagel yearn for an heir? As obsessed as I'd been with conceiving in my other world, here it was my husband. And his entire household.

I didn't realize I was continuing to stare at Ranulf until he arched a brow in unspoken question. Unable to contain the need, I reached over to caress his sleeve. His gaze drifted down to my hand.

"Where is your ring?" he asked, his expression darkening.

Left hand. Bare. Marriage band? "I gave it to the monks at St Michael's. In payment for their prayers." I responded without thinking, yet knew the answer was correct.

Thick black brows drew closer, signaling Ranulf's annoyance. I immediately felt myself shrink inside, though I resisted the impulse to remove my hand. Ranulf Navarre was not a wealthy lord. How desperate Jane of Holywelle must have been to relinquish her marriage ring in return for St Michael's intercession. More than desperate, I sensed, for Janey was taking hold of my emotions, as well as my thoughts. Desperate? Terrified? Both seemed right. But why? Such things I would ponder later after I'd settled in and understood the dynamics of Ranulf's and my relationship.

For now, I'll concentrate on being courageous. Strong. Assertive. Not weak. Never weak.

"How could I not give the Benedictines what is most precious to me in return for what is most precious to you?" I forced myself to hold his gaze rather than drop my eyes in shame. "I count that a fair trade." As if prayers could alter the insides of a woman's womb.

Was Ranulf angry that I dared allude to our lack of children? Or had that been a common topic of conversation? With the slightest shake of his head, he reached for his wine goblet, shrugging off my hand while doing so, and drank from it. Then, in obvious dismissal, he shifted his body so that he was twisted away from me in order to engage Col in conversation.

I felt bereft. Ranulf Navarre, 2nd Baron Navarre. My husband. My *raison d'etre*.

But I was an unworthy match for him. I felt it, even as I fought that feeling. That was *her*, not me.

Still...

You are a man made to war, to rule, to cause women to throw their hearts at you. Women like me who foolishly seek to tame the beast?

Absently, I wiped my fingers on the napkin resting on my left shoulder, while engaging in what would soon become second nature to me. My internal dialogue, reminding me that Ranulf Navarre belonged to me, and no matter the obstacles, I was here to claim him.

It wasn't until a page had arrived for the final handwashing and I had begun anticipating the next few hours when Ranulf and I would be alone in our chamber that I noticed a woman seated next to my maids at the lower table. Had "gypsy" been a word in that age, I would have pegged her as one. Her skin was even darker than Ranulf's, her hair blue-black, and there was something wild and exotic about her. Perhaps it was her eyes, nearly amber in color. Eyes that bored into Ranulf like a starving she-wolf.

My stomach roiled, as if I'd eaten something foul. A wave of such hatred consumed me I had to close my eyes until the feeling receded. Reflexively, my hand crept to my crystal and closed around it, seeking some sort of comfort.

Who are you? Why do you rouse such antipathy in me? Such dread?

But I knew, just as I knew the faces, if not the names of everyone in Tintagel's great hall. Gypsy was Ranulf's mistress. One of many over the years.

I could almost see their couplings even as those around me denied my accusations. "You imagine things," they said. Because of course they would.

My body trembled with a white heat. I wanted to take the contents of Ranulf's and our shared trencher and pour it over his faithless head. Or snatch the dagger he used to spear his slice of dolphin and do some spearing of my own.

"Oops!" I would say. "So sorry, *quell porc*!"

I shook my head, as if physically ridding myself of such thoughts. I was not Jane of Holywelle, not really. I might look like her and share some of her personality traits, but I was made of sterner stuff. I was not a mouse; I was not a victim, and I'd not traversed however many dimensions to repeat her mistakes.

I will make you love me. Technically, Ranulf had been unfaithful to that other Lady Jane, not me.

Knowing Gypsy would be watching, I leaned closer to Ranulf and touched my shoulder to his. Which immediately caused all other thoughts to flee. Amidst the aromas of food and smoke and tallow from the closest candles, I inhaled the faintest scent of the sea.

The same way Magdalena Moore had inhaled the scent of the Pacific Ocean on Husband Number One's skin so many years ago.

Reaching down, I rested a hand upon Ranulf's thigh, covered as it was by his tunic, and squeezed. That Janey would not have been so bold, but I was. I felt lightheaded at the very thought of what was imminent once we were alone in Tintagel's solar. *This* I could imagine quite vividly. *This* I had missed through men and marriages and eons.

Ranulf's reaction was definitely one of surprise. Another assessing glance from my face to my hand and back again.

Bringing his mouth to my ear, he whispered, "Janey, Janey. Whatever did those monks do to you, *ma petite souris?*"

My little mouse. I knew he called me that. Tonight, I would prove I was anything but.

I slid my fingers up his thigh and smiled at him from beneath lowered lashes. Provocatively, I hoped.

I love you. I want you. I've missed you. I can't wait to make love to you. For you to make love to me.

My soul trembled for his caress.

All this I hoped to relay with looks and touch. After tonight, I would be bolder with my words.

Ranulf and I finished our meal.

Gypsy glared.

RANULF NAVARRE DID NOT COME to our solar that night.

Or the next night.

Or the next.

Twenty-Four

Gypsy's actual name was Dyana. In addition to her side gig as one of Tintagel's housemaids, her main occupation seemed to be my husband's whore. Technically, as lord of the manor, Ranulf could pretty much have his way with whomever, but Gypsy/Dyana made no attempt to hide her infatuation. Or to treat me with poorly concealed contempt. Yeah, well, I might be consumed by feelings of jealousy and inferiority when in the presence of the lushly provocative creature who was in possession of my husband's penis, if not his heart, but I was still mistress of Tintagel. And Tintagel's great hall was in need of spring cleaning. On the first day, I ordered Gypsy to clear out its rushes all by her seething lonesome. After that, she was tasked with a daily sweep and scrubbing of the stone floors with a mixture of lye soap and water that hopefully left her hands red and chapped and coarse enough that my husband winced when she touched him. While Gypsy's duties as housemaid included tasks of a more personal nature, such as readying my bath, there was no way I was going to let her anywhere near me or allow her free rein in my—our—solar.

I had no idea where Ranulf bedded his whore, or even actually if he did. All I knew was that I'd spent the sennight since my arrival alone in our great bed. While it was common enough for a lord and his lady to sleep separately, save for when they had "sexual congress," Ranulf and I weren't having congress of any sort.

No wonder Janey never got pregnant. You never bedded her.

But I was not Jane of Holywelle.

I would approach Ranulf as if I were Edward the Black Prince planning a *chevauchée* against the French. Right now, I was on reconnaissance. After I'd gathered all the necessary information, I would map out my attack and then...BOOM! Ranulf Navarre wouldn't know what hit him.

FAMILIARIZING myself with Tintagel's routine was simple enough. Rise at dawn, a short walk to morning mass at the Chapel of St. Julitta, followed by the barest breaking of night's fast with bread and wine. After that, consultation with Thomas the Steward about the day's activities—which largely consisted of me listening to him and agreeing when needed.

If there was a market in town, my maids and I, accompanied by a male escort, crossed the isthmus and walked to Trevena, located roughly where the village of Tintagel was in my other world. Baskets in hand, we purchased extra staples like eggs, butter, cheese and salted fish. Sometimes merchants, passing through on their way north to larger markets, displayed their wares. It was then I purchased linen so fine it could have been silk—which was too expensive for a baron of Ranulf's means—in order to make my version of sexy lingerie. Thankfully, Janey's sewing skills were more impressive than Magdalena Moore's.

One of Trevena's merchants, who specialized in herbal remedies, also sold aromatic oils which I dawdled over, thinking to use them to sweeten my shampoos and soaps and perfumes.

"How lovely," I said, pleased when the merchant returned my smile.

But Tintagel had its own herb garden and mindful of the cost, I wondered whether I should simply discuss possible oils with Eve. She appeared to be in charge of tending our garden and was knowledgeable in all things plant related. However, the idea of such a discussion didn't settle well with me, though I could not think why. Did not *want* to think why.

"I will take this and this and this," I said, pointing to several fragrances. I was unaware that those aromatic oils would prove my secret weapon—and Ranulf's Achille's heel—in my seduction campaign.

Otherwise, during the day, we retreated to a corner of the solar where we spun wool fibers into yarn, mended clothes, embroidered and gossip. So many questions I wanted to ask about my husband, but I didn't dare, because Jane of Holywelle would know, wouldn't she? Good thing my alternate self had never been much of a talker. While performing various skills such as nalbinding—a precursor to knitting—I soaked in information about Tintagel, its inhabitants and my husband.

I was heartened by Lenota's frequent comments regarding my improved disposition.

"You be in far better spirits since your return from St Michael's Mount, saints be praised. And with a bloom to your cheeks. Now that all that nonsense is behind us!"

"What nonsense?" I wanted to ask, which would not do. I yet struggled to figure out the proper balance between Magdalena Moore and that insipid cohabitator of my brain.

Ranulf 's favorite nickname for me seemed to be *Ma petite souris*, my little mouse, which made me want to punch him.

Lenota caught me muttering, "Quit calling me that," causing her to comment, "Your lord husband once shared sweeter endearments."

"Whose side are you on?" I groused. Lenota was as lavish with her disapproval as she was with her praise.

"Ye can be a handful, m'lady, when ye've a mind."

It did feel that Ranulf had once lavished me with more tender attention, that his words had once been free of sarcasm. But whenever I tried to untangle that part of our shared past, an image of an agitated Janey flashed though my memory, shaking her head, stomping her feet and crying "No! No! NO!"

My psychic wires continued crossing. Sometimes I had difficulty sorting through what was me, what was Janey, and what was my imagination building false connections between the pair. I did know one thing. The longer I inhabited Jane of Holywelle's body, the more sympathy I had for her. Ranulf was the most frustrating man I'd ever been around, unwilling to yield, to offer me the slightest encouragement.

It's a good thing divorce is not an option here, I told myself, disregarding the irony of my many previous husbands. *You'd probably already have thrown me over for one of your floozies.* Though I wondered whether Ranulf was even capable of losing his heart to a woman.

Sometimes when we sat together at table or stood shoulder to shoulder at morning mass, I caught him watching me, but dismissed it as him sizing up me, his opponent, and figuring out how to outmaneuver me.

Or maybe, just maybe, he found me intriguing, an enigma he planned to solve in the privacy of our bedroom.

I preferred that interpretation.

It's only a matter of time, I assured myself during my long, lonely nights.

Knowing time was what we did not have.

By my calculation, this was early April 1264, which meant the Battle of Lewes loomed on the horizon. At Lewes, Simon de Montfort would defeat King Henry and capture his son, the future Edward I, effectively putting Montfort on England's throne. After that triumph, the Frenchman's end would come as swift and brutal as the downstroke of a blade.

In sixteen months, Simon de Montfort, my husband and all those who'd dared usurp Henry III would be dead.

Twenty-Five

Mid-April. On warm days I linked up several of Tintagel's children via a long leather leash and led them down a narrow path to what would later be called Merlin's Cave. Tintagel's cliffs and the Celtic Sea called me as surely as the endlessly circling gulls called to the earth below.

Although I enjoyed all the younglings, I had my favorites. Nicholas, with his wild black hair and mischievous personality, was the grandson of Sam the Dog-Boy, keeper of Tintagel's hounds; Emma, the laundresses' daughter, who carried a shabby doll with her everywhere, and Lizbeth. Ah, Lizbeth, my keeper of secrets. The daughter of a widowed chandler, the chubby two-year-old inevitably wound up in my lap as I sang simple songs, recounted well-worn fairy tales and adapted the plots from books like *Alice in Wonderland* and *The House at Pooh Corner*.

After allowing my charges to burn off some of their energy by scrambling over boulders, playing tag and hide-and-seek and tossing rocks into the tides, I clapped my hands.

"Story time!"

They immediately returned to settle around me, bare rumps unselfconsciously plopped upon the pebbled beach, legs drawn up, expressions expectant.

"Today I will begin with "Twinkle, Twinkle Little Star."

Lizbeth snuggled against me and popped her thumb in her mouth.

"I do wonder about stars," Nicholas said solemnly.

I'd just finished my version of Winnie the Pooh getting his nose stuck in a honey pot while a grumpy Eeyore accused Pooh—in Anglo-Norman French—of being a Bear of Very Little Brain when I heard the familiar thud of boots on the path leading from Tintagel's outer ward to the beach.

The moment I lived for. What a happy coincidence the children's and my excursions generally coincided with those of my husband and his squire who had incorporated swimming into their medieval version of Olympic training.

"Good morrow, m'lady," called out Col. Halting several yards away, he maneuvered his tunic over his head.

Ranulf acknowledged me with a curt nod and "Lady wife," after which both men unselfconsciously stripped down to their linen braies and short boots, folded their discarded clothing atop their towels and headed for the shallows. While the Church mandated that we women must never reveal our bare arms, more than a hint of cleavage, or God help us, uncover our hair, nakedness was perfectly acceptable in certain circumstances.

Like now.

Be still my heart!

While Col was undeniably beautiful, it was Ranulf who commanded my entire concentration. His was a warrior's body, mapped by battle scars, which only added to the perfection of his broad, muscled chest, defined arms, thick thighs and calves.

My knight *nonpareil*.

"Sweet Mother Mary," I whispered.

"Sire! Sire!" Nicholas shouted. He and the other boys immediately abandoned me for their heroes, who paused long enough to swing a few about, lift the youngest on their shoulders and pretend to lose foot races to the eldest.

"Enough!" Ranulf finally cried. "How can we best dragons if we play games all the day?"

He and Col traipsed to the shoreline, stripped naked and waded into the shallows. Carefully, until the water deepened enough that they could dive and strike out with strong, sure strokes.

Watching the flash of head and limbs as the pair receded into the distance, I thought of the Bucca—sea-spirits similar to mermen. Locals swore they haunted Cornwall's tin mines and coastline.

Here I could believe it.

Here I could believe almost anything.

Although the rest of my charges had wandered off, Lizbeth remained snuggled in my arms. Bending close to her ear, I whispered in modern English,*"Hush little baby don't say a word, Mama's gonna buy you a mockingbird."*

How ironic, I thought, stroking Lizbeth's white, soft-as-thistledown hair. *Here I am singing my favorite lullaby, just as I wished so long ago.*

Only not to my child and not in my century.

Ranulf and Col swam until they neared a scattering of small boats manned by fishermen casting their nets or twirling them overhead before expertly flinging them back into the deep.

The boats were their markers. After nearing them, the two men circled and headed back.

Bored with my attention, Lizbeth cried, "Up!", and wriggled free to join the other children who were exploring Merlin's Cave, currently at low tide.

Shamelessly, I watched Ranulf and Col rise out of the sea, drinking in every line and plane and swell of Ranulf's body, including the most intimate portion of his anatomy. Ranulf Navarre was just so achingly beautiful. Tossing his hair back with an impatient jerk of the head, he strode onto the beach. Rivulets of water plastered his body hair to his flesh, further accentuating his powerful torso and legs, and I nearly wept for the wanting of him.

The ache was so overwhelming, the compulsion to rise from my position cross-legged in the sand and go to my husband. To touch him, to bury my face against his shoulder, to place my lips against his chest so that I might taste him, breathe in his scent of sea and salt and sun in order to right the bewildering world in which I'd found myself.

Ranulf and his squire reached for their towels. In his usual lighthearted fashion, Col was finishing up some joke about a priest and a sick man, which ended with "I would appreciate it if Our Lord favored me a wee bit less."

This bizarre punch line was followed by Col's bark of a laugh and Ranulf's lower rumble.

I wouldn't quit my day job, Col, I thought, unable to hide my own smile. Not only was their laughter infectious, but the medieval sense of humor was so peculiar as to be perversely amusing. That is, until my all-too-familiar paranoia poisoned the moment.

Is this simply another pretext for you to ignore me? Or am I so insignificant you've already forgotten I'm here?

I couldn't believe that. Refused to believe that.

My hunger for Ranulf was wider than the Celtic Sea, a hunger that rippled to the farthest corners of the universe. I rose, drawn to him as surely as the sea creatures caught in the nettle-hemp of fishermen's nets. Unable to break free, pulled relentlessly, inexorably to my doom.

That ache had been with me forever, or at least since I'd been a young bride standing on Huntington Beach, inhaling the scent of the Pacific Ocean on the flesh of a man who was not Ranulf. The first of a long line of men who were not Ranulf Navarre.

Ranulf was bent over his clothing. Col watched my approach with wide eyes before swinging his gaze to his liege, whose back was to me.

"How fare ye, my lady?" Col asked politely, before quickly bowing his head, but not before I caught his half-smirk and the unhurried way he wrapped his linen towel around his hips.

Ranulf whirled around, towel in hand. Before he could react, I retrieved it.

"Let me tend to you, husband."

Col watched attentively.

"Are you my new squire, wife?" Ranulf asked. His tone was conversational, belying the sarcasm of his words.

Rather than answer, I dried his chest and pressed against him. While I could not feel his skin through my clothes and the long towel, which was more the size of a tablecloth, his nearness was a drug, feeding my addiction. I pressed closer, ignoring Ranulf's lack of response. I brought my lips to the point below his collarbone where his flesh was warmed by the sun and inhaled him.

I did not realize I'd wrapped my arms around Ranulf's neck until his hands slid around my waist, pulling me tight. I rejoiced at this small victory, reveled in the feel of him with only the press of our bodies keeping the towel between us. Until he removed his hands from my waist and raised them to my arms, firmly pushing me away.

"Janey," he breathed, one of the few times he'd actually uttered my name. His calloused hands remained wrapped around my forearms.

I stared into Ranulf's eyes, seeking what? Desire? An answer to why he ignored me? A flicker of recognition that had naught to do with wife Jane of Holywelle?

Do not tell me that you do not know, that you do not care. We had a connection. I saw you at the Chilham joust. I saw you at the Battle of Evesham.

Something tugged at my gown. I looked down to see Lizbeth, arms upraised, ordering, "Hold me!"

One last look into my husband's eyes. One last plea. "Please come to me." I begged Ranulf with my actions, with my eyes, with my body language.

What do you want from me? What more can I do? Fall to my knees like a supplicant at the shrine of a saint?

Why will you not end this game?

"Tonight?" I whispered. It was little more than a reshaping of my mouth, too soft for Col to hear.

But I'd done it. Ranulf heard me. He knew what I was asking.

~

ONCE MORE, he denied me.

Twenty-Six

I handed Ranulf his arming sword. Our hands met over its pommel, mine bare, his leather encased in mail. Dressed for traveling, he looked even more powerful, more invincible. As he would be this time.

Somewhere near Canterbury, Ranulf was supposed to rendezvous with Gilbert de Clare, Earl of Gloucester. The name Clare was familiar, though I assumed that was because of my reading. From one of England's most influential families, Gilbert de Clare was young, ambitious, and ruthless and would prove a major catalyst behind Simon de Montfort's downfall. This campaign, however, he would help capture King Henry and his son, Prince Edward.

Pondering forthcoming events, I felt a bit like Merlin—if Merlin had been a woman who could foretell the future, but only as much as she could retain from research.

I did not try to kiss Ranulf before his departure. The stings from his humiliations were too fresh. I was done rationalizing away his cruelty on the beach and elsewhere. I felt the iron doors around my heart inching closed. Ranulf's rejection hurt too much for me to continually lay my love at his feet only to have it kicked aside with a flick of his boot.

A couple of my previous husbands—they were growing dimmer,

blurring all together—had accused me of pouting. I preferred to call it brooding.

Today I was brooding.

"God keep you, husband," I said, unable to keep the sulkiness from my tone.

"You will be safe," Ranulf said, not having my convenient access to the future. "Until my return."

He gazed down at me, as if he would say more, but I refused to offer any expressions of concern or longing or weakness.

I am done with groveling.

Ranulf's men were already mounted; some carried banners, stiff on their lances, though there was no wind. Col remained close by, ever watchful of his liege. Or was he ignoring his bevy of conquests who hovered among the bystanders, including Eve, who quietly cried on Lenota's shoulder?

Ranulf swung up on his palfrey. I forced myself to place a hand on the mail-covered boot thrust into the stirrup, even though I didn't want to. Despite my bruised heart, I knew the Battle of Lewes would take place in mid-May, meaning he could be gone two months. While I was at least temporarily done with groveling, I was not willing to completely surrender after losing a couple of skirmishes.

When our eyes met this last time, I was stunned by the intensity I saw in his, like banked embers suddenly flaring to flame. Come and gone so quickly I might have imagined it.

Ranulf reined his mount, raised a clenched fist to signal his men, and they retreated in a jangle of harness, crotal bells, iron-shod hooves and the occasional curse. From the kennels, Ranulf's hounds began barking and howling as if begging their master not to abandon them.

I knew exactly how they felt.

Twenty-Seven

Time, slip-sliding away from us, like raindrops down a windowpane.

I'd finished sewing my ivory nightgown, which was more like a maxi slip with thin lace straps and a slit up the middle near my crotch. It was neatly folded and tucked away in my clothing chest, awaiting Ranulf's return.

With my husband so far away, I could think more clearly. *Once you're home, this nonsense will end,* I assured myself. *I will take command.*

Ranulf's mistress was problem number one to be resolved. I hated Gypsy, not because she was a horrible person—which I believed she was—but because she was *more* than I was. I hated the fact that she was so exotically beautiful, that she and Ranulf were shadow twins; that she was the one he chose to cuddle with, to make love to, to share private moments. While he fled from me like one diseased.

How many other women have there been? I wondered. *An endless parade?* That seemed right and yet not. When it came to Ranulf and his infidelities, to mining so much of our intimate relationship, including the early days of our courtship and marriage, my mind remained hopelessly muddled. And when I decided to call up certain parts of that, of our past so that I might better understand, I experienced a wave of nausea accompanied by such dread that I immediately backed off. Whatever Ranulf Navarre had done to me...to Janey...must be horrible indeed.

But I am no longer a victim. I'll not allow any woman to come between me and my Ranulf.

Summoning Gypsy, I dismissed her from my service and banned her from Tintagel Castle.

"I do not want you here," I said, making no pretense of politeness. The hatred in Gypsy's eyes caused them to burn with a feral intensity. Had not class traditions been so strong and Ranulf not left one of his more seasoned knights to act as my personal guard, I would have feared for my safety. I could imagine Gypsy leaping on me like a panther and tearing out my throat.

Stiffening my spine as if that would appreciably lessen our height difference, I said, "Return to your cottage and do whatever you did before becoming my husband's whore."

Gypsy seemed to grow and expand, like pumping helium into a party balloon. "You do na dare," she hissed, clenching her fists.

A protracted screaming fest would have released some of my tension, but if Gypsy really lost control, she could pin me down and demolish me with a couple of wrestling moves. Instead, I nodded to Sir Dinadan, my guard, and ordered him to remove her.

With Gypsy safely banned, I went about my wifely duties more serenely. In Ranulf's absence, I was in charge of Tintagel Castle, though Tom the Steward and our other servants, from chamberlain to scullery maid, were efficient enough to allow me to settle into a comfortable routine.

Which gave me time to concentrate on taming Ranulf. While Simon de Montfort and King Henry might be wandering about the kingdom raising their armies, I was marshaling my own forces in my non-military and admittedly scattershot way.

Although I could never compete with Gypsy's dark charms, I still believed Janey had not made the best use of her physical assets. I suspected her ability to fade into the background, to be dismissed as plain and unremarkable, had more to do with her timid personality than actual lack of comeliness. I hated sometimes feeling—and worse, even behaving—like a whipped cur, momentarily expecting the final kick that would end my misery.

Nope.

I am a woman in charge of my destiny—kind of—and I will act like it.

First, I took inventory of her/my assets. While Janey was short, she had a pleasing figure with nicely rounded hips, a slender waist and decent sized breasts, all of which would be nicely displayed in my makeshift lingerie.

Point in my favor.

My best asset was my hair, a lustrous golden brown with highlights generally only accomplished in the twenty-first century at the skilled hands of a salon stylist. When undone, the strands tumbled, thick and wavy, nearly to my waist. While a married woman's hair was supposed to be covered, I'd compromised by creating several translucent veils trimmed in ribbons and arranging my hair in one very loose braid down my back. (Upon first seeing me, Lenota had clucked and jerked like a constipated hen, while Eve vowed I looked like a princess.) Because shampoos were a dicey mixture of ashes, vine stalks, and egg whites, I devised my own, which I doused with various floral fragrances and which made my hair even more silky. Perhaps Ranulf, who, like all medieval men, was continually exhorted by priests to beware of the sexual power of unbound hair, would succumb to the lure of the forbidden and be irrationally aroused by mine.

After carefully inspecting my face in the polished metal mirror stored in a nearby chest, I wasn't horrified. Petite nose, a cupid-bow mouth, and my eyes, well, they weren't crossed or beady. Artfully used cosmetics would heighten my best features.

As I informed my less than enthusiastic maids, who saw no need for me to tart myself up.

Turning to Eve, I said, "Surely, with all your knowledge of plants and..." I waved a vague hand because I wasn't quite sure how most cosmetics were fashioned. "Anyway, mix up some herbs or something and make me beautiful!"

I smiled to let her and Lenota know I was being facetious. I did not understand the peculiar look that passed between my maids, but it made me uneasy, reminding me they were privy to secrets I should know.

However, Eve dutifully created some mixture containing soot for mascara, and using the same concoction smudged my lids after lining them with a delicate brush. For my lips, she applied a rose tincture of beeswax.

With Lenota peering over her shoulder, Eve surveyed the final product. "Lovely, my lady," she breathed, her earlier hesitancy forgotten. "When our lord sees you, he'll sweep you right into his arms." Sweet, naive Eve, who mistook minstrels' romances for reality.

Despite her earlier disapproval, Lenota voluntarily retrieved the mirror and held it up for final inspection. I had a sudden image of a distraught Janey/me weeping into the counterpane upon my bed while she and Eve stroked my back in a vain effort to comfort.

Which lessened my pleasure over the improved visage staring back at me.

"I am so happy you're no longer talking nonsense about the convent," Eve blurted, before Lenota cut her off with a warning glare.

Replacing the mirror atop a nearby chest, I turned to my maid. I had no idea what Eve meant. Was I considering making a donation to some local nunnery? Unlikely, if I'd had to relinquish my wedding ring at St Michael's Mount. Yes, desperate women could be driven to desperate lengths, but...

I can't simply question Eve. Not when I should know what she's talking about. Pretending indifference, I changed the subject, all the while cursing my hybrid of a memory, which remembered some things and erased others.

I did tuck "convent" away in my mental file cabinet, making a note to further investigate.

Twenty-Eight

April drifted by, slow and lazy. I explored as much as Tintagel as I could, from the basement buttery to the headland beyond its cluster of huts and loved it all. Only one thing gave me pause and for no discernible reason. The herb garden. Not the herb garden itself because I'd not explored it, though Eve and some of the children she conscripted spent many hours caring for the plants therein. The garden was hidden behind a stone wall bisected by a tall wooden gate, curved on top and held together by wide iron hinges. It was located past the kennels, mews, and kitchen in the southern portion of the bailey. Every time I neared it, or my eyes drifted there, I experienced the oddest pain in my skull, as though it was being squeezed in a vice.

Does that have something to do with the headaches Janey suffered? I wondered.

If so, I was glad I'd not inherited that particular affliction. Still, I was careful to skirt the area.

Most days, I took the younglings to Merlin's Cave or gathered them round to learn the alphabet and rudimentary counting since old Father Abel, their logical teacher, was obviously illiterate. Our bailiff directed the planting of new apple trees in the orchard beyond St. Julitta. Sheep were sheared and the wool readied for my maids and me to begin spinning. Lenota, Eve and I regularly trekked to Trevena, escorted by an ever-watchful Sir Dinadan, where we gathered the latest gossip along with household needs.

Life at Tintagel Castle was peaceful and surprisingly enjoyable. I seldom even glimpsed Gypsy. Her cottage was one of the largest in the cluster of huts adjoining Tintagel which housed day servants and tradesmen and the villeins who worked their small patches of land. Gypsy had placed an ale pole above her door topped by an ivy bush to proclaim that she was brewing and selling ale.

Which must be how she kept body and soul together.

One day, when feeling particularly vengeful, I accosted Father Abel. "Mayhap I should fine Dyana over the quality of her ale." With Ranulf gone, I was mistress over all of Tintagel. What good was power if you couldn't occasionally abuse it?

Father Abel, who preferred napping wherever he could find a comfortable spot to tending his flock, looked alarmed. "Is there something wrong with Dyana's drink, Lady Navarre?"

"I might say her ale's too weak, or it tastes like bilge water."

"But if 'tis not so, 'twould be a sin."

I relented because I'd taken care of the Gypsy problem and pettiness was unbecoming. Besides, I was made of far sterner stuff than Jane of Holywelle. I'd never let any of Ranulf's mistresses drive *me* to madness.

You should have cut off Ranulf's balls, I thought, silently addressing my other self, though without my previous contempt. Living with such a cold spouse and the humiliation of his full-of-herself leman would have lacerated anyone's soul. Increasingly, the lines between the original Jane and me eroded. I was Janey but not quite Janey. I found myself thinking both like her and like me, as if I had two conflicting people chattering away in my head.

On the first of May, I helped decorate the maypole and even danced around it. On May 14, the Battle of Lewes, cementing Simon de Montfort's power, took place more than two hundred miles to the east.

In the meantime, I awaited my husband's return.

Twenty-Nine

Ranulf and his men galloped across Tintagel's isthmus on their sweat-lathered stallions to the accompaniment of watchmen's blaring horns, barking dogs, and yelling children. Servants and family immediately poured out of Tintagel's various buildings to welcome home our conquering heroes. I'd barely been able to scurry to the kitchen and order food before Ranulf and his men strode into the great hall. With their coifs pushed back from dirt-streaked faces, surcoats billowing behind, and swords clanking against hauberks, I could practically see the testosterone flying off them all. God, these men. My version of medieval porn!

Disregarding Ranulf's and my awkward parting, as well as the accompanying hurts and humiliations, I searched among the knights for a glimpse of my husband. I spotted Col, surrounded by his fan club, the other men embracing wives or bairns or friends and...there he was, deep in conversation with Tintagel's marshal, no doubt instructing him on the care of their returning horses.

Pulse pounding, I approached my husband, who'd been joined by Tom the Steward and Sam the Dog-Boy. He appeared surprised when he saw me, causing me to hesitate.

Didn't Janey greet you when you returned? Isn't that customary? Am I committing a medieval faux pas?

"Welcome home, lord husband," I said, not caring. Reaching up, I cupped his cheeks and kissed him on the lips.

Ranulf raised a questioning eyebrow. Though he did not push me away, neither did he return the kiss. Still, his arms around my waist were heaven.

Col, who had sidled up to his lord, watched with open curiosity until a blushing Eve approached, dipping her head while offering a cup of wine.

Turning my attention back to my husband, I murmured against his dusty surcoat, "I worried for you." Not because it was true, but because it seemed the courteous thing to say. What was true was that I had missed him so very much. I realized the depth of it now that he was home. Overcome with happiness, the rightness of this moment, I pressed against his mail-encased body.

Ranulf drew back. "My men are hungry, lady wife. As am I."

Reluctantly, I relinquished our embrace to gesture toward the hastily assembled table topped with platters of meats and cheeses and fruit dishes.

"Afterwards, I'll have a bath readied for you in our chamber," I said. "And I'll tend you myself."

A repeat of that appraising look. Then he ducked his head and nodded.

BATHING WAS A COMPLICATED BUSINESS. A large wooden tub had to be brought out, along with several large sponges for comfortable sitting. Herb and flower-scented sheets were then draped around and above the tub, while cauldrons of water, carried from the kitchen, were warmed over a fire in the fireplace before being dumped into the tub. Much to the disapproval of everyone tasked with readying these elaborate accommodations, I insisted on bathing every other day. "Spit baths" were the norm but having to endure primitive toilet facilities was all the torture I could stand.

By the time Ranulf, accompanied by Col, opened the solar door, his bath was ready. I paused in my task of sprinkling chamomile, breweswort, mallow and brown fennel into the steaming water to watch my husband sink down on a stool.

Free of public scrutiny, Ranulf allowed his weariness to show. With the care of a mother tending her child, Col began undressing him.

When Ranulf had been stripped to his linen undergarments, I interrupted. "Thank you, Col." The sight of Ranulf's body had my stomach doing somersaults. "I'll tend to my husband from here."

Both men gaped as though I'd suggested a ménage à trois.

"What?" I wanted to say, like a pouty teen. Instead, I waited, as the lady of the manor I was, to be obeyed.

"Aye, my lady," Col said, studying me through lowered lashes. *No wonder Eve becomes moonstruck in your presence*, I thought, returning his stare. Col might not be as big and brawny as Ranulf, but the contrast of that dark hair and the bluest of blue eyes was a powerful aphrodisiac.

Col straightened and, after a final glance over his shoulder, gathered Ranulf's discarded gambeson, hauberk, surcoat and other garments, as well as scissors and razor to trim his lord's hair and beard. Bundle in hand, he exited the solar.

Leaving Ranulf and me alone. Reflexively, my hand crept up to curl around my crystal.

Ranulf rose from his perch. We stared at each other. I fancied I could hear his breathing, though more likely, it was my own. I licked my lips, as much from nervousness as desire.

What now? Dare I finish undressing you? Attend to you once you're in the water? Attempt to seduce you?

I imagined Ranulf in the tub, not quite large enough to allow him to stretch his legs, imagined sponging his back, washing that thick, beautiful hair, massaging my fingers through his scalp...

Three strides and Ranulf was upon me. Catching me by the wrist, he pulled me close enough that I could inhale his scent—sweat overlaying the sage of his deodorant, earth and leather and—I imagined—the faintest scent of the sea, which was ever a part of him.

Ranulf's fingers tightened until I flinched. "What game are you playing, wife?"

"What do you mean?"

"You know full well."

"I don't." Despite the pain, I was overcome by Ranulf's nearness, felt that hunger for him ignite in my loins.

How can you be so cold when I burn for you? How can you not know?

"Ever since your return from St Michael's Mount, you've been different. You act different. You even look different."

"Eve taught me how to use cosmetics. Do you like the change?"

Another jerk of the wrist, bringing us chest to chest. His breath smelled of wine and honeyed apples.

"You made it very clear after..." He paused, and when he spoke again, his voice was unmistakably husky, "You were eager to retire to a convent. By Easter, you said. Yet now you're all cow-eyed around me and pretending you've changed your mind?"

My jaw must have dropped somewhere to my chest. What was this? A convent? Did Jane of Holywelle want to become a nun? Could a married woman even do that? Had she been so beaten down by Ranulf's cruelties that she preferred to bury herself inside a nunnery?

"I was too hasty in my speech. That's what the Benedictines said, and that I should return to my husband."

Ranulf frowned. "Do you not understand? Do you think I've forgotten your hysterics? Your threats? Our conversation...after?" He swallowed hard and was silent, seemingly holding back...what? Accusations? Cruelties? Shared secrets we'd both agreed not to speak of?

I wished his words would spark *something* in my memory. Why was my brain overflowing with mundanities while I couldn't remember what was obviously a pivotal event in the disintegration of our marriage?

Ranulf dropped my wrist and stepped away from me. "I do not want you. You are useless to me."

I could not suppress my gasp. Never had I expected this. "Ranulf—"

"Better you embroider robes for priests or devote yourself to endless prayer or whatever you think to do." Then something seemed to snap inside him. "You were the one who said you'd rather fling yourself from Tintagel's cliffs than ever again suffer my touch," he raged, his eyes narrowed to frightening slits. "Have you forgotten that as well?"

"I do not want you...useless...", Ranulf had said.

I will not—cannot—cower before your wrath. Somehow, I have to sort out the meaning behind your accusations. Surely, Janey would not have...

But somewhere, deep within me, I could visualize that other me, face contorted, hurtling outrageous threats.

"I did not mean it. I was distraught. I've said such things before." Amidst the maelstrom swirling inside my skull, I knew that also to be true.

Ranulf's lips tightened. Yes, at times, I knew I had behaved like a madwoman. What had Ranulf Navarre done to transform docile, compliant Jane of Holywelle into a hysteric?

"Has it also slipped your memory that you approached me with your demand to 'serve the Lord?' And that you drank—" He shook his head, as if dislodging something unpleasant. With more force, he hurled the following questions: "What *really* changed your mind? What is this *really* about, wife?"

"I...I cannot lose this...lose you, not after all this time." Impossible to say more for the tsunami of tears threatening to engulf me.

Something flitted across Ranulf's face, come and gone too quickly to be read. "We've been married a decade, Janey," he said, his shoulders slumping, obviously weary of the conversation. "I need peace." More forcefully, "I need a son."

"I am still young!"

Such sorrow. Such humiliation. Such desolation.

And something more.

As badly as I wanted to deny it, Ranulf spoke truth. If we'd been married when I was fifteen, I would now be twenty-five. Not young by medieval standards. The current king's bride had been twelve on their wedding day. Eleanor of Castile, who would become Queen of England in less than a decade, had borne her Edward Longshanks his first child at age fifteen and would go on to present him at least thirteen more. Could I really blame Ranulf Navarre, who knew nothing of science, for considering me defective? (As I was, wasn't I? Hadn't at least four different husbands proven that?)

"Enough of this, Janey." Ranulf waggled his shoulders, as though ridding himself of an unpleasant memory. "I am here to bathe, not cross swords with you."

Signaling an end to our conversation, Ranulf stepped back to strip off his undershirt and braies. Fully naked, he turned his back and approached the tub. Signaling I was no longer his concern, if I existed to him at all.

"Ranulf!" I cried, ashamed of the desperation in my voice. How I despised myself for being so weak, for being just like *her*. Following him, I caught him by the shoulder.

Ranulf twisted to face me. His massive chest, dark with hair, was on full display, as were his long legs, and muscular buttocks.

I realized I was crying. How had that happened? Magdalena Moore seldom cried, but here I was desolate. No matter how I willed away the tears, they continued to flow.

"Oh, Janey," he said, his voice softer. You are too—" He let the rest of the sentence hang between us.

Too pathetic? Too stupid? Too homely? Too irrational? Too damaged?

"I would please you, husband. Let me tend you here. I would do that." I leaned over to scoop up a sponge resting atop the linen towels beside the tub. "I want nothing more than to serve you."

More gently than I would have expected, Ranulf retrieved the sponge. "I am tired, Janey. I simply wish to wash the stink from my body and sleep." He paused, then reluctantly, as if the words were pulled from him, "Later, we'll talk. When my head doesn't ache from weariness."

What now? Do I dare press you when you so clearly want to be alone?

Tears forgotten, I reached for his free hand and forced my fingers between each of his. "After you've rested, after tonight's celebration, will you come to our chamber? Spend the night with me?"

Ranulf's gaze dropped to my reddened mouth.

"Let me show you how I've changed." Softening that oh, so humiliating plea with a smile, a squeeze of my fingers. "Let me show you that I'll not fling myself off a cliff if you deign to touch me."

Unexpectedly, Ranulf reached beneath the transparent veil covering my hair to the loose braid beneath and brought it to his lips. He did not kiss it, but rather inhaled the lavender fragrance of my improvised shampoo.

"Aye," he said. Then, seemingly regretting his acquiescence, he tossed the sponge in the still-steaming water, stepped into his bath, sank down, and closed the curtains.

Shielding himself from me.

THAT NIGHT WE CELEBRATED. Flames from the great hall's hearth fire leapt high, playing upon the faces of men who'd grown lean from weeks on the march and who were as drunk on their victory as they were on wine. Though they'd washed off the grime of the campaign, most had not yet enjoyed the ministrations of a barber. Still sporting their longer hair and beards, they more closely resembled barbarians, certainly, than the vapidly pretty knights depicted by nineteenth-century Romantic artists. Reminiscent of Viking warriors pounding their cups on the table in Valhalla, each night feasting, each day striding out to fight from now into eternity.

Naturally, the Battle of Lewes dominated the conversation. An undeniable victory it had been, against a vastly superior royalist force. From their position on Offham Hill, Simon de Montfort and his men, all wearing white crosses, had watched King Henry, flying the royal banner, approach from Lewes Castle. Brutally, they'd smashed the hapless Henry, taken his eldest son Edward Longshanks hostage, and elevated Simon de Montfort to England's regent in all but name.

Like teenagers discussing their favorite slasher flicks, Ranulf's men endlessly recounted the gruesome nature of enemy deaths.

I was fascinated.

How can this be? I wondered, drunk, not on the wine, but on the scene unfolding before me. In my past life, I'd avoided any movie with onscreen violence. I couldn't even stomach boxing matches.

Yet, here I was, simultaneously horrified and fascinated.

The knights took turns speaking, all save Ranulf, who oversaw it all, his face bearing an enigmatic smile. Ranulf's men began by describing the merits or deficiencies of the weapons they'd wielded that mid-May day. From there, they'd moved on to graphic descriptions of decapitations, severed limbs, disembowelments—of both knights and horses—and...

Brutal. In the aftermath of the rout, Montfort's forces had shot Greek fire into the town of Lewes, setting thatched roofs aflame. Streets had been piled with corpses while the wounded were left to bleed out or crawl away as best they could. The rebels—meaning Ranulf—went house to house and slaughtered any survivors found therein.

For men I would have previously described as taciturn, Ranulf's knights were as gruesomely eloquent as any minstrel recounting *chansons de geste*.

Making no pretense of subtlety, I turned my head to directly study my husband. The candles caressed the hollows in his dark face, brightened the light in his eyes.

You look pleased and sated, like a vampire just finished feasting on your latest kill.

Ranulf Navarre lived for war. I knew that much. Unfortunately for my husband, while Henry III's uncle had been Richard the Lionheart, Henry's father had been John Lackland, who'd possessed minimal martial skills. Being a devout man, our present King Henry hoped to rule England via craftsmanship rather than muscle, which meant few glorious battles.

You must be doubly pleased with Lewes, carrying with it the promise of civil war. Yes, and more chaos to come.

Ranulf's eyes danced as they swept the table, finding the recountings headier, I suspected, than the unusual amount of wine he'd been drinking.

Too bad Ranulf would not be born a hundred years hence, during the beginnings of the Hundred Years War. Nor would he ride at the side of Edward Longshanks once Longshanks became king and delivered the blows to his northern neighbors that would earn him his nickname, "Hammer of the Scots."

You will be long dead by then.

Soon after, I decided to ready myself for my husband's promised visit. I squeezed Ranulf's thigh, my way of reminding him. Fearful that he needed a less subtle reminder, I leaned into his shoulder and stretched my lips to his ear. "I'll be waiting," I whispered.

Ranulf's gaze flicked to me and away.

He did not respond yea or nay.

Thirty

I wore my special gown and nervously touched the crystal pendant upon its chain, as if the stone might give me courage—or cause my husband to miraculously appear. The noises from the feasting and drinking had finally died away.

He had not come.

What a fool I was to believe your word meant something.

After Lenota and Eve had readied me, I'd sent them to sleep in the adjoining chamber.

"'Twill be just like old times," Lenota said, her lined face surprisingly soft. "Remember, mistress. Yours is not the only heart that's been bruised."

I frowned. My maid's gentle warning was both unfair and uncalled for. The only times Ranulf didn't treat me with contempt was in my fanciful longings.

I turned on my side toward the solar windows, the straw inside the top mattress whispering with my movement. The horned coverings that passed for windows had been removed for summer, allowing waves of golden moonlight to flow into the solar. The air was still, broken only by the lullaby of distant waves. A night so sweet and tender and ripe for lovemaking.

Obviously, the gods are against me.

But I am no longer patheticl Jane of Holywelle. I am the best of her and Magdalena Moore, which means I will rise above this latest disappointment.

Brave sentiments from someone who no longer knew who or what she was beyond confused.

Tossing back my sheets, I rose from my bed. The moon pooled upon the counterpane and the wooden planks with the threadbare tapestry I'd improvised to act as a carpet. Barefoot, my hair unbound, I moved to the end of my bed, staring at the closed solar door after the manner of Merlin who could conjure a person at will.

When I finally acknowledged the truth, that Ranulf had once again forsaken me, I cannot describe the depth of my sorrow, the crushing weight that settled upon my chest. If only I never had to draw another breath, if only I could expire—for then I would not have to admit the truth: Ranulf Navarre truly did not want me.

Through my misery, I thought, *Sort this through. Not the way you want it, the way it* is.

As Magdalena Moore, I'd had a lifetime of believing two things that were patently ridiculous: that somehow Ranulf Navarre had transgressed time to stalk me, first as a knight at a jousting event and then as a stranger on a battlefield. I'd woven those two events, magnified them throughout more decades than Jane of Holywelle had been alive, and concocted some sort of star-crossed relationship that had caused me to concoct a delusional familiarity, a mutual caring—*You want me enough to follow me through time*.

That assumption of a connection had led me to such unutterable foolishness.

My mistake.

I'd never felt so alone.

So bereft.

It was then I heard footsteps.

I froze, hoping that my pathetic imagination had not conjured noise from silence.

The door flew open, slamming against the opposite wall, with no heed to potential sleepers. Ranulf Navarre stood, framed in the doorway.

I didn't realize I'd been holding my breath until he strode toward me. Would he even bother to undress, or bed me fully clothed? Wouldn't that be the ultimate insult—acceding to the letter of my request while denying me what he knew I craved?

Ranulf halted a few paces away. I felt, rather than saw him scan me from tip to toe since I'd not bothered to light a candle or rushlight and it was too warm for a fire.

Two steps forward. Now I could see his expression, which caused my heart to flop like a caught fish. The look he fixed upon me.

Finally, finally...

Ranulf moved aside the hair that Eve had so lovingly combed and arranged. Slowly, he traced each of my gown straps with a calloused finger.

"What is this?" He pulled one of the straps away from my skin and caressed it between thumb and forefinger.

"I wanted to do something...special. To welcome you home. " My skin burned from the places he'd touched. "Does it displease you?"

He shook his head. "'Tis unexpected, that's all."

Ranulf traced down the front of my gown, the fabric so soft it snagged on his calloused palms. Around the curve of my hips, then upward, to circle my breasts.

My legs began to tremble. I wanted so to close my eyes, to drown myself in every sensation, but it was more important to track the expressions on his face, his incomparable face.

Ranulf continued his exploration. My breath quickened; my heart pounded so violently it must surely show through the thin material of my shift.

I felt suddenly overwhelmed by the impossibility of everything that had happened since that early March day when I'd strode into the past. When time had twisted in upon itself and coughed us up like driftwood on the shore.

Not delusional after all.

Here I was.

And there he was.

My pagan prince.

"Get on the bed," Ranulf growled.

I'd barely settled atop it when a naked Ranulf was upon me, bunching up my gown, burying his lips in the hollow of my neck, which smelled of lavender.

Ranulf raised up on his arms, his hair curtaining his face, to gaze down at me. Reaching up, I rearranged the strands behind his ears in order to better view him.

Overwhelmed with the enormity of the moment, I managed to breathe his name. All the doubts, the second-guessing, the misery had flown away at his touch.

"I have missed thee so." Fingertips traced the outline of his mouth, surrounded by his beard. "You have no idea."

"Have you now?" One side of Ranulf's mouth quirked, as if in mockery.

Ah, but if I expected a night of tender reunion, that was most definitely not what transpired.

"Take it off," Ranulf ordered, referring to my gown. He did not wait for me to obey but worked it so roughly up to my stomach the delicate material ripped.

Then he allowed his full weight to crush me, causing my crystal pendant to gouge my flesh.

Without finesse or care, he possessed me. Yet, despite the roughness, I felt such a primitive joy. *This is why I'd returned. This is what I must have.* How I had ached for this...this miracle, this second chance. With my tormentor. My betrayer. My obsession. My beloved.

Having said that, our coupling was far from epic. Or even particularly enjoyable. Ranulf claimed me the way a dog does when it lifts its leg against a fire hydrant—or its thirteenth-century equivalent. "You belong to me, Jane of Holywelle," he said through his body. "And I can do with you what I will."

The whole encounter lasted less than ten minutes. After which, Ranulf rolled off me and immediately fell asleep.

While I lay in the gradually whitening moonlight, staring up at the canopy.

Brute. So typical of you. Giving me what I ask for while withholding what I need.

Janey's thoughts leaking into my own.

Shifting upon the pillows, I positioned myself so that I could study Ranulf. Only then did I realize the enormity of the gift I'd been granted. Like fast-forwarding a flower from bud to bloom, my heart opened until I was overcome with love for this man. No wonder I'd found my way back in time.

How else could I reunite with my missing half?

The opened bed curtains caught the breath of a breeze off the sea; the risen moon caressed Ranulf's face and the area of his torso exposed above the bed coverings.

What caused Janey to threaten suicide rather than suffer your touch?

I could not fathom such hatred.

"Ranulf Navarre." I whispered his name before passing a hand over his face without touching. The profile that might have been chiseled from the rocks of Tintagel. In sleep, his mouth did not appear cruel, but rather filled with promise. Had I dared risk breaking the spell of the moment, I would have pressed my lips to his.

But I did not dare.

Thirty-One

Ranulf shared our bed for nearly a fortnight. I soon realized that my husband was not a tender or compassionate or sensitive lover. He took what he wanted without apology or explanation and with little care for my desires. When he wasn't doing his usual man thing of basically bypassing foreplay for the main event—he obviously did not buy into the medieval notion that a woman could only conceive if she found intercourse pleasurable—he was actually a rather passive partner.

Why? Later, I would look back and wonder and endlessly analyze, the way we do on the other side of some disaster, trying to figure out what went wrong, how we could have prevented the worst. At the time, I was too immersed in the wonder of being with Ranulf, of having him beside me or atop me or underneath me or sleeping next to me, to do more than note that he seemed to be holding himself back. Like a horse trainer allowing his filly her head until deciding to yank her up short.

I was so caught up in the bliss of our physical reunion that I ignored my intuition, which was screaming, "Take heed!"

You may be callous and insensitive, but I will change all that. I will fit those puzzle pieces of our souls together the way the original Janey never could.

On the most primal level, Ranulf must realize our connection, that while what was happening between us might not be magical in the fairy dust, hearts and flowers kind of way, it was certainly preternatural.

Hadn't he said, "You're different?"

That was code for "I know." Somewhere, buried deep, deep within Ranulf—that tiniest of acorns would soon burst forth full-grown as a towering oak.

"I believe you," he would say when I tearfully confessed the truth. Dark eyes filled with wonder, he'd whisper, "Your tale makes sense. Of course, we are star-crossed lovers. Didn't I also follow you across time?"

The more we're together, the more I make love to you, the more quickly that knowledge will surface.

Each night I awaited Ranulf at the foot of our bed. Each night I wore my linen slip. Each night my husband tore it from me. Each morning I mended the damage. Regarding it as a love bite, his mark of possession.

Each night Eve arranged my hair to fall free. Ranulf would bury his fingers in its strands and bring them to his lips. He seemed to love its fragrance, as he loved the fragrance of the rose or whatever flowered oil I'd add to the ointment I rubbed into my skin before each tryst. He reminded me of the Disney cartoon "Ferdinand the Bull," who wanted only to smell flowers all the live long day.

How simple men are, I thought smugly. *How simple my husband.*

"What?" Ranulf asked once, when he caught me smiling over the image of him as Ferdinand lounging among a meadow of wildflowers. He had wound long strands of hair around his fist and tugged me closer to his face.

"What, Janey?" he repeated, his grip tightening.

Shaking my head, I took the opportunity to claim his lips, for Ranulf was miserly with his kisses. Poor Janey, if only she had figured out the seductive qualities of hair! And flowers!

I imagined my doppelganger propping her prim little self in bed, her hair so tightly braided it stretched her scalp, or pulling her nightcap down over her ears and forehead until she resembled a monkey.

Jesus, Janey, lighten up. No wonder Ranulf couldn't stand you.

How naive I was, believing I had so easily tamed the beast. Having no idea that I had already wandered deep into No Man's Land and was about to be annihilated.

That last night, I felt something deeper, darker, coursing between us. As if we were on the verge of bridging that centuries' gap.

Will this be the moment you realize we're something more than Ranulf Navarre and Jane of Holywelle making love in the darkness of an insignificant chamber tucked away in the backwater of England?

Reminiscent of that scene from the movie *Excalibur*, when Merlin casts a spell over Uther Pendragon so that he will trick the Lady Igraine, who is married to another, into copulating with him? Out of that coupling would come Arthur, the once and future king.

As you and I are the blending of past and future. Tintagel is the ideal place for these myths to come to life.

While nearing the peak of our lovemaking and I moved on top of him, I was very aware of how small my body felt against his own. Which made me feel simultaneously protected and vulnerable.

Remember this. Remember this is why you traveled back seven hundred years.

Ranulf must have felt the same, for once again, he wrapped both fists in my tresses and pulled me down to him. I felt the roughness of his chest hair against the softness of my breasts, felt the hardness of his pectoral muscles, breathed in his scent, so right for me and so different from every other man's—a mixture of sea and clean sweat and sage and the oil he sometimes used to tame his hair.

While we moved together toward fulfillment, I felt a sudden surge of power, as if I'd harnessed a million volts of electricity. That I could scream his name loud enough it would echo through the castle, from Tintagel's headland all the way to Trevena and beyond. So that people in the twenty-first century who were reading in their beds, drowsing in front of the ten o'clock news, preoccupied with emptying the dishwasher, or sitting on the edge of the bathtub while their toddler splashed among the soap bubbles would suddenly pause and think,

What was that? They would feel something or hear an echo, sensing that somehow the universe had shifted.

What a spinner of tales I was.

What a buffoon.

The next evening when Ranulf approached our bed, I was dressed in a body-hiding chemise. "My courses have started, " I told him.

A quick frown before Ranulf's face settled into that familiar mask. While I recognized the mask, I could never decipher the emotions behind it. He could be furious or indifferent or thinking about the Battle of Lewes or of training his favorite hawk. Who could say?

Ranulf stared down at my stomach, as though he might directly address it before spinning on his heel and leaving our chamber.

At one time, I'd thought sleeping alone was the worst thing that could happen to me.

Not so.

The next night, Ranulf returned to our bed.

Bringing the previously banished Gypsy with him.

Thirty-Two

Dead inside. Hating him, hating myself.

If somehow you and I find ourselves together in bed again, I will withhold everything but my body.

This was a betrayal too big to be forgiven.

I retreated to the small chamber off the solar and slept on a pallet beside Lenota and Eve. Whether Ranulf nightly shared his bed with Gypsy, I couldn't say. I shut down my ears the same way I shut down my heart. Lenota and Eve's worried looks and unusual gentleness wordlessly communicated the truth of Ranulf's actions. Each in their way, they were protective of me. Eve pointedly ignored Col, as if he were responsible for his lord's action. Whenever Ranulf's squire tried to flirt, she turned her back on him, which caused Col to increase his attentions on whatever female was closest to hand. Lenota reprised her role as mother hen, this time guarding her chick.

From my maids' reactions, I knew we'd been here before, that this was far from the only time Ranulf Navarre had heaped humiliation upon his wife.

"Rest," Lenota would say after supper, gently maneuvering me up the stairs to the solar as if I were an invalid.

"Lay, m'lady." She spread her hands above the counterpane, seeming not to realize this was where my husband and his whore had so recently tupped.

After removing my slippers, she ordered me to put my feet up. "I'll fetch a warm cloth dipped in rosemary and chamomile for your headaches the way you like."

I didn't have a headache, but they apparently plagued Janey. And I rather liked being fussed over, knowing that *somebody* cared. While Lenota tended to my needs, she often reminisced about a past that was simultaneously familiar and not, about my parents and childhood memories that reminded me of a book I'd long ago read and could still vaguely recall. I felt then the loss for parents I did not know in this lifetime, had not given a thought to.

Why must everything be so mixed up?

Once, when I must have been particularly upset, she spoke in an unusually soft tone. "I remember after we first arrived here, those first years, and how much my lord...your husband... doted on ye. How sweet he was, pulling ye into his lap right in front of God or man, he did na care, treating ye like his little princess. And all the laughter and happiness between the two of ye—"

I twisted around, for I was on my back, to glare at her. "What are you talking about?" Ranulf had never been anything but a heartless bastard. I would have remembered otherwise, so why was Lenota inventing tales? Before my maid could respond, my head did indeed begin a merciless throbbing.

"Please fix me a potion," I said to Eve, cutting short Lenota's fantasies. "Something so I might rest."

Did I imagine the alarmed look that flashed across her innocent face? Apparently, some parts of my memory continued to play hide-and-seek.

Eve stumbled an "Aye, my lady," and hurried to obey. What I did not imagine was her substituting mead for a medicinal drink. While common belief holds medieval medicine was all superstition, many natural products *were* efficacious. Eve would understand how to soothe a headache, so why had she chosen a placebo? However, I was too overwrought to question her.

Like other animals, medieval man rose with the sun and bedded down with the dark. Which meant our days were much longer now, and since I slept so poorly, I did not really need any potion to doze off, at least after my whirling mind collapsed in exhaustion. Even in sleep, I fancied I could smell the betrayer and his whore on the sheets. *Our* sheets.

What a masochist I am becoming.

I did my crying alone on the parapets, letting the wind dry my tears so that no one would see. I felt myself slipping into that old Janey, allowing myself to drown in the cruelty of Ranulf, felt my soul being crushed, felt that familiar obsession, but I could not allow myself to retreat into weeping and headaches and depression.

I can't be like her.

I was not ready yet to say that I hated Ranulf Navarre, to threaten flinging myself into the tides, but I understood my alter ego's despair.

Still, I was not Janey.

I will reason through your treachery, and I will devise a successful counter offensive.

I couldn't ask how Janey had reacted to similar humiliations, if she'd done anything beyond succumbing to some form of the vapors. Whatever she'd done, it hadn't worked.

Ranulf's Gypsy was like an infestation of bedbugs, resuming her duties as housemaid while simultaneously taking up residence in my bed. Everywhere in my line of vision, gloating at her triumph—for not even deluded me could pretend that my husband had not sought her out, had not directly countermanded my banishment. Simply one more reminder of Ranulf's contempt for me.

But I remained lady of Tintagel.

I will not cower from your mistress or avoid her. I will extract my revenge.

Think "Cinderella."

And me as the wicked stepmother.

Each day I gave her a litany of tasks that kept her running from dawn to dusk.

If Gypsy complained to Ranulf, he said nothing to me. Which left me quite full of myself.

How's it feel when he's atop you and every muscle in your body aches? By the time I'm finished, you'll swear off sex forever.

Now, what to do about my wayward husband?

How best to regain the initiative in our ridiculous war? If I slept much longer on that accursed pallet, I would be permanently crippled. Nor could I forever postpone a confrontation with Ranulf unless I simply wanted to surrender, which I would never do. What then, beyond impatiently counting the days until the Battle of Evesham?

"Soon you'll be dead, you bloody bastard."

That gave me a certain morbid satisfaction, except I would be stuck here in Medieval England for no good reason unless I could figure some way back to the future. I felt so trapped, trying to dig myself out of a seemingly hopeless situation.

I am not a victim. I am not like Jane. My omnipresent litany. Though, increasingly, I wasn't exactly sure who or what I was.

~

LATE JULY. Waves slapping against Tintagel's shore, hammering against its great slabs of rock. Lizbeth nestled in my arms while I stroked her hair and crooned our private lullaby. The other children, agile as mountain goats, played upon the rocks. These daily excursions comforted me, temporarily calming my chaotic mind.

My eyes drooped while I listed by rote all the things Mama would buy her baby—mockingbird, diamond ring, looking glass, goat, cart and bull and on and on.

Peaceful. Here I experienced a level of contentment denied me in every other aspect of my dysfunctional life.

Until the oaf who was my husband intruded. Since I always timed my excursions to avoid Ranulf, he always put in an appearance.

Do you think you can still tempt me? Are you so arrogant you believe the sight of your naked body arouses me?

Hah!

In your dreams, jackass. I am so over that. And you.

Today, when I'd spotted Ranulf and his retinue descend the trail for their daily swim, I'd pointedly turned my back, ignoring Col's cheerful, "Good day to you, my lady," followed by the rest of their nonsense.

I have no idea how long I sat on the rocky shore, cradling Lizbeth, repeating the lyrics to "Hush Little Baby." Like a video loop, while my eyes drooped, and I nodded off. Until I sensed a shadow fall upon Lizbeth and me.

Cloud passing before the sun, I reasoned vaguely.

"Up!" Lizbeth cried, jerking me awake. Struggling out of my arms, she toddled off in the direction of Nicholas and the others practicing handstands along the shoreline.

"Lady wife." Ranulf's tone warned I'd best pay attention to him.

I looked up. Ranulf looked down.

We stared at each other. I hadn't spoken to my husband since that night. Should he directly address me, I responded with a nod or ignored him. Everyone in the household knew who claimed his bed. Did Ranulf expect me to pretend ignorance? That I didn't care? That I was so browbeaten I would force a smile and utter words of acceptance?

I believe I'll just ignore you.

But his tone warned I'd best pay attention to him--and I was too conditioned to disobey.

I stood and faced him, though I refused to speak first, to surrender that small concession. Ranulf's hair was wet, and he was clad only in his braies. As if the sight of his bare chest, his clinging breeches would send my heart into palpitations. I remembered the last time we'd been here together, when in my stupidity, I'd thought to tame him and taste him and bring the beast to heel.

I folded my arms across my chest. We could stay here all day before I broke the silence.

"You are pouting like a child," Ranulf said, running a hand through his hair. "I grow weary of your foolishness."

Had this been the 21st century, I would have said, "Go fuck yourself. I'm filing for a divorce." Unfortunately, here neither was an option. Well, I guess I could tell Ranulf to go fuck himself, but he wouldn't understand the idiom and the rest didn't apply.

Scrutinizing the towering brute before me, so confident in his manliness, in his belief that I was clay in his hands, the helplessness that had dogged me since Gypsy's return dropped like a cloak from my shoulders.

"You disrespect me by bringing your whore into our marriage bed and you dare call me foolish?"

My first full sentence in weeks. Sufficiently belligerent. I liked it.

Ranulf's expression signaled I'd just said something mildly interesting. Or maybe amusing.

"This time you went too far, *husband*."

Like fighters in a ring, we faced each other. Gauging strengths and weaknesses. Should I unexpectedly punch him in the stomach with the off chance I might kill him the way Harry Houdini had died when he'd received a similar blow? Or maybe kick him in the groin?

Within a millisecond, I jerked my knee to slam Ranulf in the balls, hopefully hard enough to drive them all the way to his fucking, lying traitorous throat.

I'd barely had the thought and started the motion when Ranulf grabbed my rising thigh and deftly twisted it. I immediately collapsed on my side.

Hard upon the pebbled beach.

"You son of a bitch!" It emerged more a squeak. The fall had knocked most of the wind from my lungs.

I was like a fish washed ashore, gasping for the air that would kill me. Yeah, that was pretty much a metaphor for my current situation. Dying in the open air. I closed my eyes until the spots before my eyes disappeared, and I could actually inhale without pain.

Ignoring Ranulf's extended hand, I struggled to my feet.

"When was it that you decided you could disobey your husband?" he asked, taking two steps closer in an intimidating manner.

"When I realized you're a dirty, filthy, disgusting, rutting pig," I managed, still lacking the force to make all those adjectives effective.

Ranulf did not further invade my space. Rather, he studied me, as if I were some exotic creature that had wandered into his path.

"You never give up, do you, Janey?"

With that, he chucked me under the chin, turned his back, and returned to his waiting squire.

Thirty-Three

The beach encounter awakened my inner belligerence. While it was not my nature to be confrontational, it *was* my nature to be stubborn. If I could not best Ranulf Navarre in open combat, I would wage guerilla warfare—ambushes, sneak attacks, sabotage, hit and run. If necessary, I would employ them all.

I will *win. Or at least wrestle you to a draw.*

Though I must walk a fine line lest I push my nemesis so far he packed me off to a nunnery.

I still bedded down with Lenota and Eve. For some reason Lenota had become increasingly exasperated with me, even muttering, "Ye be bringing trouble upon yourself in your usual addlepated fashion."

Instead of stopping my ears, I waited for the sound of Ranulf and Gypsy's voices, the creak of the ropes that comprised the bedframe—all the sounds of two people committing sins that, if I believed in the medieval version of God, would banish them to one of the lower circles of hell. The pair did not occupy the solar every night, which, under other circumstances, would have made me happy because my deluded self could then hypothesize that Ranulf had grown tired of his leman and would soon renounce his randy ways.

Now, however, I needed an audience.

On the nights when Ranulf and Gypsy defiled our bed—when I heard murmured voices, followed by moans and groans that I, in my fevered state, fancied were enhanced to taunt me—I put my skills as an observer/guerilla soldier to good use.

After all was quiet and I fancied I could hear Gypsy snoring—how unladylike!—I rose from my pallet and crossed to the door leading from the antechamber to the solar. It opened with a slight scraping noise, which was good. I wanted to give Ranulf, with his heightened awareness, sufficient warning so that he would not awaken from a dead sleep to knock me senseless or gut me with his dagger.

After entering, I crossed to the bed. When the night was fair, the curtains were generally open. I usually circled the bed—all with an eye to the two mounds beneath the counterpane—and then exited. After leaving my calling card. If clothes were neatly folded, I scattered them across the floor. If the rushlight on the night chest still burned, I removed it and used it to guide me back to the antechamber. If the windows were shuttered, I opened them. All things a housemaid would not do and which should play with their nerves.

When the bed curtains were closed, I poked my head between the drapes. I figured that, even asleep, Ranulf and Gypsy's subconscious would register my presence by producing nightmares of ghosts. Or enormous watching eyes, like those of *The Great Gatsby's* Doctor T.J. Eckleburg. Imagining my nemeses' perplexity, I found myself smiling, even stifling giggles. What could it be, they would wonder? Buccas? Piskies? Some sort of Cornish troll?

Once I peeked through the curtains to see Ranulf, propped on the pillows, staring back at me.

"Enjoying yourself, Janey?" he whispered.

"Very much so," I whispered back, before exiting the room.

I actually kind of was.

One night, when the moans had been particularly long and lengthy, amusement was replaced by a red-hot fury. I could not erase the images of their lovemaking, of Ranulf's betrayal, of his deliberate cruelty.

There have been other times when you've been unfaithful, when you drove me/Janey near to madness by denying it. This time you'll not gaslight me.

After lifting the lanthorn from its perch on a wall ledge, I tiptoed to the door. Though Lenota and Eve were used to my meanderings, Lenota called out, "My lady?"

"Go back to sleep," I whispered. "I know what I'm doing."

I heard her grumble, "'Twould be the first time."

Once inside the solar, I crossed to the far corner where we did our spinning, sewing and nalbinding. Finding thread, needle and a half-completed glove, I grabbed them and a stool and crept to Ranulf's bed.

Tonight, the curtains were closed. I placed my stool on my husband's side, settled the lanthorn beside it and eased down on the wooden seat. From there, I picked up thread, needle and glove and proceeded to nalbind.

If Ranulf woke, he would see a mysterious light leaking between the curtains. He would also hear a disembodied humming. Because I hummed as I fell into the mindless rhythm of passing needle through loop and shaping my glove. Running through a repertoire of Beatles songs—from "I Wanna Hold Your Hand" through their greatest hits, intending to end with "Hey Jude," because the words were so easy to remember. Basically *"Nah, nah, nah, nah, nah, nah, hey Jude"* repeated five thousand times. By the time I was into my second glove, I'd forgotten my reason for being here. Or my anger.

Finally, I heard a noise and looked up to see Ranulf, leaning, head propped up on an elbow, watching me through a gap in the curtains.

Hmmm. Were the corners of his mouth turned up? Did he find me entertaining?

"Swine!" I hissed.

Ranulf actually chuckled. Beside him, Gypsy stirred.

Point proven.

Do I even have a point? I'm not quite sure.

Gathering my sewing, I returned it to the pile of gloves on the far side of the solar and, head held high, exited the chamber.

"Goodnight, Janey!" Ranulf called after me.

"I hate you," I responded.

Thirty-Four

Two nights later, I miscalculated. While the solar was quiet, I'd heard them earlier, so I knew they were once more cohabiting. Fancying myself to be a ghost or an Avenging Angel who would scare the shit out of them, I entered the solar. I imagined moonlight upon me, causing my semi-transparent chemise to shimmer like a shroud as I glided across the floor; the gasps when I was mistaken for a spectre come to haunt the pair. While none of that was true—it was a moonless night, the coarse chemise moved more like canvas than gossamer, and I was graceless in the best of times—I approached the opened curtains. Dark figures within. But not so dark that I could not make out Ranulf moving atop his whore.

I addressed the shapes. "I hope he does a better job of pleasing you than he did me."

Both of them jumped.

Still atop Gypsy, Ranulf twisted his head to me. "Jesu, Janey!" Then, probably after deciphering the criticism of his manhood implicit in my words, he added, "What did you say?"

"I said you are a boor, Ranulf Navarre, inside bed and out. All the fine looks in the world can't hide the fact that you have the lovemaking skills of a...gopher."

Geez, where did that come from? Am I having a flashback to Bobo le Blaze?

Ranulf didn't appear particularly upset by my appraisal of his bedroom prowess.

Are you too dense to understand the analogy? Does England even have gophers?

A naked Ranulf slipped off Gypsy to face me. He stretched on his side, said, "Join us?" and patted the space beside him.

Yeah, well, I'd read my share of erotica, and when you had a threesome, it usually worked out that the third party would discover, "This is fabulous!" "I like the same sex!" "Let's the three of us set up housekeeping and have orgies every night!"

"Not interested in becoming a porn cliché," I wanted to quip. But I'd probably slipped in too many anachronistic references for one evening.

Mind whirling, I tried to think of my next move, how I might surprise him, throw him off his game.

Because that's what this is, isn't it? Our demented game?

Wordlessly, I slipped into bed beside him. I heard an incredulous "Whaaa??" from Gypsy, followed by a string of very medieval curses identifying various parts of God's anatomy.

I settled myself on the pillows— which, incidentally, are way more comfortable than the foam lumps I'd endured in the twenty-first century.

Your move, I silently taunted my husband.

Turning my back to him, I settled in, as if preparing to sleep. A shift behind me. Was that Ranulf stroking my hair? Of course! My shampoo was rose-scented, as was the lotion I rubbed on my body, immediately transforming Medieval Oaf into Ferdinand the Bull. I ignored his sniffing, as well as the hand that slid over my waist, apparently to draw me closer.

Grabbing Ranulf's wrist, I pushed his arm off me. After a minute, he settled it again. Repeat. A third time.

"Touch me again and see what happens," I growled.

A chuckle. "Is that a dare, Janey?"

More huffing from the direction of Gypsy. When would she realize she was a bit player in the drama of Ranulf Navarre and Lady Jane?

I pretended to further settle, relaxing my muscles, forcing my breathing to even out. Felt the creep of his hand, inching once again across my hip and down my stomach, imagined Ranulf's mocking smile as he teased me.

God, we're like a couple of kids.

After his hand stilled, I reached over to lace my fingers through his.

Do I dare?

I didn't know how far to test Ranulf's limits, or when a lifetime of training would kick in, not to mention the fact that he had a perfect right to hit me. One well-placed blow and he could kill me.

Yet...

I raised his hand to my mouth, as if I might kiss it. Instead, I bit into the side of his palm. Not hard, but when he didn't react, I increased the pressure until it had to hurt.

Ranulf scooted closer until he was pressed against me, his torso curved to my back. "Have you mistaken me for a haunch of venison, Janey? Do you think to feast on me?"

I bit down harder.

"My lord?" came from Gypsy.

Ranulf laughed low against my ear. "You do amuse me, wife."

"Fuck you," I replied in modern English, knowing that with his palm in my mouth, my words were an indecipherable mumble.

Harder. Harder. My jaw began to ache. If one of us didn't stop I'd end up drawing blood. Or developing lockjaw.

Apparently tiring of the game, Ranulf somehow flipped me so quickly that I was on top of him before I could react.

Gypsy bolted from the bed with a shriek. Ranulf and I were chest to chest, face to face, nose to nose, gazing at each other.

I hated him so much at that moment, but that couldn't be. I couldn't have ended up here simply to be caught in a spiral of hatred.

"So, the little mouse has teeth!" Ranulf laughed and negligently, as if flicking off a bug, tossed me off him and onto the floor.

I considered poison.

Not enough to kill you and Gypsy unless—oops!—but enough to give you diarrhea or hives or major indigestion.

Perhaps I should order Eve to turn over the key to Tintagel's garden gate which she carried attached to her girdle so I could rummage through the shed where all medicinal remedies were prepared. But the moment I thought of that simple shed I'd not seen in this life, a brutal pain threatened to crack my head open. Well, then I would enlist Eve's help in mixing some marginally wicked potion. Though when I approached her, my horrified maid gasped, "My lady! You know you are forbidden...you must ne'er even think about any such things or you'll be needing to confess to Father Abel."

All righty then.

Increasingly, I pondered the possibility that the Universe had made a mistake and I needed to get the hell out of Dodge. Hoping to recreate the right set of circumstances that would whisk me back to the twenty-first century, I retraced my original route to and from Tintagel. Ordering my reluctant maids and Sir Dinadan to stay behind, I set out as close to ten in the morning as I could guesstimate. Clutching my crystal pendant the way a Grand Dame clutches her pearls, I walked to the area that would become the Camelot Castle hotel and looped back to Tintagel's gatehouse, all the while hoping, expecting a tingling of limbs, some shifting of vision indicating I'd once more passed between two worlds.

Nothing.

The impasse between Ranulf and me *was* broken, if not in the way I could have envisioned. With King Henry and his eldest son still in custody, times had grown increasingly unsettled. To combat the spike in lawlessness, Simon de Montfort had appointed loyalists in various areas to tamp down violence. Keepers of the Peace, he called them. Ranulf had been tasked with peacekeeping in this corner of Cornwall, so he and his men, armed and mailed, rode out to patrol the byways in order to maintain law and order. Translation: harry a helpless populace and play at war games until the real thing came along.

This time when Ranulf and his men gathered in the bailey, I did not hand my husband his arming sword. I did not wish him "God speed" or anything else because I was not there. After morning mass, I'd walked to Tintagel's headland to watch the sunrise cast the seemingly endless expanse of water in scarlet and mauve. I stayed there until I was sure my nemesis was far enough away to harass others than his wife.

Nor was I there a sennight later when Ranulf returned. His favorite hounds, Sturdy and Holdfast and I were exploring a secluded glen near Trevena, cool and shadowed and peaceful with waterfalls and the ruins of an ancient heritage. Without a master to direct them, the hounds happily chased scents and barked at whatever small animals they flushed from the lush grasses. Hearing a rumble like the beginnings of an earthquake, I hurried toward the noise in time to see Ranulf and his men thundering past, destriers straining, the black and red Navarre banner taut, knights leaning forward as if in a race to reach home. Ranulf in the lead, coif pushed back, hair streaming, and, I fancied, a wicked grin on his saturnine features.

I admit my pulse spiked. "Show off," I muttered. "You do not impress me."

Even though he did.

~

THAT AFTERNOON TINTAGEL Castle held the medieval equivalent of a Super Bowl party. After the conquering heroes had been fed, bathed, shed of their military gear, and attired in their usual array, they gathered in the flat area beyond Tintagel's outbuildings to show off their prowess in skittles, horseshoes, and hammer throwing to an appreciative audience. Some of the women plucked wildflowers to weave into garlands while keeping a watchful eye on their bairns. Tintagel's usual menagerie of sheep and goats, looking little larger than cleverly crafted toys, grazed; seagulls circled and shrieked; the wind off the sea brought with it the first hint of fall.

I do not want to attend. I do not want to face you in public or in private. Nowhere, no time.

But as mistress of Tintagel, I could not completely shirk my duties. With Sturdy and Holdfast at my heels, I reluctantly approached the festivities.

Ranulf was playing skittles, a game similar to bowling. He'd just taken his turn, knocking over several pins with a wooden ball and was doing a fake strut. Maybe some easily impressed female might say Ranulf looked kind of sexy in a full-of-his-own-masculinity sort of way.

Not me. "More like a giant rooster, I muttered, which caused Holdfast, who'd been walking beside me, to nudge my hand with his nose.

"Where have you been, my lady?" Eve had come up behind me, causing me to jump.

"Jesu! You nearly gave me a heart attack!"

Eve wore a garland of flowers and her face was flushed, probably from a combination of merriment and spirits. "Your husband has been asking after ye. He was most displeased with Sir Dinadan and accused him of shirking his duty."

A frowning Lenota chimed in. "Ye canna just go wandering off alone. Particularly during these wayward times."

As if I were an Alzheimer's patient, lost on my way to the bathroom.

Ever the peacemaker, Eve placed a garland of purple and pink flowers that she'd been carrying atop my veil. "I made this for you, my lady. How lovely, the way the colors bring out your eyes!"

At that moment, Holdfast and Sturdy spotted Ranulf and raced toward him, joyfully yapping. Ranulf, who'd been taunting Col, whose turn it was to bowl, simultaneously spotted me and his running hounds. First, he snapped the dogs into obedience via hand signals. Then he fixed his attention on me.

To my left, a cluster of knights bantered over a game similar to horseshoes, where they tossed rope rings upon a peg. Farther out, Tom the Steward was spinning round and round before he let loose his sledgehammer in the hammer throw. Silhouetted against the horizon at the top of the headland, a circle of children played a dancing game.

I wished I could be with them. Or far beyond, a tiny boat rocking like a lullaby upon the vastness of the sea. Anywhere but here.

Ranulf.

I wish, I wish he'd go away.

Something jostled my leg. Looking down, I saw Lizbeth, clumsily waving a wand she'd dipped in a pot and releasing a trail of soap bubbles. "Pretty, lady," she said, grinning up at me. "Magic!"

Grateful for the distraction, I bent down to Lizbeth's eye level. "How clever you are, to make all those beautiful bubbles!" I busied myself capturing some in my open palm and laughing with Lizbeth when they popped. All the while aware of my husband...and then I spotted Gypsy clustered among the women hovering round Ranulf and his men.

The afternoon seemed to darken. Or perhaps rage had corroded my vision. "Bloody bastard," I breathed.

"Buddy baster'," Lizbeth echoed, before toddling after her bubbles.

"Here, my lady." Lenota held out a mazer of wine. I shoved it away, hands made clumsy by a sudden shaking. Beyond stricken. Enraged, like those cartoon characters with steam coming out their ears. Gypsy, dark and exotic and voluptuous and a perfect counter to my husband/her lover. Ranulf's broad back was to her, which simply meant he'd been strutting about, playing cock of the walk for her benefit.

"Lady wife!" Ranulf, standing some twenty feet away, called. Loud enough so everyone would hear, alerting our audience that the lady of the castle had been summoned to greet her returning husband.

"Calm yourself, my lady," Lenota said at my ear. "You know how ye get when your nerves be jumping all about the place."

For God's sake! I wasn't a five-year-old who'd earned a scolding for getting mud on the hem of my gown. Still, as much as I itched to spin on my heel and stalk back to my chamber, I dared not ignore Ranulf's summons.

Readying for battle, I squared my shoulders. "Lord husband." Hating him for deliberately making me a spectacle, seeking to shame me before the world.

Col, who was as much Ranulf's counselor as squire, leaned over to whisper something in his ear. Ranulf nodded, then cocked his head, studying me. I forced myself not to squirm, not to fold my arms across my chest or ball my fists. When I fairly vibrated with fury.

Ranulf beckoned me forward, as if he were king.

Back straight, I approached, willing myself to walk regally, playing my part. Gypsy had moved close enough so that little more than a handspan separated them. As if she were Ranulf's rightful consort.

Is this some game cooked up between the pair of you, your plot to humiliate me?

Halting in front of my nemesis, I dipped into a deliberately graceless curtsy. "Welcome home, lord husband," I said, loud enough for our enraptured audience to hear. Upon straightening, I murmured, "I was so hoping you'd taken a tumble from Artorius and broken your neck."

Ranulf let out a bark of laughter. Col grinned, tossed the skittles ball in the air, and, making a great show of it, resumed their game.

I was not so easily distracted. Gypsy had attached herself to my husband like a cocklebur, telegraphing the message, "I am the one who shares Ranulf Navarre's bed, not you, meek little mouse."

At least that's how I interpreted her body language.

Silence stretched between Ranulf and me. One dark eyebrow lifted, as if saying, "What are you about now, lady wife?"

Defiantly, I raised my chin. I'd not be directly crossing swords with my husband, not today. But I would strike.

"Dyana!" I craned my neck so that I looked around Ranulf to his leman. "What are you doing here? Did I not dismiss you once from Tintagel Castle?"

For the briefest of moments, Gypsy's face registered her contempt before she schooled her features.

Quiet around us, conversations ceasing mid-sentence. Gypsy's gaze swept from me to her lover, seeking his intervention on her behalf. Ranulf remained stony-faced as if watching a play that might or might not hold his interest.

"You returned like a thief in the night, thinking to cause dissent between myself and...others," I dared not directly accuse Gypsy of what she'd done, which was displace Ranulf's lawful wife. A servant could not simply crawl into her lord's bed on a whim. She must be *invited.* And we must never spotlight Ranulf's part in this sordid drama, must we? Therefore, I finished with "I could have you pilloried for this."

"My lady." Gypsy's face paled. Then, with forced bravado, she said, "Lord Navarre called me back to my rightful position months ago." Insinuating that her position superseded mine.

I snapped, "You are mistaken."

Col's eyes widened; Ranulf had bolted his mask into place.

My words could be interpreted as contradicting Gypsy—or challenging my husband's decisions as ruler of Tintagel. Tension sparked between us like St Elmo's fire. Would I dare blurt out what this society's unspoken rules decreed must remain hidden? Or would I duel with Ranulf more subtly—using sly inferences and double entendres as weapons?

Neither actually. Tintagel was a tiny planet unto its own, far too small for secrets. I could lament to the stars and beyond that Ranulf Navarre had ruthlessly crushed my heart, and no one would care. Because they already knew.

I returned my attention to Gypsy. "If you are owed any recompense for your service, I'll have it sent. For now, you are not welcome here."

"My lord!" Forgetting herself, Gypsy touched Ranulf's arm, her gesture imploring him to act as her protector.

Ranulf gazed with distaste at the fingers clutching his forearm. The eyes he then raised to his leman did not hold anger, as frightening as that would have been. Rather, they were as cold and lifeless as those in a painting. *"I do not know you, I do not care to know you,"* they said.

At that moment, I felt sorry for Gypsy. Like me, like all women, she was at the mercy of a man, of men, of a ruthless system that expected us to bow our heads and obey, no matter the circumstances.

"Go," I said, even while pitying my former competitor in the secret caverns of my heart.

Gypsy's mouth worked, but she managed a curtsy and retreated through the crowd in the direction of her cottage. Defeated, humiliated, disgraced by a champion who had proven himself false.

Before I could enjoy my bittersweet victory, Ranulf jerked me by the arm and pulled me so brutally my feet barely touched the ground and my garland tumbled from my head. Making no pretense of propriety, he dragged me toward the great hall, quite a distance away.

Upon reaching the solar, he kicked open the door. Once inside, he shoved me away from him before slamming home the bar.

Then he spun on me. "How dare you disrespect me in front of my house. If you ever—"

"Do not threaten me, husband," I said, matching him rage for rage. "You have made me a laughingstock, you who cannot keep your fucking dick in your pants." Oops, really wrong century for several words in that sentence. I rushed on. "You delight in humiliating me, and I am sick of it!"

He approached me. I backed away. He advanced. Grabbing a nearby stool, I brandished it before me like a lion tamer keeping a lion at bay. "Don't touch me."

He batted the stool aside. I picked up whatever was nearest me, which happened to be a lanthorn, followed by several embroidery hoops, working my way backwards across the solar. Ranulf swatted everything away until I was reduced to brandishing a pair of scissors from a sewing box.

"Really, Janey?" More mocking now than angry. Two steps closer and he grabbed the scissors, easily twisting them from my hand.

Face to face, breathing rapidly. I was afraid of him and aroused by him. He was a storm—all cracking lightning, roaring thunder, pounding rain.

"You will never, ever so publicly humiliate me again, Jane of Holywelle. Must I remind you that I am your lord, your husband—"

"Quit shaming me with your whores and I'll be the most docile of wives." I felt it, *knew* it, imagined I could see the faces of all the women with whom he'd lain, circling round my head, mocking me.

"Jesu." Ranulf ran a hand through his hair in frustration. "From the way you carry on, you'd think I spend all my time bouncing from bed to bed."

"Don't you?"

"Even if 'twere so, 'tis not your business."

Momentarily silenced by such blatant hypocrisy, I finally sputtered, "It's a sin."

"'Tis expected of men. Even the priests know that. A husband who loves his wife too deeply is a fool."

How would you like it if I coupled with...." I floundered, seeking a name. "With Col?"

A muscle in Ranulf's cheek twitched. "Don't be daft. You're not allowed. And do not even think to—"

"Oh, aye, husband. I would be the only wife in history to have cuckolded her husband?"

"I would kill you both," he said, and I knew he meant it.

"I'll not have Gy—Dyana back in our bed."

"Give me a son," he countered.

With that, he'd cut right to the core of our dissension. The lack of a child. I felt myself collapse internally. Gypsy hadn't given him a son either, but I dared not say, "Could the fault lie with you? With both of us?"

All fight drained away, I slumped against Ranulf. Unable to call up more anger, needing a respite from our endless battles.

I could not have been returned to Tintagel in order to recreate some bizarre version of *The Taming of the Shrew,* could I? While I'd mocked Janey for being weak, my tactics were no better.

I was too exhausted to register surprise when Ranulf did not push me away, when he allowed me to remain nestled within his arms. Even tightened his fingers around my waist.

Chest against chest, our breathing gradually slowed until finally matching in rhythm. Grateful for the momentary truce, I closed my eyes. I was so tired of our pushing and pulling, of notching yet another battle in what had become our own war of a long season. Finally, I summoned the energy to pull away.

We faced each other.

"This hurts, Ranulf," I said. "Please, no more."

Thirty-Six

The news of Gypsy's marriage to a blacksmith from Camelforde probably reached me as close to "real time" as possible in our pre-electronic era. Though Camelforde was no more than six miles to the south, I knew I'd seen the last of Gypsy. As I knew Ranulf had somehow orchestrated the arrangement. Such was his power—though in fairness, smithing was a respectable, and often profitable, trade. Gypsy would be well taken care of.

There were other changes after our fight in the solar and my pitiful plea for mercy. Something between us had definitely shifted.

We are groping our way toward a new phase in our relationship, I told myself.

Whether or not that was true, I did not imagine the ratcheting up of the sexual tension. Whenever we shared the same area the atmosphere thickened between us, drawing us closer to each other via a thousand invisible, annoyingly persistent fingers.

I made a game of willing Ranulf to turn his gaze to me and whenever he did so, experienced a silly sense of triumph. At dinner, the merest brush of his sleeve against mine caused my body to flame. When Ranulf was out hawking, I climbed to the parapet to watch his peregrine circle the sky scanning the heather and gorse and scrub for prey. Marveling at the bird's merciless beauty, the way she rode air currents, homing in on the smallest twitch from a hundred feet up, dropping like a stone to snatch up her prize. I watched Ranulf return from hunting, with Sturdy and Holdfast and the other running hounds and alaunts streaking alongside him and his fellow riders, all of them, from master huntsman to beaters, reveling in the act itself.

I found it endlessly fascinating and endlessly frustrating. In the past six months, I'd been conditioned to expect betrayal and pain as soon as I lowered my guard.

Yet I longed for Ranulf and ached for him, though watcher me viewed everything through cynical eyes. Relentlessly, she whispered in my ear, "Don't be fooled. Don't be charmed."

While Ranulf did not sleep with me—Col told Eve they bedded down in the upper courtyard barracks—I figured that was a matter of time. The anticipation would merely make the moment sweeter. Not that I expected any grand passion to be unleashed with our coupling. I was not the naïve fool I'd been upon first arriving at Tintagel. We would not be creating our own version of Tristan and Isolde, only with a happily ever after. We were not lovers or spouses. We were sparring partners.

Still, there was that other, inescapable truth: by this time next year, Ranulf would be dead.

If we had no relationship, what would have been the purpose of my return?

What if I'd only been catapulted here to witness his death?

This glitch in time *must* mean something more. Mustn't it?

Thirty-Seven

September 29. Michaelmas, the Feast of St. Michael the Archangel, was only days away. With every leaf drifting from its branch, every blade of grass bleaching out and curling in on itself, I was reminded that Mother Nature was putting another season to bed. Michaelmas was considered the official beginning of winter, which, according to current dictates, lasted until Christmas. And while some days remained summer warm, we all felt the difference. Each morning darkness arrived a wee bit earlier and lingered later, an unwelcome guest settling in for the long haul. No wonder villein and lord alike implored St. Michael and his angels to protect them from the dark things that lurked beyond the fire's light, that crept across the land beyond our sight. No wonder cottars would soon be huddling round their hearth fires and trembling as the wind raged beyond their doors. While we were safer behind our stone walls, we too would implore St. Michael to fight for us against Satan and his legions. Even I was not immune to such primal fears. With winter at our doorstep and darkness devouring the light, all things seemed possible.

Michaelmas was also a time for the collecting of rents, the hiring of new servants, the harvesting of grain and the sowing of rye and wheat for next year. After which, we would celebrate, since medieval men and women were always up for some form of a party. In truth, our ancestors worked little more than half as many days as we so-called moderns.

I decided my contribution to the forthcoming celebration would be to paint a portrait of St. Michael slaying the dragon, which was a symbol for the devil. In my youth, I'd seen many a holy card, so I was well aware of the iconography surrounding this particular saint.

"St. Michael the Archangel defend us in battle. Be our protection against the wickedness and snares of the devil..."

I felt quite proud of my artistic efforts and grateful to Father Abel, who demonstrated the proper mixture of water, egg and natural pigments to create surprisingly vibrant colors.

"I once painted a triptych," he explained. "Turned out quite a pretty sight, all praise to the saints."

Nailing the parchment to a board that doubled as an easel, I sat on a bench outside St. Julitta's, alternately painting the figures I'd sketched and enjoying my surroundings.

Fayette, the housemaid I'd hired to replace Gypsy, was helping our usual suspects gather the last of the season's blackberries. A plump, cheerful lass with a mass of orange corkscrew curls barely contained beneath her cap, Fayette had gathered all the children round, and while handing out cloth sacks, warned, "Ye must gather them afore Michaelmas. Afterward, we dare na eat them since that's the day the devil spits on 'em."

Which had certainly captured the children's wide-eyed attention.

Engrossed in painting the blade of St. Michael's sword, I didn't notice Ranulf until he'd rounded the corner of the small building and was nearly atop me.

I acknowledged my husband with the barest dip of the head before returning to my task of applying a thin layer of glaze.

"Since when do you draw, lady wife?"

So, you don't believe in polite greetings? And Jane of Holywelle doesn't draw? Good to know.

"Perhaps this is the first time I've felt the inspiration." I fixed him with a half-smile, telegraphing that I was indifferent to his rudeness and had nothing to hide.

Ranulf continued studying the painting—a winged figure with upstretched sword and a booted foot upon the head of the dragon prostrated at his feet. "Why does St. Michael look like Col?"

I stared down at my effort, not seeing any resemblance. Before I could point out that my Michael was blond and had giant angel wings protruding out his back, Col approached.

He'd obviously been watching Fayette—whose name meant Little Fairy, which she definitely was not—bounce from child to child, issuing orders and encouragement.

"Did someone call my name?" Col nodded respectfully to me, though his gaze was full of mischief.

Of course. An eligible woman is within flirting distance.

"My lady wife appears to think you are St. Michael."

Col's turn to inspect my handiwork. "More like the dragon," he countered. "Though I've not such a wicked tail, at least last time I looked."

"Actually, I patterned the dragon after my husband." I circled the eyes with the tail-end of my brush. They were red flecked and strangely slitted, more like those of the goats that wandered around Tintagel. "Something about the eyes, wouldn't you say?"

Col laughed. Ranulf studied the painting, then me. "You returned from your pilgrimage with all sorts of new talents, didn't you, Janey?"

His gaze rose from me to Fayette, whose unruly locks had tumbled free of their confines, and the children, who surrounded her with their bulging sacks of blackberries.

There it was again, that accusation that I was Imposter Janey.

Having no answer to that, I ducked my head and returned to St. Michael.

ON MICHAELMAS DAY, my painting led our procession around the Chapel of St. Julitta, past the castle orchard and in the direction of the great hall, where we would dine on the traditional feast of stubble-goose, unimaginatively named because it fed on the stubble from harvested fields.

Behind my banner, attached to a pole carried horizontally by Nicholas and Sam the Dog-Boy's other grandson, Tom the Steward held aloft a creepy four-foot corn doll, which resembled something out of a Stephen King novel. The doll represented the spirits of the newly harvested sheaves of grain and was supposed to provide a resting place for said spirits until next season's harvest. If corn spirits were not accorded proper respect, they would withhold their blessing from the forthcoming crops, leading to sparse harvests, followed by empty bellies.

In our positions as Lord and Lady of Tintagel, Ranulf and I behaved with appropriate solemnity throughout the rituals. It wasn't until we neared the great hall and our forthcoming stubble-goose feast that Ranulf leaned over and, lips brushing my ear, whispered, "Wear your linen tonight. The one I like. I mean to have you."

"How romantic you are," I replied sarcastically, even as my heart began its all too predictable acceleration. But Ranulf had already turned his attention elsewhere.

Or pretended not to hear.

Lovemaking with Ranulf was simply combat of a different kind. Adjectives like tender or gentle or erotic did not apply to our actions and I'd been a fool to have hoped, even for a second, that the dynamics between us had changed. Instead, we each grappled with the other, struggling for dominance, for possession. Even when my body responded to his caresses, my mind rebelled.

"I'll not surrender to you. You'll not bully me," I silently chastised him.

Sometimes, I caught Ranulf studying me. Was he wondering, "Who is this new Janey?" Calculating his next move so that he might conquer me once and for all?

Well, my fine lord, the time for that is long past.

~

In mid-October of each year, Trevena held a fair in honor of St. Denys. I was stunned—and secretly suspicious—when Ranulf volunteered to accompany me. Trailed by Col and an ecstatic Eve, who had several hours with her dream man, we dawdled at various booths. The St. Denys fair was larger than the norm, with hundreds of people converging from more distant places. Clusters of men, most in tunics fastened by girdles of a decent quality, lingered on the outskirts, observing fairgoers rather than participating. I did not imagine the sullen looks or the remarks in Cornish—a language I certainly did not understand—that were directed toward us.

"Why do they seem so...menacing?" I asked Ranulf, repeatedly glancing in their direction. "Are they angered over your role as Keeper of the Peace?"

Ranulf's gaze swept the watchers, his expression unreadable. Ignoring my question, he turned his attention to a display of exotic spices and oranges.

After careful inspection, he chose one orange, approximately half the size of any I'd seen in the twenty-first century.

Tiny and outrageously expensive, I thought, when the vendor quoted the price.

"For you and your sweet tooth. " Ranulf extended the hand which held the unimpressive piece of fruit.

Once again, I was surprised. The orange might have been small, but it was marvelously succulent, tasty as any dessert.

My thank you, for once, was heartfelt.

I was further charmed when Ranulf lingered over a tray of fragrant oils, unstoppering each, commenting that the blue iris smelled like violets, the cowslip like apricots, and Lent lily like spring.

"But my favorite, *ma princesse*, is rose," he said, placing that and several other pots in my basket. "Especially in your hair."

Ma princesse? Where did that come from?

After our purchase of oils, Ranulf signaled to Col, who'd been patiently waiting while Eve bargained with a cordwainer over a pair of slippers. They stepped away from us, shifting so they had a clear view of the watchers. I could not interpret their body language, but I suspected Ranulf understood the Cornish tongue and relayed its meaning to Col.

Following their return, I asked, "Are we in danger?" Ranulf's response was to position himself at my side, while Col did the same with Eve and escort us from the fair.

Once we were on the road back to Tintagel, I tried again for answers. "Please, Ranulf. Tell us what is wrong."

A glance across Eve and me to Col. "No need to fret."

By unspoken agreement, they dropped a few steps behind us. My oblivious maid, with her chatter about her obsession, made it impossible to overhear the men's conversation.

"He reminds me of that dancing bear that performed at the fair," she said, glancing back at Col. "A bit grumpy, but ye couldna take your eyes from him, could ye?"

While no one but Eve would fancy the resemblance, I wondered whether I should approach Ranulf about a match. Col was older than the usual squire and apparently meant to forever serve his lord in that capacity. Which did not preclude marriage.

Shoving down my earlier unease, I passed the rest of our walk weaving matchmaking fantasies. I was so engrossed I didn't immediately comprehend what Ranulf was saying after we reached the great hall.

"...I do not know how long I will be gone."

What? My mind raced to reconstruct his half-heard conversation and realized exactly what it was Ranulf was telling me. He was leaving again.

"Remember, I am a Keeper of the Peace," he said, as though reading my thoughts. "A few heads need to be knocked about."

Ah, the men at the market.

"I don't want you to go," I blurted. Because I hoped to spare the countryside his idea of peacekeeping? Yes. But just as importantly—and more shamefully—because I hoped the more Ranulf and I were together, the more quickly I could convince him we were well matched.

We are making progress, aren't we? Why else would you buy me that orange?

Ranulf pulled me against him. "Will you miss me, *ma princesse?*"

"If I say yes, will you stay?"

He laughed.

And rode away with the morning light.

Thirty-Nine

It was upon his return from his organized terror jaunt that Ranulf disarmed me with the cruelest weapon in his arsenal.

Kindness.

He began to woo me. While my husband was incapable of being sweet, he was more solicitous.

"Are you tired?" he asked. "Too hot?" "Too cold?"

At table, he gave me his portion of bread pudding, which had become my favorite. He showered me with little presents—ribbons, an ivory comb, sewing gloves, Castile soap, and of course, more oils. We took walks to the Chapel of St. Julitta and the walled garden beyond with its stunted fruit trees, bee boles and rows of rubbled earth that in summer would be lush with vegetables. We skirted Tintagel's cluster of huts to the highest point of the headland, where we watched the endlessly changing face of the Celtic Sea.

During such times, Ranulf linked his arm through mine, rather than the opposite, for I had ceased initiating such intimacies. He definitely became possessive, which, God help me, I liked. Every time Col spoke to me or engaged me in conversation, Ranulf called him away or stared at his squire until Col bade me a quick "m'lady" and departed. "Hands off my property," he seemed to be saying.

Treating me as your favored hound or hawk is nothing to preen about.

Yet I did. And, despite knowing better, I allowed Ranulf to plant seeds of hope in my heart, seeds that were already pushing themselves above ground in the tenderest, most vulnerable of shoots.

This time the outcome will be different, I lied to myself for the millionth time. *Because I am different.*

~

"THE DAY IS BEAUTIFUL. Shall we go for a ride?"

I hadn't gone near Tintagel's stables since my arrival. In my other life, my only experience had been as a child, riding a pony-sized pinto pastured on my grandfather's farm.

Hoping to keep the quaver from my voice, I asked, "Like on a horse?"

Ranulf looked at me oddly. "What else? One of the milk cows?"

"Why would you want to ride with me? Are you going to run me off the cliff?"

Ranulf laughed, a genuine laugh that caused his expression to appear almost human. "Mayhap I would like to spend some time alone with my lady wife. Away from...distractions."

I knew better than to be charmed, just as I knew better than to think that I could mount a horse after decades. But Janey, with all her pilgrimage jaunts, must know, and maybe some sort of medieval muscle memory might keep me from too badly embarrassing—or killing—myself. Thank God, English women would not ride sidesaddle until more than a century later.

I had seen my palfrey, a dainty bay mare with the uninspired name of Rouge, on the day I'd arrived from the future. Rouge seemed unconcerned that I was an imposter. In fact, possibly sensing my terror, she might have done her own version of interspecies female bonding by considerately setting off at a gentle pace. At least until Ranulf spurred Artorius into a lope. Somehow, Rouge and I managed to trail them in a respectable manner.

The wind verged on bitter, a reminder that I would soon be spending my first winter in Tintagel. While Tintagel's shoreline was edged in turquoise, farther out the water was a dazzling blue, matching the sky. Once in the saddle, I had removed my gossamer veil, allowing my hair to catch the wind. Soon it had loosened my braid so that it flowed about me the way Ranulf loved.

We drew rein at the Chapel of St. Julitta. Recently, Father Abel had retired to a nearby monastery, and our new priest hadn't arrived, so we had the area to ourselves. After dismounting, Ranulf tied Artorius to an iron ring attached to a wall of the portico. Then, while I was pondering how best to dismount my patiently immobile mare, Ranulf stepped to her and extended his arms to me. After easing me down, he allowed his hands to linger and maneuvered me to his side until we were hip to hip. After tying Rouge next to Artorius, he followed me as I approached the headland.

Above us, orange-beaked Herring Gulls protested our presence, sounding remarkably like yipping dogs. A trio of goats, little bigger than Ranulf's hunting dogs, raised their heads from nudging at patches of heather and gorse to watch us with disapproving eyes. As if we were responsible for their meager pickings.

Upon halting, I sensed Ranulf coming up behind me. *Flash*. I imagined him scooping me up and tossing me off the cliff. For something I'd done. Something terrible.

What did you do, Janey? Unforgivable...

I could almost remember the reason Ranulf was so angry, why he might want to hurt me.

Suddenly fearful, I stepped back, only to feel my husband's arms around my waist. Pressing his chest against my back, he murmured against my ear, "Tristan and Isolde."

As if he had no idea what that caress, that whisper did to my insides. Not only banishing my fear but igniting such a yearning. Wishing this new Ranulf was the real one, that his solicitous behavior wasn't just one more cruel maneuvering.

"What about Tristan and Isolde?" I relaxed my spine against him.

"Lovers who canna be parted even by death."

Tintagel had long been associated with the pair, who'd drunk a magic potion which left them no choice but to fall in love with each other. Following their tragic deaths, a rose tree grew from Isolde's grave while a vine grew from Tristan's to wrap itself around the tree. No matter how often the vine was cut, according to legend, it grew again, signifying that not even death could separate the lovers.

I turned then, in my husband's arms, to study him. As if Ranulf Navarre could know that I had traveled more than seven hundred years to be with him. Could he? Had there been some truth to my experience at Chilham's joust?

Are you somehow capable of tormenting me through centuries? Are you more than you seem?

"Do you remember how it once was, Janey? That day when we walked to the orchard, and you plucked apples while I serenaded you with that recorder?" He did not speak with his usual sarcasm, but something that might be mistaken for tenderness.

"You are a terrible musician," I replied automatically. "You hit so many false notes I had to cover my ears." *Wait.* How did I know that? I didn't have a specific memory of Ranulf serenading me. Of doing anything kind to me. One of those lightning flashes: teasing Ranulf, collapsing into his arms, both of us tumbling to the ground, laughing. But when would that have been? Who was that man?

Is my longing making up an entirely different version of you?

Reaching out, Ranulf brushed strands of hair tangling about my face and neck.

Of course. The siren's song that was my hair.

"*I only know the grief that comes to me/to my love-ridden heart, out of over-loving,*" he recited, before flashing his teeth, dazzling against his dark skin, and chuckling. "It took me a sennight to memorize the entire verse. I paid a passing troubadour a week's worth of wages to teach me."

Poetry? Recorders? What are you playing at? Are you trying to implant false memories to lower my defenses?

I studied Ranulf and something stirred, deep inside, that softness I'd recently kept at bay. That softness which, should I allow its release from its lair, would transmogrify into a rampaging dragon.

"'Twas a long time ago." I moved my head away from his touch. So very long ago, it resided only in my fevered imaginings. "It might as well have happened to someone else."

"Someone else?" Ranulf echoed.

"I'm cold. Let us return to the hall."

Ranulf managed to look disappointed before smoothing his features and leading us back to our mounts. Who'd have thought Ranulf Navarre was capable of such an Oscar-worthy performance? I certainly did not trust this new, solicitous Ranulf Navarre, he of the charming smile, honeyed voice and pretty words.

I would not be fooled again.

YET I WAS.

Whenever Ranulf and I were in the same room, he sought me out, sometimes with his gaze, sometimes moving to stand beside me as a reminder, I suppose, of his ownership. When we conversed, he held my gaze rather than looked away as if bored or tolerating an empty-headed creature with nothing to say. Once, during supper in the great hall, he raised his goblet to me before turning away.

What does that mean? Are you toasting me? Offering some sort of acknowledgement? Issuing a challenge?

For days, I mulled over the possibilities.

More fool I. Had there been anybody with whom to share confidences—I couldn't bare my soul to Eve and all I earned from Lenota was cryptic remarks about events I didn't really remember—I would have confessed that I craved all these kindnesses, all this attention, and more. For always, in the back of my mind, was the tick-tick-ticking of clocks that hadn't yet been invented.

With each passing hour, my soul's cry grew louder.

Please love me.

Thus, we come to the night that changed everything. While changing nothing.

It was mid-November, with Advent Season just around the corner. I'd written about Christmas traditions in *The Lion and the Leopard* and *Lords Among the Ruins* and was excited to witness the accompanying festivities firsthand, to see how closely my research matched reality.

"I've something planned for tonight," Ranulf said. "When you bathe and wash your hair, I would like you to smell of spring."

Lent lilies, then.

"Col will come for you after. Until then, stay out of the solar."

I raised my eyebrows. *What is this about? Are you planning something amorous?* Even as the thought flitted through my mind, I dismissed it.

Do not trust him.

I don't. I don't.

But my traitorous heart wasn't listening.

After Eve and Lenota brushed my hair, dressed me in my slip-gown and applied the lightest makeup, Col escorted me to our solar door.

Nervously, I pushed it open.

"Oh!"

I gazed in wonder around the room, which was bathed in candles,

candles, everywhere—upon benches, niches, ledges and the folding table beside the bed. They did not smell of the usual tallow, but of the sweet, spicy and woody mix of more expensive beeswax.

Quite an expense for one of Ranulf's station. And all the more soul-melting since it was unexpected. As was the music emanating from beyond the chamber door, where one of Tintagel's lute players strummed and plucked a hauntingly lovely melody.

Expecting to find Ranulf, I crossed to the curtained bed, feet bare and ice-cold as I trod the mix of wooden floor and worn tapestries. Tintagel's walls seemed to have inhaled the chill from the winds off the sea. Despite the candles and a roaring fire from the fireplace, my breath hovered before me like ghosts in the air.

Our bed was empty. Strange. This new version of my husband always slept beside me, as he always had his way with me. His latest routine, including his "lovemaking," was perfectly predictable. Short and coarse and unfulfilling.

Sometimes, during these less than epic couplings, my mind lit up with images of Zak Ridarelli. *He knew how to make love to a woman.* Though such memories were like the tail end of a jet stream. Soon they'd evaporate altogether. Eventually, I might forget altogether what it felt like when a man set out to please a woman.

Though, to be fair, I could not really blame Ranulf.

Why should you behave otherwise when my body always responds?

Even as I reminded myself that I deserved more, it betrayed me.

This night, however, would turn out very differently.

Settling beneath the layers of covers, I luxuriated in the enchanting music from the lute player, imagining hand-clasped lovers strolling through meadows riotous with wildflowers.

Might that be Ranulf and me someday, after all?

Drafts caused the candle flames to flicker. The fire roared more hungrily than usual, as if a servant had fed it a night's wood all at once.

I wondered where my husband might be. Until I turned my head to the left and saw Ranulf standing naked, with his back to me, in front of the long, narrow unshuttered windows. Though he must be freezing, he gave no indication. Shafts of moonlight pierced him through the paper-thin horn covering the windows, caressing his massive back, those muscular buttocks, his long, thick thighs and calves. The uncertain play of candle and firelight over those shadowed planes and indentations created a chiaroscuro more suited to canvas than flesh and blood.

From the comfort of our bed, I watched him, motionless and magnificent in the lance of moonlight. While my lips formed his name, it remained unspoken.

Yet on some level beyond hearing, he must have heard me.

Ranulf turned to me. He crossed to our curtained bed, my Caravaggio painting come to life. Carefully, he folded down the covers, rather than tossing them back in his usual haphazard fashion and sank down beside me. At the touch of his bare skin, so cold against my cocooned flesh, I experienced the inevitable surge of desire. Even while mentally girding myself for war, since our every sexual encounter was a battle.

Because I could not, would not articulate my deepest desires, Ranulf could not know what I demanded, though it was quite simple. Some sign of gentleness. Some sign of love.

A whisper of music, soft and yearning, drifted to us upon the darkness. Oddly, tears pricked my eyes. I wished, how I wished, that tonight might indeed herald an authentic change in our relationship.

Ranulf turned to me. "*Ma hérisson piquant*," he murmured, the sides of his full mouth curving upward. "My prickly hedgehog." Tonight, it emerged as an endearment.

Leaning down, Ranulf brushed his lips to mine. So light, like the fluttering of eyelashes, like the fluttering of butterfly wings. Mirroring the fluttering in my stomach.

Don't be fooled, my mind cried, bracing for his usual careless claiming.

When Ranulf drew back enough that I could see into his eyes, I was surprised that, though they held no tenderness, neither was there the usual mockery or contempt.

Ranulf continued his gentle exploration, as if I were a new country in need of mapping. Gradually, my thoughts, which were ever on guard, ever calculating, ever preparing for the next humiliation, anticipating the next hurt, simply...ceased. I forgot to worry whether this was another of his games or that he was setting me up to be the butt of some monstrous joke.

Unbidden, a sigh escaped my lips. And another. My body felt boneless, as if it had melted into the mattresses.

"Do you remember, Janey," he whispered. "The way it used to be?"

I stiffened beneath him. Why would Ranulf ruin the moment by reminding me of a past littered with mistresses and cruelties?

"Do not speak," I ordered, silencing more unwanted words with my mouth.

Ranulf became more demanding. He kissed and sucked and nibbled and caressed me until I languished in an endless sea of pleasure. My body opened completely to him. As, curse me, so did my heart.

Don't let anyone tell you that we in the twenty-first century invented lovemaking, or all its attendant, darker pleasures. Ranulf Navarre did things to me that night, which, later, upon reflection, drove me to despair. Because his actions proved he knew how to pleasure a woman. He'd simply chosen not to pleasure me.

I lost track of time. While the room must have remained chilly, our bodies were so covered in sweat we tossed aside the covers. I was so ready, so lost in him I could barely bite back my plea to end this frustrating foreplay and make love to me. To cry, "I can't bear it if you don't."

Still, the words remained captured inside me. *You'll not have that part of me*, I vowed, even as the plea rose in my throat. While I'd never craved anything or anyone the way I craved Ranulf Navarre, I still could not thus debase myself.

Ranulf continued teasing, tormenting me near to the point of madness. When I tried to reciprocate, to urge him inside me, at least with my body, he replaced my hands at my sides. Or positioned my arms above my head and restrained them with one massive hand. Or, when I attempted to match his kiss, turned his head away.

Apparently one of the rules of this particular game was that I was forbidden to initiate anything.

Rather, I was reduced to squirming and biting down on my lower lip when shaken by my inevitable orgasms. Reduced to hoping that Ranulf remained ignorant of how completely he'd unraveled me.

Still, I did not cry out his name. Following each orgasm, I did not beg him to allow me just a moment's rest in order to recover. Or order him to fuck me, for god's sake.

All the while, in the midst of this exquisite torture, my rational mind laid forth its demented case, that after tonight our relationship would be transformed.

Ranulf's stamina appeared endless. Despite what seemed like hours of foreplay, despite his continued state of arousal, despite the way I pleaded with my body, he never penetrated me. He had done everything else, which only made me more desperate for the ultimate completion.

I hadn't noticed when the music ended, when the candles guttered and the fire burned to embers. But it was only then when Ranulf finally, finally settled his sweat-slicked torso atop me. My legs immediately wrapped around his waist, and I arched up to meet him. At that moment, he, his body, this act were the only things that existed.

Then it was that his words reached across the centuries to shatter me.

"Do you like that, Janey?" he growled against my ear.

I managed an incoherent moan.

"Tell me how much you like it," he demanded, shifting himself until he was positioned to enter me.

"I do, oh, I do," I breathed.

Somewhere in my consciousness, a tocsin clamored, warning me of danger.

We have been here before... Zak Ridarelli...But Ranulf isn't Zak in another skin, I know that much...

"Tell me how much you want me." Ranulf plunged into me, hard. Before just as quickly pulling out. "Tell me you will die without me."

Was that why I'd had such a visceral reaction to similar words uttered by Zak? Had we been replaying this winter's night in Tintagel? Or were Ranulf and I riding a current of time that bore us into the future and back again?

"Janey," Ranulf growled against my ear. "Tell me!"

The atmosphere immediately plunged a thousand degrees, as if I'd been dropped whole into an Artic blizzard. Gone was the haze of passion that had clouded my senses these past hours. The pretty stories I'd woven these past weeks, the lies I'd allowed myself to spin.

This whole elaborate charade had simply been another of Ranulf Navarre's games.

To remind me that, with or without him, I was nothing.

The nerve endings in my body shriveled. As did those tiny shoots of hope that I'd so naively imagined he'd planted in my heart.

"Go to hell," I sputtered against Ranulf's ear.

He laughed then, and before plunging into me a final time, whispered, "*Ma princesse*, we are already there."

Forty-One

That was the night I conceived. I knew it—the very moment it happened, during that demonic coupling.

This was a new twist. Never before had I experienced the knowing, because there'd been nothing to know. As Magdalena Moore, I'd hoped. I'd counted the days between menstruation. I'd tracked my fertile periods. I'd consulted doctors. I'd virtually chosen some of my husbands the way a prized stud is chosen to service a broodmare. Janey had prayed to St Margaret of Antioch, patron saint of pregnant women and childbirth, and bent her knee at shrines the length of Cornwall.

Both of us bargaining, in our own way, to a God who'd decided the answer was "no."

This was different.

I knew that Janey had been barren. But had she conceived, only to later miscarry? That didn't seem right, not with Ranulf taunting her about her diseased womb.

I clutched my secret close to me.

Certainly, I will not tell you, my accursed husband. You will find out along with everyone else when the fit of my clothes betrays my condition.

I owed him nothing beyond my eternal hatred.

Following the mockery of our lovemaking, the very next night, in fact, Ranulf brought a new woman to bed. This time it was our chambermaid, Fayette, who later slunk about her duties with downcast eyes and flushed cheeks.

"I do not blame you," I wanted to say. *"My brute of a spouse is simply making the point that I am worthless, that one vagina is interchangeable with another.*

Well he knew he'd broken what was left of my foolish, foolish heart.

If God were just, Ranulf Navarre would never live long enough to hold his son. (I fantasized carrying a boy.) The Battle of Evesham would occur a few weeks before my due date. And this time if monks brought me Ranulf's head the way I'd imagined in the dream scene of *The Landlord's Black-Eyed Daughter,* I would spit upon it. After which would I, like the original Janey, crawl off to die even as she'd cursed Ranulf Navarre through the centuries?

Apparently, that is how our script's been written. No reason to rail against what cannot be changed.

Which meant it was only a matter of time before my pregnancy, my phantom son, would take their leave of me.

Forty-Two

Despair gradually replaced anger.

I imagined taking a dagger to my wrists.

Sneaking into Tintagel's herbal garden and its shed where I would mix myself a concoction that would stop my heart.

At my lowest, I fantasized pressing a button that could blow me to bits, the way mortar rounds had atomized soldiers during WWI.

Over time, even despair leached away until I was simply numb.

I'd lost my ability to fight, to give a tinker's damn about anything. I was as beaten as Jane of Holywelle had been at her lowest.

I could not stand Fayette's unhappiness and assured her I did not blame her, but she was like a crushed kitten. Even her curls had lost their spring. Therefore, I changed up my response. I quit sleeping in Tintagel Castle.

Despite the colder weather, I was too humiliated to return to the antechamber and my maids a second time.

I was done, done, done. Beaten, beaten, beaten.

While Ranulf was holding manorial court away from where he might monitor me, I removed a pallet from a storage room and carried it the short distance to Tintagel's chapel. Later, I added blankets and a few foodstuffs. St. Julitta's new priest had not arrived, so I had the place to myself and needn't worry about being disturbed. Each morning I laid out the usual household tasks before disappearing until supper, for I dared not completely stir Ranulf's displeasure. Lenota and Eve tried to persuade me to put matters into perspective, alternating between pep talks and overelaborate acts of pity disguised as kindness.

"M'lady, 'twas only a handful of times," Eve said. "Ye mustn't dwell on it. Ye mustn't despair. Last time—"

"Ye know how flirtatious is that one," interrupted Lenota, referring to Fayette. "Making cow eyes at everyone that looks her way."

"I'll not blame a poor, hapless, *powerless* lass half my husband's age for seducing him. And you'll not either." Fayette was simply an unfortunate byproduct of the toxic sludge that was our...whatever it was.

Weather permitting, I sat atop a giant boulder jutting out from the rest of the cliff, a short distance from the chapel. Or stood on one of the great slabs of rock beyond the kitchen and great hall, where I'd watched Ranulf play skittles. Always with my gaze to the sea, observing the water hover and settle, rise and fall, before rushing inward to break upon the rocks. The ever-changing panorama overhead—the sun arcing across the sky like Helios in his golden chariot; the winter moon ghosting clouds stacked upon the horizon. The wind, cold enough to freeze my cheeks or rummage through my hair like a playful child. All of it vast and terrifying and beautiful, all of it reminding me of my insignificance. Yet, in my misery, I still felt myself to be the loneliest creature on the planet, not properly belonging anywhere, out of place and time, without anyone who cared whether Janey, Magdalena, or an amalgam of us both, existed.

I was ashamed of acting as though my suffering was unique. I knew better than anyone, certainly in this present century, what the future held—endless wars, marching one after the other; the annihilation of thousands of species; the despoiling of a planet that was far more beautiful in the thirteenth century than the twenty-first. The diseases and epidemics and all the attendant sorrows that accompanied the human condition. So much more horrendous than anything I could even dream of experiencing.

I have no right to hurt, I reminded myself a thousand times a day.

Yet I did. The universe had narrowed down to me, and out under the velvet blackness, I sometimes imagined that the rest of the planet had exploded, leaving me as its lone survivor. I was reminded of a "Twilight Zone" episode, where a henpecked husband who wants to be left alone with his precious books is below the surface in a steel vault when a nuclear war erupts. Upon emerging from the vault, the man realizes he's the only human left alive. He's ecstatic. He can do as he pleases! All those books to read, anything he wants to say or think or do without his nagging wife or mocking co-workers. Then he breaks his glasses. His eyesight is so poor that he can't see anything. Specifically, his beloved books. The one thing he most craves is forever forbidden to him.

"It's not fair," he cries.

As did I, in my selfishness, my absurdity.

Yet, that's how I felt. A creature without a century. Without boundaries or guideposts or clues explaining what this was all about. Why I was here. There must be a reason beyond something so inconsequential as reliving a failed relationship.

Mustn't there?

I wondered whether God or the gods or whoever mocked us were forcing us to trudge in an endless circle of humiliation, reconciliation, rinse, repeat.

How pathetic are we that we can't even invent new torments? That you have no arrows in your quiver beyond bedding other women and taunting me with your infidelities.

To which I reacted as predictably as Pavlov's dogs.

Are you right, Ranulf? Are we both in hell?

The only thing I knew for certain was that Ranulf Navarre would be dead in less than a year. Beyond that, what? Would I somehow end up back in the twenty-first century, then back here, bouncing back and forth, a pinball in some cosmic pinball machine?

If that were the case, maybe I should short circuit the entire demonic process by flinging myself off Tintagel's cliffs into the vastness below.

Forty-Three

Tintagel's Chapel of St. Julitta was always dark and cold, though colorful frescoes somewhat brightened its walls. Even during the day, the handful of narrow windows let in minimal light. The interior was largely bare, save for an altar, a railing separating priest from worshipper, and a couple of benches positioned near the portico entrance.

As usual, I drifted to the window overlooking the altar where mass was celebrated. Unlike the rest of the windows, which were covered with horn, this contained stained glass, its colors scattered like precious jewels upon the floor. I rather liked the idea of standing in the sanctuary, where Father Abel had officiated daily mass. Where women were forbidden. I generally slept here, very aware that the real Jane of Holywelle would never have dared such blasphemy.

"Lady Navarre?"

I turned. A short, slight stranger dressed in the grey habit of a Franciscan stood framed in the portico. A bright orange fringe framed his tonsure, which only added to the impression that he was impossibly young.

"Where is Father Abel?" I asked, suppressing the urge to retreat from the sanctuary.

"He remains in poor health. Lord...your husband asked that I attend to your spiritual needs. Particularly with the Advent festivities. So that..." He appeared nervous, shrugged, and blushed. "It being the holy season...and..."

Taking pity on him, I exited the sanctuary while he warily watched my approach.

Did Ranulf tell you I am violent? Mad?

The young friar licked his lips "I...I am Father Peter."

"Well, Father Peter, I suppose I will have to find another place to sleep." Though that would not be my husband's bed.

There was no way I would go anywhere near the cluster of cottages where Fayette slept when not with my husband. Where villagers would carry tales to Ranulf. Tintagel's stables, at least the hay loft, would be warm, but much too public. Tintagel had two caves—Merlin's, which filled with the tides, and a second located high on the promontory, which I'd nicknamed Lover's Cave since it was supposedly a meeting place for Tristan and Isolde. Lover's Cave would have to do. While I blustered I would rather freeze than slink back to my husband's chamber, I often fantasized about central heating and cranking up the thermostat in my Colorado cabin past ninety degrees. It had been months since I'd felt gloriously, gluttonously warm.

In the meantime, the Christmas season was full upon us. St. Julitta's was hung with violet, matching the violet vestments Father Peter donned to celebrate mass.

The first morning he welcomed us all at mass, Ranulf planted himself beside me. After that, I vowed not to attend again.

Father Peter did not scold or threaten me with damnation, but I often caught him watching me in the great hall during grace. His expression was unfailingly earnest, his words gentle. Sometimes he parted his lips, perhaps to initiate a conversation wherein he would offer advice or censure, though he never followed through.

Did you hear Ranulf's confession? I wondered. *What do you know?*

Since private confessionals were centuries in the future, everyone standing in line would also be privy to Ranulf's misdeeds. But since my husband didn't consider his treatment of me sinful, he'd have no need to list any transgressions. More likely, Father Peter simply pitied me as openly as he dared without earning the displeasure of the lord of the manor.

I enjoyed overseeing Christmas preparations—the spread of seasonal greenery about the great hall and instructing Nicholas, Emma, Lizbeth and all the other children to tie apples to the twisted trees beyond Tintagel's outer ward.

"Shall we reenact a Nativity Scene?" I asked Father Peter. "We certainly have the animals, and the younglings can portray all the rest."

"Such a clever idea, m'lady. St. Francis was the first to introduce Nativity Scenes, you know. I've been wishing I might recreate one. As a reminder that even the Blessed Savior was born in the humblest of surroundings."

I was pleased that Father Peter was pleased. He had a way of making me feel warm and comfortable which had become all too rare.

For that I was as grateful as my wizened heart allowed.

THE FORTY DAYS of fasting would end Christmas Eve, so Cook and I readied a sumptuous feast. Rather, he suggested various traditional dishes, and I assented. Ranulf and his men had recently killed a boar, which meant the customary boar's head would be prepared for the Christmas feast. Thomas the Steward directed the pantler, butler and the rest of the staff all the way down to the laundresses and scullery maids so that everything would be in readiness.

"I appreciate your skilled hand," I said to my steward. I was probably over the top in my praises, but with Thomas in charge, Tintagel could continue running smoothly with me only ghosting around the edges.

Allowing me to continue wallowing in self-pity, which suited me just fine.

With the worsening weather, I did spend more time in the solar with Lenota and Eve, while Fayette was kept busy elsewhere in the castle.

"Our lord sleeps alone," said Eve, as if that might make me forgive him. "And Col"—she blushed at the familiarity of his given name—"laments he is in the foulest of moods."

"Do not carry tales," Lenota warned. But every other day, she readied a bath I no longer cared about—smelly armpits were the least of my concerns—and experimented with yet more fragrant shampoos, which she methodically worked into my hair. As if a concoction of lavender or cherry or honeysuckle could somehow waft its way to Ranulf's nose and entice him into behaving like—oh, I don't know—a facsimile of a human being.

"Ye must cease your foolishness," she said to me once. Her mouth was drawn and dark circles marred the skin beneath her eyes. "Ye drove him to this—"

"Do not even think to blame me!" I snarled, behaving foolishly indeed. "He is cruel and heartless and—"

"There was a time—"

"How dare you take his side when he is the one who treats me with such contempt? What did I do to deserve this other than being a woman?"

Lenota compressed her mouth and said nothing.

Nightly, Ranulf and I, side by side, presided over simple entertainments. Canticles about angels and wise men and other seasonal themes. There were pantomimes, as well as simple plays which were done in the Anglo-Norman tongue rather than Latin, as was customary in larger households.

These nights leading up to Christmas and the Twelve Days of Christmas were magical. Save for the presence of the man seated beside me. A plethora of emotions radiated from him, enveloping me in ...what? His rage? Contempt? Amusement? I was so poor at reading him, though I reminded myself it was no longer my business to care. Over the course of an even, Ranulf would never fail to ask me questions or directly engage me, probably to keep up appearances. My responses generally consisted of grunts and sighs. I was also careful to never grant him the courtesy of looking directly into his eyes. Letting him know I'd welcome lepers, who had to warn the "unpolluted" of their approach via bells or clappers, before I'd suffer his presence.

After the entertainment, after the trenchers were gathered, the tables cleared and broken down, I slipped away, out into a darkness that, with each day, came earlier and lingered longer.

Wrapped in my fur-lined mantle and carrying a lanthorn, I made my way to Lovers' Cave. Often, Father Peter stepped out of the darkness, where the light from the great hall abruptly ended, retrieved the lanthorn, and guided me to my destination.

"You know you can sleep in the chapel," Father Peter said once, while positioning the lanthorn to provide the best light for our footsteps.

"You are too kind," I replied in a tone that made it clear I would not.

Father Peter simply nodded and held the lanthorn higher so I would not stumble in the dark.

Christmas Eve. The Nativity scene, which would be enacted in Lovers' Cave, was ready, thanks to the hard work of Tintagel's younglings. Father Peter and I readied our volunteers for their parts as Mary, Joseph, the angels, wise men, and shepherds. Sam the Dog-Boy's grandson, Nicholas, was Joseph. With his crazy mass of black curls, dark, snapping eyes and exuberant manner, he was irresistible. Mary was played by Cook's youngest, while baby Jesus was the cloth doll that the laundress's daughter Emma dragged everywhere. We'd prettied the doll up and made a half-hearted attempt to make her look more like a boy before laying her/him in a manger. Of course, there was an ox and an ass and even a couple of goats that Lizbeth insisted must be included.

Torch lights in hand, all of Tintagel made its way to Lover's Cave. The winter solstice had just passed, causing darkness to drop at an impossibly early hour. The Big and Little Dippers crouched low on the horizon, while the rest of the stars stood out, white as moonstones.

Father Peter waited for us at the entrance. The children, faces glowing in the smoking flames, were angels come to life. Since medieval man had no concept of "history," in the sense that people of other ages might dress or fashion their hair or speak differently, all the actors wore regular clothing. But the shepherds carried crooks, the angels sported wings of starched linen, the wise men wore crowns of a sort, and a charcoal beard darkened Nicholas/Joseph's cheeks.

Viewing the tableau, with all of us gathered round and the night perfectly quiet save for the occasional lowing of the miniature-sized animals, the ox, the donkey and the goats nudging at the straw, I was struck by the simple magnificence of the scene.

Here, in Tintagel, with Lizbeth snuggled in my arms, I felt as if I could stretch high enough to brush my knuckles against the heavens. Out here in the vastness of stone and sky, I, who'd long ago lost my faith, could almost believe in discarded childhood tales. Could almost believe in Christmas miracles.

Maybe a child really is growing in my womb. A child that will break the curse. A child I will someday hold in my arms and rock to sleep with lullabies.

Everyone performed his or her lines prettily, though the Virgin Mary began hiccupping halfway through, causing Father Peter to put comforting hands on her shoulders while coaxing her to finish. Afterward, the young friar led a short round of singing before we trekked to St. Julitta's for Christmas Eve mass. The air settled sharp in our lungs, and when I lifted my gaze to the heavens, I was once again overwhelmed by a sense of my insignificance. But tonight, I felt comforted as I felt a rush of tenderness for all those who inhabited Tintagel.

Save for the human ass walking beside me.

Earlier, before the children had begun preparing the Nativity scene, Father Peter had bundled up my bedding, removed it from Lovers' Cave and hidden it outside St. Julitta's underneath the stained-glass window, his way of signaling I could sleep in the sanctuary after everyone had departed.

At mass's end, Ranulf and I stood outside the portico as if we were an actual lord and lady of the manor in an actual relationship. I felt quite daring wishing everybody "Merry Christmas!" since the actual greeting was hundreds of years in the future. When several echoed it in return, I delighted in the idea I was doing something seditious.

Once the crowd thinned, I decided to take my leave. Mentally, I went over my to-do list before evening's end—help Father Peter return the Nativity animals to their pens, supervise the children removing their costumes, and finally, dole out animal-shaped marzipan cookies as rewards. However, when I stepped away from Ranulf, he caught me by the wrist and pulled me back around. Jerking me against his chest, he pinned me there.

I shoved against him. Had he wanted, he could have crushed me. Instead, he allowed me to arch away from him.

"Your temper has lasted long enough. I expect you to warm my bed tonight."

"You already have someone. Probably several someones."

"You're my wife," Ranulf said, his tone warning that ended all debate.

In the soft light spilling from St Julitta's, I was reminded once again of how perfectly formed my husband was, every part of him. I could not have conjured a more desirable man. Like Lucifer, who had been the most beautiful of God's angels.

Perhaps he still was. Perhaps the "Morning Star" stood before me in human form.

"I've been remarkably tolerant," said Ranulf Navarre. "Even Col mocks me."

I sincerely doubted Ranulf's squire would do any such thing.

I lifted my chin and fisted my hands inside woolen gloves. "I'll never share your bed again."

Ranulf dropped my wrist. "I'll expect you tonight."

"If wishes were horses, beggars would ride," I retorted, feeling quite clever. This was the second time in the past several minutes I had uttered an anachronistic expression.

Surprisingly, Ranulf laughed. Reaching beneath my headdress, he tugged at my hair, expertly loosing my braid. As it tumbled free, he ran his fingers through it before giving it a gentle tug.

"Do not disappoint me, *ma hérisson piquant*."

With that, he strode in the direction of the churchgoers who were returning to Tintagel's great hall.

That night I slept in St. Julitta's sacristy.

I WAS CURLED in a fetal position on the stone floor of St. Julitta's, with the air like shards of ice slicing my lungs, wrapped up in the wolf pelts that had miraculously appeared after I spotted Col exiting the chapel.

Col's kindness? Eve's nagging Col? Col acting as his liege's proxy?

Gingerly, I forced my body to a sitting position.

How long can I continue this charade?

Carefully I flexed my aching joints. Each day it became more difficult to persuade my wayward body that a trek to Tintagel's great hall was doable.

It was when I eased myself to standing position that I saw it. In a corner above a far larger chest containing Father Peter's vestments and extra clothing.

A reliquary.

The reliquary. Though the painted figures on its surface were bright as jewels, its wood a warm chestnut and its steepled roof topped by a dainty cross. The cross I'd intuited when Felix Eastoft had presented the reliquary to me in Glastonbury.

"There you are," I whispered, heart racing with excitement. "I think I'm beginning to understand."

Inside that reliquary, on a parchment discovered centuries later, a thirteenth century someone had written, *"I mourn for my love."*

Not someone.

Me.

Forty-Four

On the Feast of the Epiphany, we distributed pouches containing cloth dolls to the village and castle girls, wooden tops for boys and ginger cookies for all. In an age devoid of so many entertainments we take for granted, I'd had no trouble finding volunteers eager to alter their routines in order to craft the toys. Even Col had lent his carving skills and helped dispense the gifts.

"You are so kind, my lady," Col said, smiling into my eyes. "I hope this means you will grace us more often with your presence."

I returned his smile. Col the Charmer. Increasingly, since Ranulf's and my disastrous night, I'd wondered about Zak Ridarelli. I knew Zak wasn't Ranulf—that didn't feel right, but even though Col and Zak looked only marginally alike—I linked so many of their actions, attitudes, and even some of their gestures.

"Eve deserves more praise than I do," I said, dragging my attention back to the present. "'Twas she and Lenota who fashioned most of the dolls."

Today was the ending of seasonal celebrations. The yule log, which had burned continuously to keep the baby Jesus warm in his manger and to usher in a year of good luck, had crumbled to ash. The prior day, Twelfth Night, we'd removed all the Christmas greenery from

Tintagel's great hall, and today we were consuming the last of the wassail, which I much preferred to eggnog, or "posset," as it was called. No matter the name, no matter the century, it tasted hideous.

As the afternoon waned, I was filled with equal amounts of lingering Christmas cheer and dread. The wassail, which bubbled in a cauldron above the hall's central fire, warmed my insides and engendered a good feeling toward most of those around me. Dread because soon I would sneak away for whatever abode was least likely to turn me into an icicle by morning.

My concerns centered more on the dusting of snow that had greeted me the last two mornings, the ice that crusted the trio of springs dotting this part of Tintagel's headland.

How long until I'm forced to return to that loathsome chamber?

Pride was one thing, but freezing to death in order to prove a point only I cared about was something else altogether.

~

"PRESENTS!" announced Ranulf, and then, like a proper liege lord, he distributed his largesse saving mine for last.

"'Tis a rune ring," Ranulf said, upon handing me a wide carved band. "It has magical powers." I looked for signs of mockery in his expression but found none. He slipped it on my left middle finger. A reminder of my absent wedding ring?

I held out my hand to inspect the band, which was thick and heavy and quite beautiful. Even as Magdalena Moore, I would have admired it.

"What sorts of magical powers?" I asked because I had to say *something*.

"It can predict the future."

I thought of my Glastonbury crystal in its familiar place around my neck. However, I didn't need rune rings or crystals to guess our future.

"I didn't get you anything," I said, a bit unnerved by the ring carved with odd symbols. Why would Ranulf have chosen this particular charm? I covered my discomfort with sarcasm, made easier by the generous amounts of ale in the wassail. "You, husband, have not been a good boy." Okay, I was mixing up my Christmas traditions, but Ranulf grinned, as if pleased that regardless of the century, he qualified as the quintessential bad boy.

He next handed me a long, folded piece of ivory silk, far too expensive for a baron of his rank.

"I want a garment like you used to wear," he said. While my linen gown had been mended until it looked like a patchwork quilt, of course I hadn't worn it. Because I hadn't slept in our bed in a month.

Ranulf ran a huge, calloused palm across the thin fabric and leaned closer. Moving aside my gossamer veil, he whispered, "You will either come willingly, or I do not mind a spirited claiming, *mon chaton*."

Hmm, from mouse to hedgehog to kitten. Willing my body not to respond to his breath against my ear, to ignore the shiver that could be mistaken for arousal, I turned my head away.

I'll not obey you, I told myself, even as my fingers stroked the silken material. *I'll not be fooled again.*

Forty-Five

The next day, while I was helping Father Peter remove the Advent decorations from the chapel, we heard the blast of a trumpet from Tintagel's outer gate announcing visitors.

"I can finish, my lady." We'd been reciting the prayer of his mentor, St. Francis of Assisi. *"Lord, make me an instrument of Thy peace. Where there is hatred..."* I'd memorized it in my former life and felt a special sort of awe, to be so near its inception. And how appropriate the words were, here in this lovely chapel. *"Where there is despair, hope... Where there is darkness, light..."* A hushed sense of wonder and gratitude for this hiccup in time.

I shrugged. "My husband can take care of any guests." Carefully, I folded each of the violet hangings we'd taken down from the walls.

"I wonder if the visitors might be some of Simon de Montfort's liege men, here to travel with your husband," Peter commented from the corner of the makeshift sacristy where I'd first spotted the reliquary.

"Why would that be?"

Father Peter returned with a chest large enough to store the hangings. "Parliament. They were summoned mid-December. It opens near January's end, I believe." Retrieving one of the folded hangings, he arranged it into the bottom of the chest. "You know the roads this time of year."

Now, this was interesting! While my memory wasn't perfect, I could mark off many of the events that would lead to Simon de Montfort's bloody end. This Parliament was one of them.

"And my husband will be in attendance." I said it as a statement, though it was an assumption.

While I wrestled with the last of the cumbersome hangings, I felt the heaviness of the rune ring upon my finger.

How curious this all is. To be as certain of the future as though I ***do*** *possess magical powers.*

"Janey."

I spun around. Ranulf stood in the portico's doorway, so big he nearly filled the entrance. My traitorous heart increased its rhythm. After handing the final square to Father Peter, I crossed my arms across my chest and addressed my husband. "What do you want?"

"You are needed. Gilbert de Clare has arrived."

Ah, Gilbert de Clare again. Gilbert de Clare, 7th Earl of Gloucester. A powerful Marcher lord with the mindboggling number of two hundred manors to his name. Clare was also one of the men who would be most responsible for Simon de Montfort's defeat—and thus, the death of my husband.

"Have whichever woman you're currently sarding greet him," I said. "I am otherwise occupied."

Even in the dim light, I saw his mouth tighten.

"Gloucester asked specifically after you, as you must know he would. Do not keep our guests waiting."

"No. Make up an excuse or tell the earl the truth for all I care."

I turned my back, pretending to inspect one of the uncovered wall frescoes that possessed biblical figures and boats and animals I had no idea how to interpret.

"Montfort has called a parliament," Ranulf said, echoing Father Peter's earlier remark.

The words caused a chill down my spine, a supernal touch reminding me to pay attention.

I loved the names assigned to England's Parliaments—Parliament of the White Bands; the Good Parliament; the Bad Parliament; the Wonderful Parliament; the Merciless Parliament; Parliament of the Dunces; the Fire and Faggot Parliament. In contrast, "the Great Parliament of 1265," as labeled by historians, sounded prosaic. But it would be the first time in English history that common men would be brought together to have their say on how their kingdom should be governed. Previously, their duty had been restricted to giving consent for the levying of taxes.

I'd spent a career reconstructing the fourteenth century—battles, parliaments, baronial quarrels, the pomp and pageantry of coronations, royal marriages and deaths.

Now here I am, nearing the denouement of one of medieval England's most important events, and I waste the opportunity sparring with my husband?

Ranulf called my name again, his tone demanding obedience.

From the corner of my eye, I noticed Father Peter scoop up the chest and retreat in the direction of the sacristy.

I heard my husband's approaching footsteps.

"What do you have to say that could possibly convince me?" I imagined the rune ring growing warmer on my finger.

Ranulf halted behind me. "I need say nothing. I need command you."

Simon de Montfort. A historic parliament. The names and places I so loved spread before me, mine for the taking. How could I resist such an offering?

I twisted to face my husband. "I will act as your dutiful consort on one condition."

The corners of Ranulf's mouth lifted, as though amused that I thought to dictate to him.

"And what might that be?"

"You take me with you. To London."

Forty-Six

D*ear God in Heaven, I have never been so cold, so sore, so miserable in my entire life.*

What had ever possessed me to voluntarily spend days in the saddle during a wet, miserable winter, as all English winters were wet and miserable? Perhaps not so much with central heating and, I don't know, cars and public transport that allow you to travel to London in half a day. Unfortunately, our journey would take more than a week—if everything went well. And how could everything go well in January of 1264? (Or 1265. I could never figure out exactly when New Year's began in medieval England. Nor, apparently, could some chroniclers.)

Not that Ranulf had acquiesced to my request to accompany him. In fact, he'd forbidden it.

"You hate long rides," he'd said dismissively. "And I'm of no mind to listen to your whining for days on end."

So, Jane of Holywelle wasn't an accomplished equestrienne. Good to know.

"I'll be quiet as a mouse," I'd responded, which only caused him to roll his eyes. I'd dressed like a man in tunic, surcoat, and mantle so that travel would be more comfortable and packed what I hoped would keep me alive during my journey into the unknown.

"You are ridiculous," he hissed, possibly referring to my clothing, probably referring to me as a whole. Still, I'd not be denied. I gambled that he wouldn't dare beat me in front of Gilbert de Clare, who was apparently some sort of relation, or Col, who increasingly risked his lord's disapproval by being openly solicitous, even protective. (Also, I did not miss the way he eyed my butt when I appeared in my "ridiculous" outfit.)

You definitely need a wife.

With a shake of his head, Ranulf swung into the saddle, followed by the rest of his men. They set off at a brisk pace, Gilbert de Clare's men in front, their yellow and red pennons fluttering prettily behind them. Ranulf followed, undeniably mouthwatering in his hauberk topped by his vermillion surcoat. I could look at him all day—and probably would —since I brought up the rear.

Because Rouge was a palfrey, as were most horses used for travel, I could theoretically maintain a pace that alternated between a trot and a lope without too much damage to my backside.

Theoretically.

A half-day in the saddle and I imagined bum blisters, if there was such a thing. Ranulf showed no mercy. Occasionally, he maneuvered his stallion, Highstepper, away from his usual position and wheeled around so he could view me struggling along, lagging behind even the sumpter horses.

Obviously, he was hoping that, in the quarter-hour or so since he'd last checked, I'd admitted defeat and slunk back to Tintagel. Or fallen off Rouge and was sprawled in a ditch somewhere or half-buried in a latrine pit overflowing from recent rains.

Despite my already stiffening muscles, I forced Rouge to maintain a pace allowing me to stay in sight of my companions. I was terrified that somehow they would vanish *en masse*, leaving me to maneuver this hostile world alone. Should I become lost, I had no ideas of landmarks or how to interpret makeshift signs or anything else that might point the way to the next village, let alone London. I couldn't even really tell the four directions. And even if I could, without frames of reference, what good would that do?

I felt totally useless. Not to mention overwhelmed.

When travelling at a pace where forty miles a day was as impressive as Chuck Yeager breaking the sound barrier, England stretched vast and formidable as the Amazon Rain Forest. Currently, we were passing through desolate moorland, covered with heather and an occasional scruffy-looking tree, bent in the shape of prevailing gales. I imagined wolves tracking our progress from behind the misshapen tors rising from granite plateaus.

Strange.

Why am I terrified of animals I championed as Magdalena Moore?

Yeah, but everything looked very different in the thirteenth century.

Stop this silliness.

I had way more reality-based concerns—like the need for shelter and food and bathing facilities. And why hadn't I brought changes of clothing? Or a maid? As dead as I already felt, I wasn't sure I'd be able to do more than curl up and groan my misery.

Yet I could not shake my canine obsession. Maybe hunger had made me light-headed. While my traveling companions had no trouble eating while riding, I didn't dare. If I tried to dig around in my saddlebag for my ration of bread and cheese and dried fruits, I'd probably lose my balance. Mastering two things simultaneously? Not today. When the terrain was smooth enough and the pace slow enough, the best I could do was open the top of the costrel lashed across my chest and swallow a bit of watered-down ale.

Meanwhile, my senses were alert for signs of my latest nemeses. "There!" I imagined Alpha Male saying to the rest of his pack, in whatever way wolves communicate. "That straggler is the weakest in the herd. Let's take her down."

By the time we reached the monastery where we would lodge, I nearly wept with relief. Thankfully, my fellow travelers had not simply struck out with no idea as to routes or accommodations. There was a method to this medieval madness. I was so cold and tired and stiff, however, that even though the others easily dismounted and began tending their horses, I remained stuck atop poor, patient Rouge. My husband was speaking with the abbot, so there'd be no help from him. And, yes, by now, I would have shamelessly begged his assistance.

"M'lady." Col gently reached up to remove the reins from my stiff hands.

"My savior," I managed as he led me to a mounting block. Once there, however, I wasn't sure my thigh muscles would respond to my commands to swing me up and over the saddle.

Ranulf suddenly appeared, growling for his squire to tend to their horses, before reaching up and pulling me none too gently from my perch. Though, in fairness, any movement would have been too rough.

Unable to suppress my groans, unable to move, I collapsed against my husband. With a muffled curse, he scooped me in his arms and carried me to the abbot's lodgings, where we would spend the night.

I'd like to say that I stayed aloof from Ranulf, but I was so exhausted I collapsed on the provided pallet, and when I woke up the next morning, I found myself wrapped around him and all that wonderful body heat.

Ranulf Navarre had won this round. Once again he had me in his bed.

TWO DAYS LATER, we separated from a reluctant Gilbert de Clare.

I didn't understand the young earl's hesitancy at splitting up, or indeed his familiarity toward me, though I'd deduced we were cousins. (Probably because he kept calling me *"cousine."*) Despite all I knew about Gilbert de Clare, Earl of Gloucester, I found it impossible to dislike him. He was lean and wiry with the ruddy complexion and mercurial temper associated with redheads. However, he laughed as easily as he frowned and possessed an endearing enthusiasm that caused him to jump from subject to subject. I was surprised that one so young—he could not be more than twenty—had been Ranulf's commander at the Battle of Lewes, but Clare already carried himself with an air of authority. He'd also been the one who'd led the recent massacre of Jews at Canterbury, though since my husband had also participated, I could not reserve my revulsion for Clare alone.

Like most people, the Earl of Gloucester could not be easily labeled.

Throughout our journey, Gilbert de Clare often sought me out to talk about people and places and events that were unfamiliar and yet familiar. Most likely relatives.

It was all so confusing.

Our last evening, while enjoying the hospitality of a local lord, Clare engaged me in a round of riddles. Apparently, this was something he and Janey enjoyed, though I generally had no idea about answers involving moons, tides, cupboards and needles. I pretended my sudden stupidity was an act, which seemed to add to Clare's amusement.

I did guess one riddle—or recalled it—which might have said something about Jane of Holywelle's sense of humor.

The riddle began with...

"It swings by his thigh – a most magical thing!"

And ended with

"...shoves it into a well-known hole

That it fills completely when stretched out.

It has often been there before. And now it sticks there again."

I laughed and clapped my hands. "A key!"

Just another reminder that our ancestors enjoyed...earthy wordplay.

Upon leaving, Clare kissed me on the cheek, a gesture reserved only for family members, and said, "We will meet again in London."

Ranulf had the good grace to refrain from blaming me for his troupe's slower pace. Twice, when I'd been so weary I actually fell asleep in the saddle, Ranulf scooped me from Rouge and positioned me behind him so I could ride pillion. Highstepper's smooth, ambling gait had a way of rocking me into a half-waking, half-dreaming state until the roughness of Ranulf's hauberk dug deep into my cheek, and I remembered who it was I was embracing.

I was too sore and exhausted to care.

In addition to the rigors of travel, my stomach had become queasy of a morning.

Could this be another symptom of my pregnancy? I wondered even as I scoffed at the notion. My barrenness was simple, brutal fact. If somehow I'd conceived, it was simply a snag in the tapestry the fates wove for mankind which would soon be rectified.

So, we rode. There was no denying that, even in winter, England was beautiful. Most fields were not yet edged by stone walls or hedges but rather consisted of acres of open land, outlined by smaller plots, all lying fallow. In areas where it hadn't yet snowed, the earth would be a rich chocolate or as emerald green as if it were spring. Away from villages topped by their inevitable smoky haze, the skies were more intense, whether clear or ominously black with an approaching storm. In the vastness of unbroken countryside, the animals that had escaped autumn's slaughter looked even more like cleverly constructed toys—oversized cows, sheep, and, nearer a manor or farm, horses. I found the mix of man and nature endlessly fascinating, though I tried not to stare overmuch, since none of this would have been new to Jane of Holywelle. Still, I sometimes caught Ranulf watching me, as if puzzled/annoyed/suspicious?

Increasingly, I was too tired to care. More than once, I nearly blurted the sixty-four-gazillion dollar question: "Why isn't parliament called in summer, when we have a better chance of not freezing to death or being swept away by winter storms?"

"The weather is fickle as a whore's heart," Ranulf commented in a colorful and pre-politically correct way I rather liked. Sometimes rain, sometimes wind, sometimes sun, sometimes bone-chilling cold, and sometimes all of them within a few hours of the other. With each passing day, I more admired the physical prowess of Ranulf and his men. Knights were raised to be fit; that was their job, like contemporary athletes—though knights worked from childhood into middle age and under far more brutal conditions. If we couldn't find an inn or stand of trees or shed or abandoned building during one of the inevitable squalls, we had to continue riding. While this was a one-time nightmare for me, Ranulf and his men endured this every extended outing. It was beyond miserable. Although my woolen mantle was surprisingly rain resistant, my hands, even inside fur-lined gloves, were icy stumps an hour out, as were my feet in their ill-fitting, leaky boots. Yet Ranulf and his men were, for all intents and purposes, encased in metal. Other than uttering an occasional muffled curse, however, they simply pulled their traveling cloaks closer, flipped up their hoods, bent their faces to the elements, and pushed forward. During a time when a cold could settle into pneumonia, a cut could turn gangrenous, and a broken bone prove fatal, it was a miracle anyone survived to old age.

We'd been traveling at least a week, staying primarily at castles and religious houses, and while we were largely strangers, all were dutybound to house us. Monasteries had the best accommodations—efficient systems of providing water so we might wash up, cook a meal and bed down on decent pallets.

The Romans, those remarkable Romans, had built roads that remained the finest in the kingdom, but we were still too far south to make much use of them. Some of the royal highways were little more than trails, often cutting through pastures and fields. Bridges were rare, though rain-swollen streams and rivers became increasingly common the farther inland we rode. Unfortunately, we seemed fated to cross every one of them. Sometimes we found places to ford, but other times, well, that was the part of the journey that later lived on in my nightmares. The river, slithering along like an enormous serpent, was eager to suck me under. Approaching the bank, eying that rolling menace, I'd never felt such terror. I imagined being pulled off Rouge by its relentless pressure and, weighted down by my clothing, immediately sucked beneath the surface.

I can't do this. I will find my way back to the nearest monastery and wait there until the troupe's return.

I'd been wrong when I'd assumed Ranulf had disapproved of my accompanying him simply to thwart me.

Before the first crossing—and all the subsequent ones—Ranulf wordlessly dragged me off Rouge and settled me in front of him as best he could in the uncomfortable saddle. Eyes closed, I buried my face against his surcoat while he wrapped his voluminous beaver-lined mantle around me, pretending my limbs shook from cold rather than terror. Gently, easily he urged his reluctant stallion into the current. Thankfully, there were only a handful of times when Highstepper was actually forced to swim. When the current crept past our boots to our thighs and Highstepper's muscles bunched, I could feel him running beneath us, though his hooves struck only water. Then I knew, I just knew, we'd go rolling and tumbling downriver like sticks in the current.

Yet we never did. It gave me a new appreciation for the relationship between our ancestors and their horses. As well as knights, at least when they actually lived up to their role as protectors. For, in this world, muscle and might really were primary survival skills.

How easy it is to adapt to you as my defender, I thought, silently addressing my husband. *And how instinctively you fill that role.*

Simply stated, I could never have survived on my own. Inch by inch, day by day, I surrendered, allowing Ranulf Navarre to be my champion. While I bobbed along, rather like those aforementioned sticks in the current. I didn't understand how I could be so physically miserable while feeling so safe.

The ground rules were shaking under my feet. What had seemed so certain at the beginning of our journey had grown far murkier, and I didn't like it, not at all.

~

THE DAYS WERE LONG. To break the monotony, the men sometimes talked, though seldom of consequential things.

Is that because of my presence? I wondered. *Do you think me incapable of grasping anything more complicated than a "Good morrow" and "Fare thee well?"*

Maybe their own minds simply didn't run that way. They certainly didn't discuss politics, though I'd already discerned that Ranulf was indifferent to such things.

"I am Simon de Montfort's man," was his attitude. *"Beyond that I am not interested in the whys and wherefores."*

Col often unlashed his lute from his saddle and played to pass the time. The men enjoyed singing—bawdy ballads, and sometimes mournful ones, and sometimes those filled with blood and gore and things that would have been rated R.

While the men entertained themselves, I called up repertoires of songs I'd known. More than anything, I missed music. Everything from Big Band artists like Glenn Miller to Peggy Lee to the Beatles and the Animals to blues, modern and old. Women singers with sultry voices, and whenever I was pillioned too long behind Ranulf, I recalled Stevie Nicks singing "Landslide."

Aye, I built my life around you, didn't I?

On this particular day, when the sky remained cloudless, when there wasn't the hint of a breeze, when the snow in the fields sparkled like diamonds in a sun warm enough that I could remove my cloak, I slipped into a folk song, "The Gypsy Rover." A handsome gypsy, who whistles and sings till the green woods ring, captures the heart of a beautiful lady. The lady leaves her castle gate, her servants, her velvet gown and shoes of Spanish leather to sleep on the cold, cold ground with her gypsy lover. Who turns out to be the lord over castle and lands, because some songs *do* have happy endings.

I remembered Sherralinda and I googling "handsome gypsy men," and felt a pang for my friend.

Are you frantic over my absence? How many months have passed, or in that other world, has it only been a few hours? Have I fallen and smashed my head? Am I lying comatose in a hospital hooked up to machines?

Suddenly Father Peter's face flashed behind my eyes. Something about his eyes reminded me of Sherralinda.

Wouldn't that be something, if Sherralinda had somehow been reverse reincarnated into a Franciscan friar?

Lost in my daydreams, I didn't realize I was still singing about my handsome gypsy rover until I caught Ranulf, who rode beside me, staring.

"What? Is there something wrong with my voice?"

"Never heard that song before," he said.

Of course not. *Particularly*, I thought with a shiver, *when I've been singing it in modern English.*

Forty-Eight

Near Bath I found the castle of my dreams. Or my regression.

"We will be staying the night at Adford Castle," Ranulf said, looking expectantly at me. We'd just splashed through another one of the streams that made up the River Avon, which spread around this area in a thousand annoying fingers.

I nodded but didn't reply. The name meant nothing to me.

"I thought you'd be more excited," he said, which immediately put me on alert.

"I'm too bone-weary to get excited over anything," I responded, hoping my explanation sufficed.

A lingering look before Ranulf grunted and returned to his man thoughts.

Adford Castle appeared to be even smaller than Tintagel, though there was something charming, almost feminine about it. Perhaps it was the way the afternoon sun turned its painted walls the faintest rose.

"Adford." I rolled the word, which felt right and comfortable, on my tongue. After our troupe passed the huts clustering around its outer curtain, crossed the drawbridge and rode beneath the barbican with its portcullis raised in welcome, I remembered. Adford Castle was my childhood home.

As I suddenly remembered my parents, my beautiful parents.

How could I not have given you more than a passing thought? I wondered, momentarily overcome by a wave of grief. *Did I assume I was like Aphrodite rising full-grown from the sea?*

Two sets of parents centuries apart. Two more deaths to mourn.

Upon entering the bailey, we were greeted by a smiling group of servants.

"Last time we saw you, you were a wee one," said the Reeve. *Dann the Reeve.* Forgetting all protocol, he addressed me first and wrapped me in a hug. I felt oddly teary as I realized yet another part of my past had been dropped down a deep well.

The other household members crowded close, questioning me about Lenota and a dozen other subjects without waiting for answers I could not supply. Mercifully, each of their names popped into my head when I had need of addressing them individually.

While Adford's marshal ordered the care of our horses, and Ranulf and his men stretched their bodies, my former household swept me into the great hall.

Memories bubbled to the surface, bubbles on an inky lake. I'd last seen this room as a frightened child gazing up at my parents seated upon the dais. Before I'd dared allow my gaze to slip to Ranulf Navarre. My first glimpse of my tormentor, my nemesis, my obsession.

What were you thinking that day? Were you impatient for me to reach the proper age for marriage? Impatient for me to give you your sons?

The whole experience caused another of those floaty feelings, reminding me I didn't fit anywhere.

We spent the night in the solar I'd once shared with my parents. So much coming back to me. Adford had been part of my pitiful dowry. I wondered why a man so magnificent as Ranulf Navarre would have chosen me and just as quickly deduced the answer. The Clare family. We were related to one of England's most powerful dynasties. As I remembered playing with a red-haired five-year-old when I'd been a mature girl of ten. When Gilbert de Clare had been chased by an ill-tempered goose and hid behind my skirts; when we'd floated homemade boats down the stream by the grain mill.

I felt nostalgic for something I hadn't known I missed.

Too many worlds, too many memories, I thought, before falling into my usual exhausted sleep.

With Ranulf beside me.

Much has been written about the filth of London, and yes, it was an assault to the senses. Depending on the wind or the direction of the gate through which one entered—Newgate in our case—you smelled London well before your arrival. Everything imaginable was dumped into the River Thames, as well as on the narrow streets, though there was some effort to keep areas, at least in front of households or businesses, clean.

Yes, there were rats, horrible, slinking, filthy rats. Dogs, pigs and cats rutted about the refuse-clotted ditches. One had to be careful where one stepped.

Still, I was in London. *London!*

What immediately appealed to me was its compact size. Despite being England's largest city, everything was within walking distance. Its buildings possessed a certain pleasing symmetry—unlike contemporary London, which sprawls forever in a discordant hodgepodge of architectural styles.

We stayed in one of Gilbert de Clare's residences along the Strand, which linked the city to Westminster, where Parliament was being held. Gloucester's Inn was an imposing stone two-story, though Ranulf settled in with no more comment than when we'd slept on straw in a pilgrim's hospital. He did not appear envious of Clare's mindboggling wealth. In a time when property was all, Ranulf seemed passionate about two things—producing an heir and fighting.

Gilbert de Clare visited after we'd settled in. Over supper, he recounted the opening days of a Parliament that was already being referred to as Montfort's Parliament. Ranulf listened politely, but while Clare genuinely seemed to care about reforms and King Henry's abuses, Ranulf soon became restless, shifting on his stool, fiddling with the dagger at his belt, and finally, flinging his arms back and yawning, a rude signal he was ready to retire.

Whoever Gilbert de Clare was, whatever his sins, he was always kind to me. Before leaving that first evening, he provided me with a maid, Gertrude, and promised to send a pair of dressmakers to replace my totally inappropriate—not to mention filthy—clothing.

"I will order them to use material from Flanders," he said. "Only the finest for you, *cousine*."

"You must not—"

"If you're in need of more gowns or whatnots, Threadneedle Street is the place. And to purchase your slippers and pattens, Cordwainer Street is close by."

Grabbing my purse, the earl filled it with coins. "For anything you need. Enjoy your first trip to London."

While one of the marks of a great lord was his largesse, I protested, fearing Ranulf might be humiliated.

Gilbert closed the drawstring on my purse and returned it gently to my girdle. "Have you forgotten, *cousine*, that your husband saved my life?"

I shook my head.

I hadn't forgotten because I didn't *know*.

That...or so much else.

THREE DAYS LATER, I was out and about, outfitted in one of my beautiful new gowns and a fur-lined mantle, another gift from Gilbert de Clare. I gauged from the finished size of my kirtle that my shape had not changed, just another indication that pregnancy was a figment of my imagination, though in truth, it was probably too early to tell.

Gertrude produced an actual glass mirror which I used to apply cosmetics. After surveying the results, I decided that, while I would never be a beauty, I would not disgrace Ranulf.

And immediately chastised myself for caring about my husband's opinion. Or basing my self-worth on my physical attributes. Or lack thereof.

A notion that would probably never have occurred to the real Jane of Holywelle.

Our first outing was to West Cheap, London's principal marketplace. Gertrude accompanied me, as did Col, per Ranulf's instructions. I didn't mind. Gertrude was familiar with every area of the city and knowledgeable about various sellers—who used inaccurate scales, who sold questionable meats, who watered down their ale. Had I been the actual Jane of Holywelle, I would still have felt like a bumpkin. The area, which contained feeder streets with names like Milk Street and Poultry Lane to describe their products, was uncomfortably crowded. Noisy, with hawkers crying their wares and far too much pushing and shoving, which made me particularly grateful for Col's watchful presence. Cutpurses were ever a worry, and Gertrude, for whatever reason, seemed obsessed with kidnappers. She reminded me of my mother, who had ever admonished me to "watch my purse."

From one side of West Cheap, we could see St Paul's Cathedral with its magnificent spire thrusting hundreds of feet above the city. Its very presence filled me with excitement. What I'd written about in *A Child Upon the Throne* I would soon see in person. The opposite end of West Cheap was Old Jewry Street. After we'd worked our way through the carts and stalls and press of bundled bodies to that particular area, I received yet another lesson in medieval prejudices.

Large buildings, all in ruins, ran from the conduit bordering Old Jewry into its heart. Stone walls, like those of Gloucester's Inn.

Had Gloucester's Inn been destroyed in a conflagration.

When I commented about the ever-present danger of fire, Gertrude snorted.

"Jews!" My maid's thin lips pursed, as if ready to spit. "Five hundred killed here; last year it was. Their houses burned. I've not seen a yellow band since."

Col walked beside us, his air indifferent. My stomach lurched, as if my usual morning queasiness had been transferred to afternoon.

"We're well rid of Christ's killers, I say." The expression on Gertrude's pinched face, unflatteringly framed by a muddy brown wimple, turned venomous. "They've a greedy finger in every pie. Soon they'll own all the kingdom." She frowned down at her basket of sundries as though fearing some Jew might momentarily appear and snatch it away. "I've not even mentioned all the Christian children they butcher! And the kidnappings, grabbing good people off the streets!"

Sweet God in Heaven!

The real reason Jews were persecuted was because they'd loaned out lots of money to powerful people, including Simon de Montfort. Rather than repay those loans, Montfort and the others had slaughtered their Jewish lenders and burned all relevant bonds and contracts, forever wiping out their debts.

"Let's be off to Cordwainer Street," I said, my voice tight. "I am in need of shoes."

It was not only Jews that the English hated. Unsurprisingly, foreigners—in this case Henry III's powerful Lusignan relatives, who were referred to as "aliens"—were pretty much responsible for every evil Jews and women hadn't already committed.

Later that afternoon, after we'd returned to Gloucester's Inn with full baskets and aching feet, I decided to further question Col about this alien business. The thirteenth century didn't have a monopoly on prejudice, so I adopted my best neutral simply-seeking-information-without-judging manner.

"I am puzzled, Col."

Col leaned in, his expression concerned. "How might I help, my lady?"

"Everyone hates the...aliens." I stumbled over the word which reminded me of bug-eyed creatures in flying saucers. "Yet Simon de Montfort was born in France, as are the Lusignans, and has as many ties there as here. Why would you choose a Frenchman to lead you when you hate Frenchmen?" I was not sowing seeds. I simply wanted to understand this particular example of cognitive dissonance.

Col shrugged. "We all come from somewhere. We've a run of monarchs from Anjou, do we not?" He was referring to the Plantagenets, who would not hold that name for centuries. I could tell from Col's manner that he wasn't interested in further discussion.

"The Earl of Leicester does have a sincere heart for the poor," I pressed, suppressing my annoyance at what was, truth be told, Col's patronizing manner. "And he is very devout, isn't he? And idealistic. Still, I do not understand the difference between Montfort and the Lusignans."

Why should I not be curious about the man who would lead my husband to his death?

While Col did not literally pat me on the head, he did so metaphorically. "You think deep thoughts, my lady." He handed me the bundle of shoes and pattens he'd carried from Cordwainer Street, mumbled something about the stables, and departed.

Leaving me more curious than ever about the man who would lead my husband—and possibly Col--to their deaths.

Fifty

For the next three weeks, weather permitting, I played tourist. Gertrude, Col, and I visited the Tower of London—though I refused to view the exotic animals caged in the king's menagerie—watched horse races at Smithfield and cogs docking and departing from Queenhithe and Billingsgate. London Bridge was a must, with its houses built right above its stone arches and its drawbridge which was raised and lowered with the passage of the tallest ships. In its center was the Chapel of St. Thomas on the Bridge, from which pilgrims, endless pilgrims, officially began their trek to Thomas Becket's shrine in Canterbury.

Canterbury. I imagined visiting it on our return to Tintagel. Would Ranulf grant me that? He might, as thanksgiving for my pregnancy.

Too early. Do not think such thoughts. Do not be deluded.

The highlight of my stay was St. Paul's Cathedral—England's largest church with the tallest spire. Londoners, including those herding animals to various markets, used its transept as a thoroughfare. Upon entering, I was captivated by its soaring ceilings and frescoed walls and columns as overwhelmingly garish as any Renaissance art. A cacophony of noise—thousands of human and animal voices overlaid by the clamor of ongoing construction. Paul's Walk, the cathedral's breathtakingly long nave aisle, was like a mini town. Youths chased footballs in a rough equivalent of modern-day soccer; soberly dressed guild members conducted business and intrigues; merchants displayed everything from furniture to religious trinkets to puddings and pasties; lords and ladies paraded about with hawks on gloves and hounds on leash; harried friars shouted, "Make way," while guiding pilgrims to the grave of St. Paul's saint, Bishop Erkenwald.

A feast for the senses that eventually became overpowering. While my stomach remained sensitive in the mornings, that usually passed by this time of day. "I just need to sit for a few moments," I said to my companions, feeling lightheaded.

It was Col who expressed concern. "Are you ill, my lady? Should we return to the residence?"

I shook my head. "It's just...no. From here, I can admire all the lovely stained glass." After sinking down on an available bench, I pointed to an exquisite rose window located in the apse. "Breathtaking, isn't it?"

Col smiled into my eyes. "Breathtaking!"

What a dog!

While Gertrude wandered among the stalls looking to purchase more of the fragrant oils and soaps I'd requested, Col kept watch at my side until I felt well enough to exit into the courtyard. At Paul's Cross, an outdoor pulpit, some firebrand was exhorting a small gathering about the dangers of false kings. He was obviously referring to Montfort's Parliament, a subject I avoided with Ranulf, who seemed alternately bored and irritated by the whole business. How well I knew that anything happening at the Palace of Westminster was simply a raging against the dying of the light. Like watching news footage preceding the assassination of Franz Ferdinand or Hitler's invasion of Poland or the fall of the Berlin Wall. You knew the ending. Archduke Franz Ferdinand would not take an alternate route and arrive safely at Sarajevo's city hall; Hitler would not decide invading Poland was a stupid idea, and Gorbachev would not turn his back on Soviet reforms.

As this parliament will not change the fate of Simon de Montfort. And, I thought, that familiar sense of dread returning, *by extension, you, my husband.*

It was imperative to listen, to better understand, even though *Simon de Montfort: Father of English Democracy* had chronicled the entire tragedy.

The Benedictine at Paul's Cross raged. "Under his insufferable cloak of self-righteousness, the Foreigner has cast aside, killed or imprisoned all those who dared cross him."

Unconcerned by this criticism of a man who was his liege, or at least one of his lieges, Col turned away to chat up a pretty face.

"Aye, the Foreigner will say to you, 'Obey this,' 'Do that,' all the while disregarding those same rules when they run counter to his ambitions."

I arched my back, easing an ache that had lodged there. Some of this was frightening stuff and some of it I'd heard a thousand times over on political podcasts. Different people, Different century, same complaints.

"The Foreigner disguises his and his family's selfish ends under the guise of "common good." Heaping more power upon himself and lands and titles and riches upon his offspring of vipers."

As if weary of the Benedictine's diatribe, St Paul's bells began ringing, followed by other bells. While the priest continued waving his arms and shouting, it was like watching television on mute.

"Please take me home," I said to Col, who immediately obliged.

Simon de Montfort, his greeds, delusions, lofty ideals and visions, might all make a spellbinding chapter in English history, but for me it meant only one thing: that my husband, Col and thousands of others would soon die because of them.

Fifty-One

Generally, Ranulf returned to Gloucester's Inn before St. Martin's le Grand rang its eight o'clock curfew, signaling the closing of city gates. Following a light supper, he closeted himself with Col and his other men before coming to bed.

Ranulf's presence was the highlight of my day, particularly since the weather had turned unrelentingly miserable. I spent most of my time hovered near the fire or experimenting with the pen, parchment and paints provided by Gertrude and seated before a desk scrounged up by Col. While my movements were made clumsy by gloves with fingertips cut off, I began sketching the things I'd seen on our walks—guild signs hanging above doorways, cunningly carved finials and gargoyles, a packhorse at rest and faces, always faces. Handsome Col, a profile of Gilbert de Clare, of Gertrude bent over the fireplace. After each, I wrote a paragraph or so, but those I scraped from the parchment since they were written in contemporary English and *verboten*.

Still, the days dragged.

I missed my husband.

Truth was the way my fingertips ached of the winter cold, my soul ached for Ranulf Navarre. After spending every moment of our journey together, after coming to think of him, God help me, as my champion, I often daydreamed about our past fortnight. The times he swept me off Rouge, set me in front of him and guided us safely across raging rivers and swollen streams. How he fed me before himself and even acquiesced to my desire for boiled water, which had been a quirk at Tintagel and a pain in the ass during the journey. The rumble of a voice that transformed into a lovely tenor when he sang, the way he spooned against me on those narrow pallets in hospitals and monasteries, as if sheltering me even in sleep.

I need not call up memories of my five other husbands to be reminded not a one had ever, ever really protected me.

How ironic that an actual knight had proven to be my "knight in shining armor."

WHEN RANULF WAS LATE, jealousy flashed through me like heat lightning.

He's with another woman, I would think, pacing our chamber, wringing my hands like a madwoman. *He's played me for a fool. Again. Again.*

But each evening, he returned, his jaw tight, his expression tense, and I knew his attention was on parliamentary doings rather than some doxie. Increasingly, I suspected that, while I might be consumed by Ranulf's wandering eye, he himself thought little about sex beyond sating the urge when needed. Otherwise, once the act was decoupled from his desire for a child or to taunt me, I doubted he thought much about sex at all.

After my husband climbed the stairs to our chamber and began readying for bed, I chattered inanities about my day. On and on, while Ranulf performed his evening ablutions. Watching the play of muscle while he washed himself in a basin and brushed his teeth. His body always so tense, as if he might burst from his skin.

How difficult it must be for a man of action to stand around for hours on end listening to quarreling and speechifying.

Despite the hardships of our journey, I wished we were once more on the road, returning to Tintagel.

Soon it would be spring.

My second spring with Ranulf Navarre.

And my last.

I still hate you, I reminded myself, watching him cross to our bed. Inwardly laughing at the emptiness of that declaration.

Once beneath the covers, Ranulf would slide to me and bury his head in my hair.

"You smell like cherries," he'd say. Or apricots. Or lavender. "My favorite," my Ferdinand would murmur, no matter which fragrance. Soon he sighed, his breathing deepened, and he relaxed into sleep.

So many nights I lay awake, listening to Gloucester's Inn's timbers settle, to the winds whistle or howl and rains hammer upon the clay-tiled roof. Soothed by the warmth of Ranulf's body, touched by how little—a few drops of fragrant oil—it took to please him.

I did not allow my thoughts to dwell on the fact that the man beside me, so large and warm and powerful and invincible, would have his life snuffed in less than twenty weeks.

It cannot be so. Something will happen.

Pretending that wishful thinking could alter what had been written in the stars.

Inevitably, my hands crept to my stomach, imagining it was slightly rounded.

Despairing because I could not give Ranulf Navarre the one thing he desired above all.

Two things, really.

A child.

And a longer life.

Fifty-Two

Crash!

Our chamber door slammed against the wall, and I jumped, causing my quill pen to smear the letter I'd been forming on my parchment.

Ranulf entered, a whirlwind of energy, and strode to me. "Come along, wife. We've a feast to attend."

This was the first I'd heard of it. While Ranulf probably knew about my current artistic endeavors, I hid the results from him under the bed. More alarming, from my perspective, I doubted Janey could read and write. She certainly wouldn't have formed letters in Modern English.

"What are you doing?" Ranulf grabbed the parchment and stared down at it, brows drawn in a frown. Even if he was also illiterate, the shape of the words would be alien to anything he'd seen in a psalter or other contemporary work.

My mind was more blank than the parchment. I could think of nothing.

He ran a finger across the word, which had been "costermonger," the final "r" ending in a blob. Finger pausing, or perhaps frozen there.

My pulse quickened; I struggled to breathe. How could I explain? What plausible story might I concoct?

Before I could speak, Ranulf tossed the square back on the desk and shook his head, as if to say, "Wasting your time on such nonsense!"

"Have Gertrude dress your hair," he ordered and reached out to lift a strand, for I let my hair fall free when alone. He brought it to his nose and inhaled, but rather than his usual "Name the Fragrance" game, said, "Also change into your finest gown."

I finally found my voice. "Why? Where are we going? What is this about?"

"To your cousin's. He has invited us to a feast. With Simon De Montfort as our honored guest."

~

SIMON DE MONTFORT, 6th Earl of Leicester, was exactly what I expected him to be. And not.

Montfort was in his late fifties, his dark hair streaked with grey. The earl was not so tall or broad as Ranulf, but he carried himself like the warrior he was. Recently, Montfort had fallen from his horse and broken his leg, so he walked with a limp, but even dressed in a russet of middling quality, one would never mistake who ruled this room—or the kingdom.

Our introduction was so quick and unexpected it was only following my curtsy and after I stared up at Montfort that the enormity of the moment hit me. Here, this man standing before me, had successfully challenged the unlimited power of the king; his actions would pave the way for *every* man and woman to be politically represented.

And he would lead directly to the death of my husband.

I cannot say what we spoke of during our short conversation. Surely, the usual banalities. Montfort had a natural charisma, hardly surprising, having raised himself from almost nothing to *de facto* King of England. His speech was clipped and precise, each utterance sounding like a command. I needed not the verdict of historians to tell me that Simon de Montfort was intelligent and shrewd. Also, in that lean visage, with those bright, dark eyes lit by an inner fire, I saw the face of a religious zealot.

A divine madness, I found myself thinking. *And not in a good way*. I was relieved when he moved away, and a chamberlain blew the horn announcing our first course. From our position at a lower table, I could more discreetly study the man who would alter the fate of so many.

Gilbert de Clare's entertainment might be described as "intimate," with no more than twenty lords, not all with a female companion. Montfort sat in the center of the dais on an elaborately carved chair, almost a throne, with Gloucester at his right.

As the courses were set before us, jongleurs did a shortened version of a *Cirque du Soleil* performance followed by the recitation of a chivalric romance called *King Horn. King Horn* included the usual—wicked Saracens, mighty battles, lots of betrayals and endlessly thwarted lovers.

Beneath it all, the murmur of conversation, most of which, I suspected, centered around the man in the throne chair. I wondered at the real reason for this feast, or at least our invitation. *Has something happened in Parliament?* Ranulf had spoken with enthusiasm of a tournament that Gilbert de Clare was organizing. He wasn't the only knight eager for physical action. Beyond that, did tonight's feast hold some larger meaning?

King Horn was reaching its conclusion, which included a happily ever after for our long-suffering lovers, and I was beginning to droop. I wasn't used to so much food and my gown fitted more tightly than it should.

Could this be a sign we have been blessed with a miracle?

Despite my physical discomfort, I forced my attention to Simon de Montfort. This was a significant moment in my—our—lives, in history, and I must memorialize it, if only to myself.

Whether reaching for his goblet or retrieving a slice of meat from a proffered platter, the Earl of Leicester's every movement was measured. He ate and drank abstemiously. Simon de Montfort was legendary for his devoutness, which included inveterate fasting. He surrounded himself with more priests than knights and counted high-ranking clergy among his most trusted advisors. Each midnight he awakened in order to pray through the wee hours. He probably confessed his sins as often as he attended mass, which was daily—sometimes more than once. He had even taken an oath, it was rumored, to abstain from sexual congress with his wife.

All this I'd heard. Watching him seated so regally upon the dais, his dark eyes ablaze with that peculiar light, I believed that and more.

Perhaps because I knew what would cause Simon de Montfort, Earl of Leicester's downfall, of the venality that lived alongside the ascetic, I found myself comparing him to modern-day televangelists. You either buy their schtick and think they're wonderful or you question their every word. That's how I felt about Simon de Montfort.

I had been so focused on Montfort that we were well into our third course before I noticed the tension between him and Gilbert de Clare. Their body language had turned stiff, their conversation more heated.

Leaning in toward my husband, I nodded in the direction of the pair. "What is wrong?"

"Leicester is upset because Gloucester invited his two younger sons to participate in the tournament. Montfort believes that with all the warring factions his boys are in danger of being murdered. Montfort all but accused your cousin of wishing for their deaths."

Ranulf twisted his shoulders, as if trying to loosen his muscles, his attitude clearly proclaiming, "A pox on these intrigues." After taking another drink from the loving cup, he studied the two earls, whose expressions were tight, their jaws clenched. "I'll wager Montfort just ordered Gloucester to cancel the tournament, as he has long threatened. Your cousin will not take kindly to that. "

That's when I remembered.

Here in this timbered hall with Clare family banners proudly displayed upon plastered and painted walls, with the light from smoking candle wheels gleaming upon expensive silver tableware, with richly dressed barons who were sworn to the cause of parliamentary reform drinking and feasting, we were witnessing the beginning of the end of the alliance between Gilbert de Clare and Simon de Montfort. All too soon, "The Red Earl" would transfer his allegiance to King Henry. A move that would irrevocably splinter the rebels' loyalties.

I felt a chill, as if an artic wind had blown in through an opened door. Without realizing, my fingers dug into Ranulf's thigh. I wanted away from all this—this jockeying for power, these petty quarrels and, yes, even mighty matters of state. What I longed for was the banality of a life quietly lived. To play out my—our—days on a tiny stage. To arrive and depart this world as softly as a sigh.

And then the most peculiar thought came to me—one that must have been percolating in the recesses of my mind from the moment I first saw Ranulf gazing out upon Tintagel's ramparts. One that I'd openly contemplated when Ranulf caught me with my writing.

Tell him.

Could I warn my husband without revealing the actual truth? Maneuver around the time travel part, but somehow persuade him of the rest? Could I convince Ranulf to turn, as Gilbert de Clare would turn? If Ranulf did switch sides, would that save his life? Perhaps even alter our destinies?

Later, after we returned to Gloucester's Inn, undressed, and slipped into bed, I decided I must try.

If I fail, if I stumble when presenting my case, will you mock me as mad? Pack me off to a nunnery? Dismiss me as a fool?

Ranulf turned to me, lying on my back, and curled his fist into my hair.

I licked my lips. "Lord husband—"

"Tonight, you smell of apples," my Ferdinand said. "Sweet and tart." He tugged my hair to bring me closer, grasped my hips and positioned me atop him.

I did not tell him that night.

We left London in the spring of 1265, on the heels of Parliament's adjournment. Ranulf's men—all of us—were in high spirits, laughing and jesting, glad to be free of the city with its pall of pollution and its endless intrigues.

"Might we visit Canterbury?" I'd asked the previous night. "I would worship at Thomas Becket's shrine." That wrecking ball of all things Catholic, Henry VIII, had destroyed the saint's shrine and scattered his bones. This would be my opportunity to see the elaborate shrine in something other than ancient sketches.

Ranulf quoted in a soft voice, *"Such as thou art, some time was I; Such as I am, such shalt thou be. I little thought on the hour of death; So long as I enjoyed breath."*

While the words were familiar, I couldn't place them. Before I could question him on his seeming *non sequitur*, he said, "Aye, lady wife. 'Tis a good time of year for pilgrimages."

Which is the reason Ranulf, his men, and I were headed south on Watling Street, the old Roman road and the same route Geoffrey Chaucer would later memorialize in *The Canterbury Tales.* Kent, all of England, had shaken loose from winter. New-born calves and lambs tottered about in fields already lush with wildflowers. Birds called from hedgerows, traveling pilgrims sang their hymns, Col strummed his lute and sometimes, above it all, I caught the distant trill of a shepherd's pipe. The sun was warm on our faces and thinking ahead to tomorrow's visit to Canterbury, I fairly vibrated with excitement. Still, something felt off, though I couldn't think what it was, even after we'd bedded down in a priory near Rochester Cathedral.

The route from Rochester to Canterbury was familiar, not only as part of Pilgrims' Way, but for another reason. What? The answer teased my memory, refusing to show itself.

Though Ranulf immediately fell asleep after stretching out on our pallet, I could not. My muscles were sore from unaccustomed hours in the saddle, but that wasn't what caused this lingering unease. I had the most peculiar image of the ground having crumbled beneath me and pitched me into...something...that would leave me more adrift than I already was.

What is it? What is wrong? What am I missing?

Ranulf had wrapped himself around me as he always did when traveling. Since arriving in London, I'd worn a chemise to hide any changes to my body, which had become undeniable. Easy enough to keep my rounded stomach and larger breasts from a husband who was not overly interested in exploring the finer points of my body—at least beyond my hair. Right now, this very moment, yes, I *was* with child. But, even though I knew the illogic of it, I feared that once I revealed the news to Ranulf, I would miscarry. How could we possibly rewrite our scripts? Until I could no longer hide my condition, I would hold my secret close.

Even after the priory bell called monks to their early morning vigil, I stared dry-eyed into the darkness. Comforted by Ranulf's massive body, loving him and denying that I did, pretending, while knowing otherwise, that we might yet escape our destinies.

My increasingly muddled thoughts settled upon that unfortunate Tudor queen, the first Mary. While history might remember her for her nickname, Bloody Mary, and her persecution of Protestants, I was fixated on her phantom pregnancies. Exhibiting all the physical signs, Mary Tudor had even retired to a lying-in chamber—only to emerge empty-armed after her eleventh month.

Have I also deluded myself into a false pregnancy? Is this why I feel so uneasy? Why I can't sleep? Why I'm reluctant to share my news with Ranulf?

Because I know... I know...

Abruptly, with an almost audible click, everything fell into place. Like a giant set of moving gears, its teeth sliding from one to another.

Of course.

It wasn't my pregnancy that was keeping me awake, or my anticipation of tomorrow's destination.

Though it *did* have to do with our destination. Rochester to Canterbury was not only part of Pilgrims' Way, but the route the Black Prince's funeral cortege had—would—follow to bring Edward of Woodstock to his final resting place.

Which led me directly to Ranulf's response when I'd asked him if we might visit Canterbury Cathedral.

"*Such as thou art, some time was I...*"

Goosebumps erupted the length of my body.

I remember.

The source of that quote.

But that makes no sense.

I twisted in Ranulf's arms so that I could lay upon my back atop the uncomfortably thin pallet. Ranulf adjusted himself in sleep, repositioning a leg atop mine. Tears leaked from beneath my eyelids, their salt burning my aching eyes. Even through my chemise, I felt the heat of his body, the gentle puff of his breath against my ear. I wept because Ranulf Navarre didn't love me, because I was bewildered and frightened and didn't understand anything at all. Certainly not the revelation that had just zapped me with the force of a lightning bolt.

I must be mistaken. Could I be trapped in some sort of extended dream? Dreams had their own internal logic, which crumbled upon awakening. But I wasn't caught in some hypnagogic state. I was awake.

*This makes **no** sense.*

It can't be.

But it was.

The first lines Ranulf had quoted were not from a verse. They were from an epitaph describing Death, that great leveler of men—whether they be peasants or cardinals or kings.

As Magdalena Moore, I had seen that epitaph several times during my trips to Canterbury. It was inscribed in Latin on the tomb of Edward Woodstock, England's Black Prince.

Who died in 1376, more than a century in the future.

EVERY SPRING, a fictional Fordwich Castle held a fictional cherry fair in the middle of a fictional cherry orchard in the real-life village of Fordwich, within walking distance of Canterbury. Here it was that my *Knights of England* characters fell in love, married, nursed broken hearts and wept over cheating lovers, rejoiced in births and mourned deaths, all the while trying to survive political intrigues, plagues, and rebellions.

The overarching theme of the series is: "Life though pleasant is transitory, even as is the Cherry Fair."

I was certainly aware of the fleeting nature of life, of how quickly Magdalena Moore had run through her years, and how few weeks remained for my husband and me.

This lovely spring afternoon Ranulf, Col, and I were riding through the actual village of Fordwich. Improbably, fantastically.

Here. I am here!

Ranulf's men-at-arms had ridden ahead to Canterbury, though Ranulf had indulged me my side journey without complaint. I could not fathom why he was being so accommodating, but there was so much about Ranulf Navarre I didn't understand. While I'd applied clinical labels to him—narcissist, psychopath, misogynist—I'd generally simply described him in my head as "asshole."

I was no longer so sure.

Who are you? was a question that increasingly flitted through my brain. Last night remained another riddle in need of solving, though I had concocted a plausible explanation for the Mystery of the Epitaph. Simple, really. The epitaph had been in circulation well before Edward the Black Prince's death. Once we visited Thomas Becket's shrine, I was sure I'd find those very verses carved somewhere in the depths of Canterbury Cathedral.

Our jaunt through Fordwich—beginning at the Leopard's Head Inn on its outskirts, past the quaint Church of St. Mary the Virgin and ending at the road leading to the docks abutting the River Stour—might have taken five minutes.

Imagine my astonishment when, right beyond Fordwich's boundary, we happened upon an actual cherry orchard. Larger and more beautiful than anything in my imagination.

In full bloom. As the trees were always in bloom during my fictional Cherry Fairs.

"Oh!" I breathed, drawing rein. Clouds of cherry blossoms, row upon row, shimmered in the late afternoon sun.

"Isn't it enchanting?" I asked, too distracted to note whether Ranulf or Col responded. I felt as I had the moment I'd strode from Camelot Castle into the thirteenth century. As if I hovered between two worlds—as if when I peered into the orchard's heart, I would glimpse my fictional characters, like pale torches wavering among the trees.

Logically, I knew that finding a cherry orchard—or apple, pear, or plum—in a county nicknamed the "Garden of England" was hardly unusual.

Still, I could almost hear a whisper, beckoning me to *"Come. Have a look. Anything might happen."* Raising a hand to my necklace, I clasped the crystal, warm from my body heat.

"Might we explore?" Without awaiting Ranulf's permission, I managed a dismount so graceless that my teeth clacked together, and I had to grab Rouge's stirrup for balance.

Lifting my skirts above the tangle of grasses and wildflowers, I struck out across the meadow. I heard Ranulf order Col to watch our horses before reaching my side.

Those who have near-death experiences or are somehow transported to heaven say mere words cannot describe its beauty. Which is how I felt upon reaching the orchard. The trees, which were staggered rather than planted in neat rows, were so heavily weighted with white and pink blossoms that some branches caressed the ground. The air was redolent with their scent. As we stepped past the first rows, my vision filled with blossoms, so numerous they rivaled raindrops in a summer shower. A stillness descended, as if all the insects and woodland animals—even the trees themselves—had paused to measure our approach. That feeling again of stepping into a painting, of being participants in something supernal. Did Ranulf feel it too? I could not say, but somehow we were holding hands, which was an uncommon occurrence.

When we reached what I gauged to be the heart of the grove, Ranulf paused to bring one of the low-hanging branches to his nose. Closing his eyes, he inhaled its perfume, his expression blissful.

Watching him, I felt such a tenderness. How darkly beautiful he was, highlighted against the clouds of petals.

Remember him, my heart whispered. I wished we *had* entered a magical place, where we could be characters of my making, filled with hope and love and yearning and misunderstandings and challenges that I, as a writer, could manipulate into a happily ever after.

"*Mon Ferdinand le taureau,*" I whispered.

Ranulf slowly opened his eyes, as though drunk on the fragrance. "Who is Ferdinand the Bull?" He released the branch, breaking the spell.

Once more, I reached for his hand. "Come, let us sit. I would tell you a story."

Mindful of my sore muscles, I eased down against the trunk of a nearby tree, my rune ring catching on the rough bark. Ranulf dropped gracefully next to me. Cocooned in our bower, I allowed my shoulder to touch his. Through the trees, I spotted Col, legs apart, arms folded, watching over our grazing horses.

"Imagine," I began. "A very long time ago, in a faraway place, there lived a bull named Ferdinand. While Ferdinand was the biggest, fiercest-looking bull in all the kingdom, he possessed a gentle heart. All he wanted to do was lounge about among the flowers and the bees and the butterflies and all the rest of nature."

While I spun my story, Ranulf reached around him to pluck flowers and place them in his lap.

Knowing it would please my husband, I emphasized how menacing and strong Ferdinand looked in the bullfighting ring and how his human opponents quaked at the sight of him. Of course, bullfighting was several centuries in the future, and I couldn't mention words like "matador," so I improvised, the way one can in tall tales.

"So, Ferdinand was very fierce," Ranulf said, obviously pleased by my characterization. His thick, scarred fingers deftly twisted the stems resting atop his surcoat into a flower garland.

"He was by far the biggest and strongest of all the bulls, and he could be mean-tempered. But only when he accidentally sat on a bee and found himself with a stinger embedded in his arse. Then his bellow was heard throughout the kingdom."

Ranulf's teeth flashed white against his tanned skin, and he laughed, a lovely sound I heard all too seldom. While he bent over his wreath, I noticed more strands of silver amid the black of his hair. Because Ranulf was such a force of nature, I tended to forget he was fifteen years my senior. I balled my hands into fists in order to keep from reaching out to touch his hair, to rearrange the strands and run my fingers through their softness.

A cherry blossom drifted down to settle like a kiss upon Ranulf's shoulder.

I swallowed down the wave of emotion tightening my throat and blinked away the sudden prick of tears. This moment was its own form of magic.

Leaning over, Ranulf removed my head covering and placed the finished garland atop my hair. We sat in comfortable silence, interrupted only by the distant bells of Canterbury Cathedral and voices from sailors loading and unloading cargo on nearby docks. Over time the effects of a night with too little sleep, as well as the perfumed atmosphere, caused my eyelids to droop. I suppressed a yawn, and then a second.

"Let's rest, for just a few minutes," I murmured. So tired, almost as if I'd taken a sleeping potion. Vaguely, I thought of the scene in *The Landlord's Black-Eyed Daughter* when Plucky Bess had fallen asleep in the Vale of Evesham so she might dream her dream of another Lady Jane's betrayal of another Ranulf Navarre.

If I fall asleep now, might I have a similar dream, something that made sense of this past year?

Removing my garland, I stretched out, placing it atop my stomach.

Ranulf followed. Had I not been so tired, I might have burrowed my head against his chest to cushion my head from the ground. But I was already drifting into that state between awareness and oblivion.

I barely registered Ranulf's removal of the garland from my stomach. Or his exploratory hand across it, signaling an amorous mood.

My brain was too hazy to realize the danger, that, even through my clothing, Ranulf would be able to map the changes to my body.

Ranulf paused in his exploration. "Janey?"

That one word yanked me back to the present. My eyes flew open and met Ranulf's, which were wide with shock.

Before I could think to speak or move, Ranulf was on his knees, straddling either side of my legs. He yanked up my gown and chemise, revealing the leggings I wore for riding and my bare stomach.

Carefully, he ran a hand over my exposed flesh.

"You are with child?" His eyes never left my stomach.

My heart began a staccato hammering, as if, now that Ranulf knew, the babe would abruptly disappear like the puff of smoke heralding the climax of a magician's trick.

"Can it be so?" Placing both hands upon my stomach, Ranulf continued his careful exploration.

I so wanted this to be true, so wanted the wonder of his expression to remain rather than crumble to grief when the gods turned against us.

"Speak to me, Janey. Are you with child? Why haven't you told me?"

"I didn't want to disappoint you if I wasn't really...if it was a mistake."

Ranulf threw back his head and laughed. "A son!"

For now, I would share Ranulf's happiness. I could grant him that much. "I..I am glad you're pleased," I said, suddenly shy.

"Pleased?" He shook a fist at the heavens and bellowed, "My son!"

Grabbing my hand, he pulled us both to our feet. In so doing, he knocked against a branch, causing blossoms to tremble around us and their scent to envelop us.

Ranulf wrapped his arms about me so tightly I struggled to breathe before abruptly loosening his grip. I could almost hear his thoughts. *Careful...must not hurt my babe.*

"When?" he whispered.

"Late August, I think." Shoving down the horrible event that would accompany that landmark.

"You are carrying my son, Janey!"

I found myself laughing with him, and when he picked me up, willingly slipping my arms around his neck.

"Col!" he called to his watching squire. "Congratulate me. I am to be a father!"

Fifty-Four

While Ranulf Navarre would never be a hero from the pages of a romantic tale, he was almost worshipful, not because of me, but because of the treasure I carried.

He insisted that I ride with him rather than separately, which meant a few extra days in Canterbury to have his saddle properly modified. During our wait, I was allowed to enjoy a town I dearly loved, parts of which have not so greatly changed over the centuries. I *did* visit Thomas Becket's shrine—an enormously gaudy monument of gold and silver studded with precious stones, some the size of a fist. Unfortunately, so many pilgrims packed the cathedral that our black-robed Benedictine guides hurried us past so quickly I was unable to test my hypothesis concerning the Mystery of the Epitaph.

Once we struck out from Canterbury, our hours in the saddle were halved, partially due to Ranulf's determination that we give thanks at every passing shrine. "We can't have you jostle our son," he said, his arm wrapped protectively above my stomach as we rode. He seemed to take particular pleasure in the phrase "our son."

Ranulf's men good-naturedly adapted to our glacial pace. We in the future might gush about "living in the moment," but our ancestors largely *did*. When one could not bend nature to one's will, when entertainments largely had to come from imagination rather than electronic devices and other manufactured distractions, patience ruled the day. As did simple amusements.

So many times between bouts of singing and conversation, much of it teasing Ranulf about his behavior as a proud papa, my husband slipped his hand to my stomach and murmured against my ear, "*Hush little baby, don't say a word*," in a reasonable facsimile of modern English. That had surprised me since I'd prided myself on being discreet when singing to Lizbeth.

Ranulf also serenaded our child with an older lullaby that began, "*Lullay lullow, lullay lully*," in a voice so sweet it melted my heart. There were times, amid his whispered endearments, that I was undone by the purity of his happiness. I could not be pregnant, but somehow, I was. I could not carry this babe to term, but I was four months along. Still, if I did successfully deliver a child, Ranulf would not live to see it born. How could God—something, someone—grant him the deepest desire of his heart, only to see that it would never be fulfilled? Was this some sort of punishment? I didn't believe in hell, but I did believe in karma.

Still, while I would never describe Ranulf Navarre as a "good" man, what did the word even mean? Wouldn't that depend on one's interpretation of good, as well as the century? Moreover, in the long arc of history, Ranulf Navarre, like most of us, was a flawed human being rather than a monster.

When such worries overwhelmed me, I rested my head against my husband's chest, imagining I could hear the beating of his heart through several layers of clothing, and swallowed back sobs.

Naturally, Ranulf noticed, as he now noticed everything about me.

"Are you tired, Janey?" he would ask. "Should we rest for the day?" Even when it was not yet afternoon.

I'd shake my head. "You know what emotional creatures pregnant women can be."

Which caused him to grin proudly and—I imagined—puff out his chest like Mussolini standing on a balcony, basking in the adoration of his *fascistas*.

Or perhaps Ranulf Navarre was simply like most every other man who had been granted the desire most precious to his heart.

~

We did not reach Glastonbury Abbey until well into our second week. Glastonbury! A little over a year ago, I had met Felix Eastoft and begun my journey down the rabbit hole.

Since *this* Glastonbury Abbey was one of England's wealthiest, our accommodations were better than normal, though Ranulf was not important enough to receive personal attention from its abbot. Such was reserved for lords the caliber of Gilbert de Clare.

Once we were fed and rested, I could not resist asking Ranulf if we might visit the tombs of Arthur and Guinevere in the abbey church. Nearly three centuries later, under the reign of Henry VIII, they would be destroyed, and while the tombs were the medieval version of a hoax, I could almost believe them to be true. Because everyone around me did.

Afterward, we walked to Glastonbury Tor. As Magdalena Moore, I had trod the path to its summit and visited the ruins of St. Michael's Church, which was now intact, the silhouette of its bell tower darker than the twilight settling over Somerset. All of it seeming normal and yet not. Centuries yawned between this and my contemporary visits and yet much of the landscape, many of the landmarks, fit one atop the other.

That untethered feeling, as if I were floating between two worlds, returned. I clasped Ranulf's hand to ground me.

We visited Chalice Well located at the foot of Glastonbury Tor. Here it was that Joseph of Arimathea had buried the holy grail which had caught drops of Christ's blood at the crucifixion, thus turning the water red.

Because of the lateness of the hour, the area was blessedly empty. Ranulf knelt beside the well to scoop up a handful of water. Knowing that the red color was due to all manner of foul-tasting minerals, I declined to follow him in drinking. Afterward, he stood, bowed his head, made the sign of the cross, and murmured an Ave Maria.

Who is this stranger? I wondered. This could not be the same man who avoided morning mass at Tintagel and glowered at Father Peter if the priest's pre-meal graces extended beyond short and sweet.

I felt such tenderness toward Ranulf, even when I knew better. This quiet bower—renowned for its Christian holiness and before that, pagan magic—seemed to stir...unusual...albeit misguided emotions. Was it my imagination, or did my crystal pendant feel extra hot upon my skin? Wouldn't it be lovely if Glastonbury Tor was indeed a gateway to fairyland, where beautiful faerie men and women could sometimes be glimpsed riding into the side of the hill? Or perhaps Druids, dancing naked to welcome the summer solstice?

Glastonbury Abbey's bells rang compline, reminding the faithful of Night Prayer and then bed. And that it was the Christian God who now laid claim to Glastonbury.

Ranulf and I remained wrapped in the gloaming, with only the gentle murmur of a nearby pipe feeding into the well. Once again, the atmosphere possessed a hushed, expectant quality. As if waiting for me to speak...

Say something!

The knowledge of Ranulf's impending fate had been like a giant boulder upon my chest these past weeks, slowly, inexorably crushing the life from me.

"Simon de Montfort is sowing the seeds of his own destruction." The words flowed from me the way Chalice Well's sacred waters flowed into its basin. "He is behaving the way so many do when seizing power, by repeating the same transgressions of his predecessors. Can you not see that? Do you not know where this is headed?" I paused, breathless—and excited—by the beginnings of my confession.

Ranulf studied me through narrowed eyes, his body language telegraphing his dismissiveness. I rushed on. "Montfort is showering his family members with lands and titles and behaving as foolishly as King Henry. The only difference is that Montfort is skilled enough to move swiftly to consolidate his power. Which will only hasten his downfall."

"So says my wife, the soothsayer." Ranulf's lips curved in a mocking smile. "Has my ring been whispering to you about the future?"

"Montfort's power numbers in weeks, not years," I continued stubbornly, moving closer to him. A dusting of stars had appeared behind the tower of St. Michael's Church along with a fingernail moon. A breeze sprang up, causing leaves to rustle around us and a strand of Ranulf's hair to inch toward his mouth.

"It is easy enough to observe human nature. Montfort has a grasping family. His wife. His children. Lord Almighty, but their greed is boundless."

Ranulf continued studying me. Rather than more sarcasm or engaging in a pointed round of questioning, he snaked out an arm to pull me against him. Raising my left hand, which held the rune ring, he ran an index finger around its design, as though its secrets might indeed whisper to him.

"I am a baron of middling importance," he finally said, dropping his hands to my rounded stomach. "We are far away from the Marcher lands, which Montfort most covets and where his barons are most dissatisfied. I will have my sword arm speak for me."

"That is a non-answer. You must—"

"The night is turning chill. You're not dressed for it." Ranulf wrapped an arm around me and pulled me away from the well, to the entrance of the grove. "Let us return to our lodgings," he said, clear in his dismissal. "We've a long ride tomorrow."

I was nearly six months along. The babe remained nestled safely inside, and I allowed myself to hope that God had granted us a miracle. Even as I knew better. However, "Hope springs eternal" is a cliché for a reason. Hope, no matter the circumstances, can prove impossible to kill.

Upon our return from London, Ranulf moved us from the solar—stairs!—set up a series of privacy screens and disassembled and re-assembled our bed in a corner of Tintagel's great hall.

"We will sleep here until my son arrives," he informed me. "It will be safer for you to move about."

Nightly Ranulf shared our bed, retreating when I did, even tending to some of Lenota and Eve's duties such as undressing me and combing my hair. With my increasing bulk, settling me into bed had become a bit of an undertaking. Ranulf mastered it by scooping me into his arms and depositing me gently atop the mattresses, followed by a final rearranging of pillows that had already been plumped. "You feel heavier, wife," he would say, or "Your belly has grown," with such pride, as if he were responsible.

While Ranulf continued administering his daily duties, he always kept an eye on my whereabouts. When my maids and I went to market, Ranulf accompanied us, retrieving my empty basket to carry under his arm. Throughout the walk, he asked whether I needed to rest, was hungry or thirsty, or should be carried across a rough patch of ground. (Earning a rather smug smile from Lenota and envious sighs from Eve—at least the few times when Col was not at her side.)

"I am thinking you should stay in bed until your birthing," he said during one sojourn.

"Three months of bed rest? Eve would have to knock me out with one of her potions to keep me sane." I said it lightly and was stunned when I could swear his face paled. Quickly, he changed the subject; I shrugged it off as my imagination.

A dozen times a day, Ranulf beckoned me to him.

"How is my son?" Oblivious to those around us, he splayed his fingers atop my belly.

If the babe was active, Ranulf grinned his delight. "He is a lusty one. What a fine warrior he'll be." When it was quiet, Ranulf's dark brows drew together. "When did you last feel him? Why is he not moving? I told you to rest more. If you overtax yourself, you'll harm our boy."

At night, with the smells of the evening meal warring with my Ferdinand's omnipresent bouquets, we settled into bed. Ranulf inevitably rested his head upon my stomach and when our babe kicked, talked to him. "You will be the finest knight in history, as renowned as Arthur, as loyal as Lancelot, as pure as Galahad..."

I laughed. "Let's not get carried away. He is your son, after all."

"You will be the first of many Ranulfs," he promised my stomach while gently stroking it. I'd not thought a man could be so tender, certainly not Ranulf Navarre. I could not resist running my fingers through my husband's hair, so thick and lustrous. "We will call him Ranulf the Younger," I promised, fighting back tears.

Behind everything I did—every smile, every conversation, the smallest act, my every interaction with Ranulf—was that storm on the horizon. Slowly, inexorably the clouds would pile one atop the other until the deluge was loosed.

I experienced such a tenderness toward him, made more bittersweet with the knowing that, as big and skilled and dangerous as

Ranulf Navarre might be, he was still a man. His façade of invincibility could—and would be—pierced.

My Ferdinand would bleed out alongside all the rebels who, before summer's end, would engage Henry III and Edward Longshanks on the field of Evesham.

Fifty-Six

Something was very wrong with sweet Eve. Her expression was drawn, and she had dark smudges beneath her eyes. Rather than attend to her duties, my maid often disappeared or spent long hours locked away in the herb garden. I often caught Lenota studying her, eyebrows drawn in a worried frown.

After coming across Eve crying, I questioned her, only to have her shake her head. "Has Col done something?" I had been remiss postponing talking to Ranulf about a match. Without asking permission, she simply spun on her heel and scurried away.

I don't know when I realized the devastating truth—that Col was not the object of Eve's affections.

Ranulf was.

Once I realized, a thousand damning images assailed me with the force of a smithy's hammer. The blushes, soft looks, and sighs, the flirtations aimed at the wrong target. Col was always with Ranulf and I, fool that I was forever and ever, had mistaken the object of Eve's affections.

Not Ranulf's handsome squire.

No, not at all.

"How could this be?" You might ask. "How could you know?"

I caught them.

Oh, they thought they were so clever! As if my pregnancy rendered my legs unworkable! Ranulf might treat me like an invalid—now I knew why, and it wasn't because of care for my condition—but I was far from that. So that when I lumbered from the great hall to the kitchen in order to inform Cook that stewed apples should be added to tonight's menu, I saw them. Beyond the kitchen, by the gate leading to Tintagel's herb garden. The pair chest to chest. Ranulf looking down at her, while Eve gazed intently up at him, saying...whatever while waving her arms about. Obviously distressed, as she should be for betraying her mistress. Ranulf reaching out to still her hands. And then to wrap his arms around her waist, she folding herself into him.

Of course. Since I can no longer service you, you've found a substitute.

I closed my eyes. *No wonder you drove Janey mad.* I imagined my alter ego at the edge of one of Tintagel's bleak promontories, alone and tiny, raising her fists to the heavens and screaming, screaming, screaming...

I'd allowed myself to be tricked ten times over. Nothing had changed.

I will retire to a nunnery, and if we indeed thwart the fates, give birth behind its walls. To hell with you. I hope you go to your death believing I denied you access to your child.

I fantasized miraculously returning to the twenty-first century. Having my baby in a clean hospital, surrounded by actual doctors and something other than quack treatments or sketchy herbal remedies.

Driving Ranulf mad with my sudden disappearance.

But I'd tried the reverse glitch in time bit before. And, after pondering all the implications, I realized I'd return, not as pregnant Jane of Holywelle, but as Magdalena Moore, an old, barren woman...

So... there would be no escape. But this time I would confront Eve and then my husband. After that I would retreat to a nunnery, ridding myself forever of Tintagel.

I HAD NEVER ENTERED Tintagel's private garden. Because of others' reactions, I sensed I should not. I had no actual idea why beyond my own instinctive reluctance and those peculiar headaches that seemed to warn me away.

I had become clever with my condition, substituting little Nicholas for my eyes and legs.

"Eve is now in the garden," he informed me one afternoon.

"Climb over the gate and unbolt it from the inside." Not questioning how I knew the gate was locked by a key on the outside and locked by sliding a bolt into a hole on the inside.

"Then tell Cook you are to have an extra doughnut as a reward." I ruffled his dark curls. "Let's make that two."

Upon approaching the garden gate, I felt a curious churning in my stomach, a lightheadedness. When putting my hand on the solid wooden gate held in place by large iron hinges dusted with rust, I *knew* I had once tended this garden alongside Eve. As I'd helped mix and minister potions for everything from diarrhea to heart palpitations to cold remedies. Before touching the gate, I'd not remembered any of that.

Inside. The garden was planned chaos, with the taller aromatics such as balm, the marjorams and mints on the edge and the lower plants growing around the border of a meandering path leading to a thatched wooden shed.

I inhaled deeply, identifying various herbs like angelica that we used for cooking, medicines and perfumes. Once these scents had soothed me...and then they had not. I remembered Eve and me and a handful of other women weeding and raking, hoeing and staking out the raised beds, the various carefully grouped varieties, all planted in accordance with the cycles of the moon.

My gaze snapped to the corner opposite the shed and there it was, the bench where Ranulf sometimes sat when he'd time to get away or seemed in need of peace and the calming fragrance of various plants.

So real, I could almost see him. Eyes closed, face upturned to the sun. I'd witnessed that scene many times.

Why did I not remember before this moment?

Since the garden appeared devoid of people, Eve must be in the shed. With each step in that direction, I felt invisible fingers press against my throat, making swallowing painful.

I don't like this.

My heart beat against my chest like war drums calling knights to battle. *Boom, boom, boom.* Panic. Half-turning, thinking to leave.

Eve's voice drifted from the shed's interior.

Is this where you and Ranulf meet? Where you're meeting at this very moment?

No, that couldn't be right. Today, my husband presided over manorial court.

I crept as best as I could toward the wattle and daub structure. Since the windows were no more than holes and their shutters open, I had a clear view inside.

Bundles of drying plants hanging from the ceiling, shelves filled with jars and bowls. In the center of the tiny room, a scarred wooden table was cluttered with plants and various implements.

Eve ground a pestle into a mortar of herbs while reciting in a small, shaky voice, "Sage, rue, pennyroyal." Over and over, like a mantra.

A peculiar feeling, a sudden flash, as if lightning had gone to ground inside my head.

"Sage, rue, pennyroyal..."

Something is very wrong. Something I mustn't think about. Something terrible that happened inside that shed.

"Sage, rue, pennyroyal."

I knew that the combination of those particular herbs was used for abortions. *What is this?* Was dear sweet Eve thinking to poison me? Scheming to abort my baby at this late date? So that she could have Ranulf all to herself?

To abort my baby.

That flash inside my head. Images. The truth came to me, what everyone had been hiding from me.

"No," I breathed. I reached out to steady myself, causing a shutter to thud against the wall. Eve jumped before turning to face me, her face the color of bleached muslin.

"My lady?"

Little things suddenly slotted together. Flash. Flash. I saw it all. The real reason for my visit to St. Michael's Mount. The real reason Ranulf was so angry.

"Oh! You're not to be here, my lady."

Janey had missed her courses. I *had missed my courses. Scarce believing, I'd not told anyone. I'd been late before, but they'd always been false alarms. Never this many days. And Ranulf was so cruel to me. Ignoring me or accusing me of hysterics, of being possessed. Refusing to understand. To love me. I knew everyone in the household hated me, knew I was all alone, that all of Tintagel carried tales to Ranulf regarding his mad wife. I knew they did. My thoughts... violent...toward myself and others. There were certain things... but it was Ranulf's fault. All his fault.*

Aye, once he'd pretended to care, to treat me tenderly, to call me his princess rather than his mouse, sworn his eternal love...

Don't remember! Don't remember!

Even God was mocking me. After all this time when I'd petitioned Him and haunted shrines begging for a child, He'd given me one when it would have been like delivering the spawn of the devil.

Eve beside me, her hand on one of my wrists. Saying something, but I was deep in this other memory.

I would not, WOULD NOT have this child.

When the area was deserted, I slunk into the shed. Cold. Near All Hallows Eve. Searching through various ceramic pots and herbals, fumbling through jars arrayed on the shelves, mumbling "Sage, rue, pennyroyal" like the lunatic I was. Until I found the herbs. Pennyroyal was the key. So innocuous, smelling like mint rather than the death dealer it could be. In high enough doses, it induced labor.

The moment I curled my fist around the jar, I became aware of a cramping, the kind I experienced before my periods. A second, then a third. I knew then I'd no need to get rid of anything. Not pregnant at all. Sliding down to the ground. Weeping and then...

Eve was leading me away from the shed, an arm around my waist while the scene played before me.

Madwoman. Screaming, crying, smashing containers, anything within reach against the wall. Picking up a jar of nightshade, knowing what I would do...

Deadly. Good. End it. End my misery; end the infinite torment of loving, loathing him. *But I'd gotten the proportions wrong. Only enough nightshade to act as a purgative. Terrible stomach cramps. Vomiting. Days and days. Father*

Abel administering Extreme Unction. Weeks of convalescence. Weeks when Ranulf had not left my side, Lenota later told me. And that I'd ignored him. Refused to speak to him or anyone. Until I came to grips with the enormity of my sin and what I must do to redeem myself.

I hadn't gone to St. Michael's Mount to pray for a child.

I'd gone to St. Michael's Mount to receive absolution for my attempted suicide.

COL AND EVE were married within the week. It had been Ranulf who had taken note of her pregnancy, who had ferreted the truth from her that his squire was the father. While Eve, in her despair, had unwittingly decided to choose a similar path to mine. Rid herself of an illegitimate child.

As for me?

I knew not what to think or to feel.

Or to be.

Fifty-Seven

We each write our autobiographies, if only in the recesses of our brains. And, while we embrace it as the truth of "our life"—we lived it, didn't we?—it is fiction. It has to be. We rummage through billions of random thoughts and experiences in order to pull out the few necessary to concoct a coherent story. Humans are hardwired to create order from chaos. In other words, we are the ultimate unreliable narrators.

As was Jane of Holywelle. And since I was mucking about in the sludge of Janey's psyche—since I was kind of, sort of her—I'd been duped. As Janey had been duped, viewing her world, particularly her husband, through her own damaged lens.

"Why do you keep staring at me?" Ranulf asked, interrupting my musings.

Of course, I had been. As if the entire complicated truth of Ranulf Navarre and Lady Jane had been stamped upon his visage. I had missed so much. On the heels of Eve and the herb garden incident, the window to my subconscious had been flung open, releasing a flood of memories. Ranulf's tenderness on our wedding night; love songs sung to me in those early years, sweet as any troubadour's; pulling me on his lap when I'd find him on his bench in the garden... image after image, layer upon layer, all the building blocks necessary to create a happy marriage. They'd all been there. Until, gradually, over time, it changed. **I** changed.

Even now, my head ached to think of it—the suspicions, accusations, jealousies that, along with my barrenness and his obsession with bearing a son and heir, had driven me to a breakdown. I realized now Ranulf's infidelities largely existed in my imagination. Even with Gypsy. He'd not taken her to bed until after I'd made my threats about the nunnery, had threatened suicide if he touched me, and later... the things Janey—I—had done. Too painful to face all at once, this sorting of fact from fiction. Ranulf Navarre the flawed human being vs. Ranulf Navarre the monster fashioned from my pain and sickness.

"You surprise me at times, husband," I said, finally responding to Ranulf's question. "In pleasant ways. There is more to you than a pretty face."

He frowned at the unfamiliar phrase but did not further question me.

There were times I wanted to cradle his cheeks between my hands and kiss him; to twine his fingers through mine so I might feel his strength and warmth; to apologize for misjudging him, for hurting him.

How selfish I've been. How deluded.

Ranulf Navarre might not have been the romantic hero of my—or Janey's dreams—but at one time, at least, he'd tried.

May marched inexorably onward. I was very aware that political events were continuing apace, days away from our tiny pocket of England. In less than a sennight, Edward Longshanks would escape his rebel captors, which would start the Doomsday clock inching toward Armageddon.

An important marker I preferred not to ponder.

It has naught to do with Ranulf Navarre, I soothed myself.

But it did. On the heels of Prince Edward's flight, Simon de Montfort would call up his supporters for his final campaign...

Before we'd all scattered to complete our morning duties following daily mass, the outside world appeared in the form of a pilgrim. I knew the stranger wasn't who he professed to be for he rode a mule, whereas pilgrims generally walked. Mules were hardier than regular horses, and since this one looked well worn, I deduced the pilgrim had traveled a fair distance. Furthermore, he carried the look of a fighting man.

After closeting himself with my husband and Col, the stranger departed. When I questioned Ranulf, his response was a terse "Not your worry."

Even after we retreated for the evening, Ranulf remained taut as a bow string. When the bedside rushlight finally flickered out, he sighed, turned on his side and pressed a hand to my belly as if grounding himself.

"What is it, husband?" I whispered. "Please tell me."

Ranulf was quiet for so long I thought he would not answer. Then he said, "These are unsettling times."

Which wasn't exactly news.

I must have drifted off, only to awaken when Ranulf eased from bed. I watched his shape in the darkness, slipping on his clothes, exiting the chamber.

I had no choice but to follow.

Wrapped in a dark cloak, I fancied myself invisible, though my bulk made my movements clumsy. I stayed close enough to keep Ranulf in view but far enough away he'd not hear me stumble on the rough terrain.

He was headed toward the Chapel of St. Julitta. Beyond that lay Tintagel's orchard and the handful of huts.

"What are you up to?" I muttered, before realizing I needed to save my breath and concentrate on avoiding falling on my face.

After passing St. Julitta, Ranulf headed in the direction of Tintagel's walled garden.

I ducked inside the church portico. Father Peter must be spending the night in Trevena, where he sometimes served double duty as chaplain of St. Materiana's, an ancient Saxon church overlooking the village.

A figure emerged from the garden area, his height and bulk clearly identifying his sex. The man's mantle billowed in the wind that had sprung off the sea. I grasped the stone facing of the portico, wincing when my rune ring caught upon a rough spot.

Who are you? Why the secrecy? What is this about?

Ranulf and the stranger stood silhouetted against the skyline. Drew closer. Their heads inclined together, as if sharing secrets, though who could hear anything above the pounding waves, the rustling wind? And who other than me would be watching?

I waited in the shadows until the pair embraced, ending their assignation. While Ranulf watched, the figure walked toward me in the direction of Tintagel Castle. The stranger's hood was thrown back; his cloak swirled around him with each step. His stride was familiar, though I couldn't place it. Until, in passing, his face was revealed in the light of the half-moon. I even fancied I could discern his red hair.

Gilbert de Clare, Earl of Gloucester. The pilgrim had been a disguise for one of Gloucester's men, obviously seeking an assignation.

Which made no sense. Gilbert de Clare should be way north, monitoring Prince Edward's escape.

I tried to puzzle out a reason for this clandestine visit. Did Clare consider events too dangerous to be openly spotted in rebel territory? But baronial loyalties, particularly my cousin's, shifted with the shadows. Ranulf had shrugged off Clare's change of heart.

I should have told you everything. Even though Ranulf would simply dismiss me again.

Still, for an important man like the Earl of Gloucester to travel halfway across the kingdom, he wanted something from my husband. What?

Gilbert de Clare's boots thudded soft upon the earth, gradually fading as their wearer vanished.

My breathing sounded far too loud in the enclosed space of the portico. I'd not realized my hands were balled into fists, my fingernails digging into my palms. This meeting must have something to do with Clare's turning. Was Ranulf trying to persuade him to reconsider his treason? Or the reverse: Was my cousin somehow thinking to use Ranulf? Betray him?

After a time, Ranulf followed Clare, only to abruptly veer toward St. Julitta. "What are you doing out here?" he challenged.

So much for my stealth abilities.

Before I could formulate a plausible response, he joined me. Predictable as the seasons: "You'll harm my son."

"Why is Gilbert de Clare sneaking about in the dead of night? What does he want?"

"Let's get you to bed. I can feel you shivering through your mantle." Ranulf had put his arm around me to guide me, but I refused to move. I gazed up at him, trying to read clues to...something...in the planes and hollows of his face.

In ten weeks, you'll be dead.

The reality struck me full force, the accompanying sorrow nearly knocking me to my knees. "Gilbert de Clare will help Prince Edward escape his captors," I blurted. "Simon de Montfort will then try to align himself with the Prince of Wales to increase his fighting force, which will only further alienate Marcher lords—"

"Do not fret matters you know naught about," Ranulf interrupted.

"I **do** know." Beyond that, I could only manage a pathetic wail. "I don't want you to die!"

"I have no intention of dying." Ranulf's fingers dug through the thick wool of the mantle into my shoulder. "Come along, Janey. Nerves are bad for our baby."

Is this how cows feel when being forced through the slaughterhouse chute?

"We need to talk, Ranulf. You must listen."

He led me back to the great hall, undressed me and carefully put me to bed.

When I tried to speak, Ranulf put a rough finger against my lips. *"Hush little baby, don't say a word,"* he singsonged and kissed my forehead.

After which, he crawled into bed beside me and cradled me in his arms until he, at least, fell asleep.

Our last night before Ranulf and his men rode away to their fate. *Doomed, doomed, doomed.* Prince Edward's escape had unleashed the hounds of hell. The Marcher lords were in open rebellion, flocking to King Henry and his son, the prince.

Seven weeks until the hounds would tear apart the hares.

After retreating to our makeshift bedroom, Ranulf had washed my hair—this time with apple scented shampoo—over a basin to spare me the awkwardness of contorting my body. Dried strands now covered his chest in a silken shawl.

Each day, Evesham, with all its name represented, tormented me. I felt myself fracturing, each part smaller than the previous, like a house of mirrors stretching into infinity. I could no longer erect emotional barriers between us or pretend that I did not love Ranulf Navarre body and soul. I did. After accepting that, through a misfire or gift from the universe, I had become pregnant and might yet become a mother, other perceptions had also shifted.

Not only about Janey. My previous behavior, my "love" increasingly struck me as having more to do with my needs than any genuine devotion toward Ranulf. More my outsized ego complaining because it could not have its way. I'd wrapped obsession in its cloak and called it love, but it was still obsession. I'd been more determined to break Ranulf Navarre to my will, to win at our demented game than to care for the actual man himself. He'd been an object I needed to possess rather than flesh and blood.

Is that what I was sent back to learn?

Our babe began moving more forcefully than usual. Ranulf slid a hand down to rest his palm upon the bump, following its track across my flesh. I felt his smile in my hair and tears leak from beneath my closed eyelids. What good would this child do, for me, for us, when it had no father? When what Ranulf most wanted in the world would be denied him? Why would God so punish him?

Foolish, foolish me. It wasn't about punishment; it was simply the casting of the runes...

"There is going to be a battle, early August," I began, feeling the steady beating of his heart against my ear. "The rebels will lose. Simon de Montfort will be killed, and most of his men. You... Please, please do not fight, Ranulf."

"How do you know these things?" He changed position so he could view my face in the summer's moonlight. For once, he appeared curious rather than dismissive.

"Dreams," I lied. "Or mayhap it's the rune ring."

"One need not be a prophet to guess where this will end," Ranulf said, reverting to his usual flippancy. "Montfort is daily losing support, and your cousin Gloucester was the only thing keeping the Marcher lords in check. Simon de Montfort ought not to have been as grasping as the king. He ought not to have repeated Henry of Winchester's mistakes."

"Is this why you met with Gilbert de Clare? Was he trying to persuade you to join the royalists?"

"Enough, Janey." He sighed. "This is not a matter for women."

"It's a matter for me when you will leave me a widow and your son without a father," I wanted to scream.

But I'd said all I dared. Once again, he'd refused to listen.

Through the night, with Ranulf slumbering beside me, I railed against God, the fates, whatever was toying with us. What scales were being balanced? Had we expiated our sins, whatever they might be, so we'd be granted our hearts' desire? But, if that were so, why would Ranulf be punished in the cruelest of fashions? Leaving me a widow with a child who would be labeled the progeny of a traitor? I *knew* our future in Henry of Winchester's England—shunning, confiscated lands, at least until the rebels' punishment was lifted, which would occur at a ruinous financial cost. Would I be forced to marry again, *need* to marry for protection? But who would wed a woman with a minor title and a bit of land, if I was lucky, and who was past her prime childbearing years?

Aye, the runes had been cast.

And it was not only Ranulf Navarre who was doomed.

WHILE COL HELD Ranulf's stallion, my husband approached me. Tintagel's household was clustered about the bailey, most looking solemn, the children sleepy but excited. Father Peter had already blessed Ranulf and his retinue.

I extended Ranulf's arming sword. A sliver from the true cross rested inside the pommel, or so went the story. With trembling fingers, I belted the sword across Ranulf's hips.

My eyes felt as if they'd been scoured by sandpaper. I gazed up at him. For the last time...

The last time...

Slipping the crystal pendant from inside my gown, I handed it to him. "Please wear this. Beneath your armor. For protection." A futile gesture, yet I made it anyway.

After, Ranulf placed his hands on both sides of my stomach before sliding them to the front, over my belly button. Leaning down, he kissed the spot through my kirtle.

He straightened, and once again our eyes locked. Words were pointless. To tell him I loved him meant nothing. To admonish him to stay safe was a mockery. He was a knight going off to war. Answering his call to duty without whining or complaint. I could not deny there was a certain nobility in facing your fate with unflinching determination and courage. At least in novels and histories and ballads and in the abstract. In real life, it was not nearly so glorious. Not when the survivors would have to live with the aftermath.

"I will be back before the child is born," he said finally, his voice husky, his expression tender.

Ranulf raised a hand to where he could feel my heartbeat and pressed a final kiss upon my forehead before turning to mount his palfrey.

In moments, the bailey was empty of men and horses. A fog had rolled in, obliterating all sign of them save for the distant clop of hooves, a fading jangle of harnesses.

I heard the muffled sounds of weeping and knew Eve was nearby.

Father Peter appeared at my side. "Never fear, my lady," he said softly. "Your husband will return."

I did not doubt that he would.

Though Ranulf Navarre would return as a ghost.

July. While we received intermittent word, I didn't need stale rumors to know fate's unfolding. At twenty-six, Prince Edward was a more formidable warrior than his father, relentlessly pursuing rebel forces throughout the Welsh Marches. Simon de Montfort might be a skilled tactician, but he was being harried like a stag run to ground. His two sons, Henry and Simon the Younger, who were supposed to be rushing to reinforce their father's forces, were far less experienced commanders. And because of their cruelty, avarice and arrogance, engendered little loyalty among their own troops.

These things I knew, and while I tried to block the accompanying images, they haunted my dreams. I took to napping rather than risk a deeper sleep in which the Battle of Evesham replayed behind my eyelids like scenes from a horror movie. Similar to the scene I'd written in *The Landlord's Black-Eyed* when Plucky Bess dreams of Ranulf Navarre and his traitorous Janey.

Don't want to think of it, don't want to relive it in any shape, form or fashion.

While waking I had some control, but after slipping into unconsciousness?

That way led to madness.

We've all known situations where time seems to drag yet simultaneously races past. That's how it was with me.

Tick-tock. Tick-tock.

Another second, another minute, another hour had been sheared from Ranulf's allotted number of days.

I had not the words to express how much I missed my husband. The ache was as constant as my heartbeat. For more than a year, I'd seen Ranulf nearly every day. And, before that, the husband who'd loved me once—at least a little. Now he'd been erased as thoroughly as footprints at high tide. Yet, Tintagel *was* Ranulf Navarre. Everywhere I looked—the brutal rocks, the battering waves, all of it—was an extension of him.

"Torment" was a word I'd once thrown around. Only now did I fully grasp its meaning. How could anyone survive the weight of such grief? And, yet, somehow we trudge on, don't we, dragging our sorrows behind us?

I'd searched for Ranulf Navarre across the centuries. Among my five husbands, in the face of every man I saw, down to those I passed on the street or glimpsed in a crowd. Ever seeking the jolt of recognition that would signal, "There you are."

I cannot lose you. I cannot.

My increasing bulk was a convenient excuse to miss morning mass, though I still enjoyed spending time with Tintagel's younglings. While I could not follow them and Father Peter to Merlin's Cave, they often set up a makeshift bench and pillows for me against a wall of St. Julitta's. Daily, I found myself sketching portraits of my husband, remembering, remembering that piece of parchment in the reliquary from another time and place.

Knowing, not caring.

Maybe I was simply a puppet at the mercy of larger forces, but I felt compelled to draw my husband, to create a portfolio while his face and form were still fresh, a portfolio that I would someday share with our son if the fates allowed him safe passage to Earth. My version of a photo album, accompanied by captions, generally a line or two from a nursery rhyme to jog my memory, to resurrect a father his child would never meet.

When not drawing, I recounted fairy tales to the baker's dozen of boys and girls who seemed to trail me everywhere, or listened to Father Peter's Bible stories. Watching the children run and skip and play their games, my heart lightened, though even that lightening was bittersweet.

My mental conversation with my husband consisted of: *You will never see your son.*

When Lizbeth attached herself to my side—I was too big to cuddle her in my lap: *You will never hold your son.*

When the bairns sang their songs or laughed or called to each other: *You will never hear your son.*

I was so very tired. Increasingly, the scene I'd written from *Landlord* haunted me, but I must not think about it, think about Evesham. Sitting in the coolness of St. Julitta's shadows, I found myself drifting off, only to jerk awake the moment certain predictable images intruded —that first fork of lightning across the roiling sky of the killing field, that first line of advancing troops...

I set aside my parchment with its portrait of my husband and beneath it those familiar words, "I mourn for my love..."

I'd finally figured out the line that had niggled me since my time with Felix Eastoft. A line from "Who Killed Cock Robin," which my mother had read using all sorts of funny voices for the sparrow, the fish, the fly...

Who'll be chief mourner?
I, said the Dove,
I mourn for my love,
I'll be chief mourner.

Exhausted, I closed my eyes until I felt a cooling shadow above me. Swimming back to a semblance of alertness, I looked up to see the concerned visage of Father Peter. After preliminary greetings, he settled beside me.

"You need not fear, my lady."

His shoulder touched mine. Around us, girls braided flowers into each other's hair while several boys sparred with makeshift swords.

"Our lord will return to us. I know it."

"You know?" I echoed, my voice measured, though mentally, I dismissed him as a simpleton.

Father Peter retrieved the parchment and board, studied it, ran his fingers across the letters of Ranulf's name, the line of verse. He made no comment about the odd writing. I was beyond offering explanations.

"Life is filled with miracles. We need just open our senses to it. Or so says Roger Bacon."

Father Peter's reference to his fellow Franciscan piqued my interest. I'd written about Bacon in *A Child Upon the Throne* and knew a bit about him. One of the great medieval minds, Roger Bacon advocated science as the means to learning rather than magic and superstition. He counted the magnifying glass among his inventions and had deduced such future mechanical marvels as cars, airplanes, steamships, hot air balloons and even helicopters.

While watching the absent journey of the priest's fingers, I repeated, "Open our senses to miracles?"

"What a world Father Bacon lays before us in his writings. Cities with buildings a hundred times taller than the tallest tree and illuminated more brightly than a billion candles. Devices that hold all the knowledge of mankind at our fingertips and can transport our voices from one end of the Earth to the other."

His words caused goosebumps. Well I knew that world, had ***known*** that world. I also knew Roger Bacon had made no claims of being a seer. Where was this peculiar talk coming from?

"How marvelous are the feats of man," Father Peter mused. "If we can harness our pride, which is no certain thing."

I turned to study him with his cherubic face, fringe of orange hair and gentle mien.

Something is not right here.

"I didn't know you were versed in the works of Roger Bacon."

"He *is* a fellow Franciscan."

A raven settled upon a nearby outcropping to survey us out of obsidian eyes.

"Have you met him then? Doesn't he sometimes teach at Oxford?" I couldn't imagine Tintagel's diffident priest mixing well with sophisticated academics.

"Father Bacon believes that mankind's prime sorrow lies in our inability to accept things as they are," Father Peter replied, ignoring my questions. "To ever be in search of something else. Which means happiness will forever remain beyond our grasp."

Echoes of Sherralinda and her New Age philosophies! Wouldn't it be an interesting twist if my friend had somehow made her way to me in the form of Tintagel's priest?

"Inner peace is the source of all true happiness," I agreed. "Learning to live in the present." Which was not only New Age jargon but Buddhist philosophy. From the corner of my eyes, I studied Father Peter, hoping to register a change in his demeanor. All the while feeling ridiculous. What did I expect? That a mystical veil had been ripped aside to reveal Sherralinda slouched beside me?

Father Peter, however, was watching the children and looking not a whit like my best friend. I, too, watched them, along with my maid, Eve, who was teaching them a clapping game. The wind blew against her blossoming stomach, and I was warmed by her all too rare laugh for she—we—were all melancholy for our men.

"...there will always be war," Father Peter was saying, "'Tis because of man's fallen nature."

"Original sin." So much easier to blame outside forces than take responsibility for our cruelties.

The slant of the sun had banished the shadows on this side of St. Julitta, signaling an imminent end to my outing. Gulls circled overhead; the discordant barking of seals wafted on the breeze.

"At least here in Tintagel, the air smells of the sea and the sun is just warm enough and the children are happy," I said dismissively. Usually, Father Peter's presence was comforting; not so today.

Our raven emitted a caw, flapped its wings, and departed.

"My back hurts. My babe and I are going to return to my chamber."

"M'lady." Father Peter stood and extended a hand to grasp. Though I clutched my quill and paint pot in one hand, I didn't mention the parchment that remained on the ground beside Father Peter. If that was the clue that would lead Magdalena Moore back here, so be it. "Eve," I called to my maid after struggling to my feet. "Please escort me home."

Much later, after Tintagel's household had settled, I replayed the afternoon's conversation. So many odd things. Was I leaving bread-crumbs for future me, trying to manipulate events, or merely acquiescing to immutable reality? Would Father Peter tuck the parchment in the reliquary box thinking to return it to me at a later date, then forgetting? But beyond that, the entire tenor of our interaction had been unsettling. There was something beneath our conversation, something involving our discussion regarding Roger Bacon that was particularly skewed.

What?

My eyes snapped open when I remembered fragments from my research.

This much I knew.

Roger Bacon would never refer to electricity, computers, skyscrapers or telephones. His "prophecies" involving mechanical marvels were all the result of meticulous scientific observation. Nothing supernatural about any of it, despite later attempts to label him a medieval Nostradamus.

Yet Father Peter had sketched out the world that I had so recently inhabited, a world he could not possibly know.

How can that be?

Furthermore, Roger Bacon's *Opus Majus*, his "Greater Work," had not yet been published in this year of our Lord 1265.

But Father Peter pretended familiarity with its contents.

I felt as befuddled as when my husband had quoted the Black Prince's epitaph.

What is happening here?

"*There are more things in heaven and earth, Horatio, than are dreamt of in your philosophy*," I whispered.

I certainly felt the truth of Shakespeare's words. Still, there must be an explanation, plausible or otherwise.

But if so, my exhausted mind could not find it.

Finally, finally, out of Father Peter's and my entire conversation, two sentences emerged.

Naturally, they involved my husband.

"Our lord will return to us. I know it."

However, my prognosticator had not specified that Ranulf Navarre would return to us *alive*.

Sixty

Leaning over her, he smiled.

His beard was raven-colored, as was his hair, thick and curling below his ears, covering the coif which rested upon his nape. A black hawk was emblazoned across the front of his wine-colored surcoat. His long sword was belted low on his left hip. He grinned at her as he bent to kiss her good-bye. She hated him. Hated him and clung to him, sobbing into his hauberk. "Don't go! I'm sorry! Don't leave me!" She loved him, even if she had betrayed him, betrayed them all.

She didn't stand on the parapet and watch him ride away, though she usually did. She would watch him die, instead.

From the coolness of the abbey, where the monks chanted the Hours of the Dead, she viewed the battle. The royal forces outnumbered the rebels so completely, that it would be murder rather than battle, but he would not have chosen any other way to die. She had given him that much, at least.

The fighting was savage and disjointed. Above the chants of the monks, she heard the cries of men and horses, the ringing of swords. She spotted his lord's banner near the crest of the hill—the red vertical lines angled across the gold. She knew he would be there, where the fighting was fiercest. Fighting not so much for his lord's cause but because he loved war more than life. He loved war more than food or drink or beautiful women or sunsets, more than swift horses, land and friendship. Certainly, more than her.

The sky blackened and a wind sprang up, howling through the abbey. She began to cry. She wanted to call him back and tell him she hadn't meant to betray him, but she could not reclaim the days. Instead, she must reap what she had sown in all its bitter harvest.

Around him, knights dropped as suddenly as if felled by the lighting that cracked across the sky. One hundred sixty knights on the rebels' side, but only a handful remained. He was one, of course, fighting as if were a new knight and it was his first battle. But he was a man of forty-one and it was his last.

Knights surrounded him. Knights that belonged to the king. Twenty knights for every rebel. The sky grew darker and darker until she could see only two things clearly—the flash of lightning and the flash of swords. His horse reared above the other mounted knights. She glimpsed a blur of red just before the surcoat disappeared and his horse toppled over, and the knights closed in on them.

"Ranulf!" she screamed.

I WOKE up bathed in sweat. I was sure I'd been screaming, but Lenota and Eve, who slept nearby, had not come rushing to my side. At long last, I'd not been able to keep the dream I'd first sketched in *The Landlord's Black-Eyed Daughter* at bay.

Only I am not that Janey, I reminded myself. *This time around we changed those dynamics. I did not betray my husband.*

Truth and fiction blurred together until I imagined circuits shorting, popping in the air as our pasts tumbled along a riverbed which veered off into endless tributaries. Had I tapped into one of many parallel universes? Were there infinite permutations of the Battle of Evesham containing some version of Ranulf Navarre and his Lady Jane?

Perhaps, but I could only concentrate on this one where a blend of Jane of Holywelle and Magdalena Moore loved this Ranulf Navarre.

Increasingly, I worried about the delivery of our child, which I estimated to be in approximately three weeks.

Will I die in childbirth? Am I a second Bloody Mary, destined to carry a mirage into infinity?

While I could not unravel that particular sequence of events, I knew this much: In one week, my husband would be dead.

Is any of this even happening? Am I bound in a straitjacket of madness?

Had I conjured Ranulf and Janey, in all their permutations, out of my imagination?

What is real? is anything *real?*

I remembered a Chinese tale about a man who dreamt he was a butterfly. When he awakened, he could not be sure whether he was a man dreaming that he was a butterfly or a butterfly dreaming he was a man.

Which was the question I increasingly pondered: "*Am I a woman dreaming I am a butterfly? Or am I a butterfly, dreaming that I am a woman?*"

Death had proven himself a capricious lover, just like Ranulf. She wanted Ranulf so badly. She missed him more than the children she'd never borne. Without Ranulf, her life had lost all meaning, like a summer without sun. Life would be forever gray and black and white, without the green of tree leaves, the red of roses, the pinwheel colors of excitement and laughter. Soon she and Ranulf would be reunited. In hell, most assuredly, for their sins had been great. Her soul floated upwards, beyond the canopied bed, past the shadows hiding the ceiling rafters, into a blackness pricked with stars...

Everything was gray, as if viewed through a fog. She saw herself from a position directly above the bed where she lay. Her pale hair spread across the pillows, dwarfing the delicate features of her face. She had wasted to little more than a shadow. Finally, she was dying. Upon Ranulf's death, she had willed herself to die, but it had taken far too long. She welcomed Death. More than welcomed him. Hungrily embraced him.

The words of the other Janey's death from *The Landlord's Black-Eyed Daughter* came to life in a second dream. Now all of it was out there. I no longer need fear sleep.

A good thing, since this butterfly was, oh, so very weary.

Sixty-One

Lammas Day. This year no celebration, and tomorrow, tomorrow was the Battle of Evesham. These past few days I'd ordered the solar cleaned and readied for the birthing. This afternoon I'd waddled to the promontory overlooking the Celtic Sea. Hoping to avoid Father Peter, I'd detoured around St. Julitta. After our peculiar interaction, I imagined him suddenly disappearing from Tintagel and after making inquiries being asked, "Who is this priest of whom you speak? We've ne'er heard of him." But Father Peter continued his duties and treated me as if nothing had changed. No return of my parchment drawing. No mention of its peculiar writing. No more odd conversations or uncomfortable glimpses into matters I could not understand and might have conjured.

Therefore, I didn't avoid him because he made me uncomfortable. I avoided him because I wanted to be alone.

I stared out at the sea, bumping up against an endless horizon of more water met by sky. But beyond my vision lay Ireland, whole continents, though they remained invisible to anyone standing at the edge of Tintagel's cliffs. If my mind weren't so scrambled, perhaps I could have conjured a fitting metaphor.

"My lady?" I recognized Father Peter's voice and heard the rustle of his cassock as he moved to stand beside me. "I smell rain in the air. And the wind is sharp for this time of year."

I nodded. *One more day. Tomorrow there will be terrible storm at Evesham. You will fight in that storm. You will die in that storm.*

"Let us get you home."

Home?

I was too devastated to weep.

Reckoning

AUGUST 1265

"The murder of Evesham, for battle it was none."

— ROBERT OF GLOUCESTER, CHRONICLER

Sixty-Two

Simon de Montfort and his men died hard. Exactly as Ranulf would have wanted. The battle had first been waged on horseback until the rebels' destriers were cut down. With a storm pounding the combatants and lightning flashing all around—just as in my dream—the men had continued fighting on foot. I imagined frozen frames of combat—a raised axe illumined by a jag of lightning; a mace or arming sword in a downward arc, the broken and blunted lances that were used as makeshift weapons making contact with the side of an enemy head. There was a magnificence in the rebels' hopelessness, that they would die for the leader they respected and his sons whom they did not.

Simon de Montfort was protected by a ring of his household knights. Once that ring was breached by twelve knights handpicked by Prince Edward to dispatch the earl, Montfort was doomed. Montfort's horse was killed beneath him; Montfort continued the fight on foot. Snapping and snarling and feinting after the manner of a wolf pack, Edward's assassins closed in, wearing down a fifty-seven-year-old soldier with a bad leg who wielded his weapons with desperate efficiency. The *coup de grâce* was finally delivered from behind with a dagger slipped between the rings of his mail. Were Simon de Montfort's last words really, "Thank God?" Could anything have been heard above the royalist butchers who, undone by bloodlust, stripped Montfort—even past his ever-present hair shirt—and set about mutilating his corpse?

While Simon had lived long enough to see his oldest son Henry split by a sword, in turnabout Simon the Younger, who had dawdled overlong in order to eat dinner, arrived just in time to see his father's head displayed atop a pike.

All this I already knew, though actual news remained sporadic. I suspected much of what Thomas the Steward did hear from the village bellman during daily trips to Trevena was sanitized or kept from me. When facing the worst, our universal reaction is to deny or minimize, so it wasn't surprising that most of the household expressed hope that Simon had ultimately prevailed. Or, if the worst had happened, that Ranulf and his troupe had miraculously survived.

Though I knew my husband was dead, I did not *feel* it. On the third or fourth night following the battle—so hard to keep track of time—I lay quiet in my bed. Since Evesham, Eve had slept with me, crying herself to sleep over Col and her fears for their babe.

A sight we must have been, two ungainly pregnant women going about our duties as if the world had not changed, as if we might still be wives rather than widows.

This night, however, was too hot to share a bed, and Eve's tears made me just the opposite, as if I were a parched wasteland.

Why do I not feel more? I wondered. *Am I simply numb?*

This particular even, a peculiar thing happened. I felt a gentle hand settle upon my brow, after which I was enveloped by a blissful peace.

"Choose love. Or choose fear," said a voice.

Not exactly audible, but it was not mine.

I knew, of course I did, that most of our decisions are based on fear.

The fear of hell if we sin.

The fear of starvation if our barns aren't overflowing.

The fear of death if our child sickens.

The fear of poverty if we haven't stored a chamber of gold.

The fear of loss if a loved one rejects us.

The fear of grief, of our own spiritual annihilation if our beloved dies.

I'd lived life, perhaps many lifetimes, with fear as my baseline. And yet, hadn't my forays into other spiritualities taught me that love cannot co-exist with fear? I'd been so caught up in my dramas I was ruled by it. Giving lip service to love when my every action was motivated by its opposite. Shouldn't I, of all people, understand that there is more to us than our bodies? That giving into our terrors would never bring peace? Shouldn't I know by now that most of the worries I'd dreamed up at three o'clock in the morning were never those that materialized in the light of day?

My child is safe, waiting to be born. I have been granted my heart's desire. I will not cower and hide my face from a future that will never arrive.

Right now, I choose peace. I choose love.

Tomorrow, the other will intrude.

But for now...

And Ranulf?

I would mourn him tomorrow.

Sixty-Three

Word spread from Evesham outward like the aftershock of a nuclear bomb. While I'd had time to process events, those around me moved like zombies, immobilized by grief. Eve was undone and Lenota little better. Even Fayette's corkscrew curls drooped pitifully. We were a small household, and whether the dead were friends or lovers or something else, all were familiar and dear.

Following his daily trek to Trevena and the latest tidbits of news, Thomas the Steward returned with "A few rebels escaped the slaughter and followed Lord Montfort's middle son to Kenilworth Castle. They remain holed up there." He gazed at me meaningfully, as if silently urging me to make the leap from that to Ranulf's survival.

Eve made the leap for me. "Perhaps our lord is at Kenilworth." By Ranulf, of course, she meant Col.

"Perhaps," I agreed, though that could not be the case. Either Thomas the Steward or the village bellman had omitted several pertinent facts. Such as: In Evesham's aftermath, when those few surviving rebels had tried to flee, Prince Edward's men had speared them like fish with their lances. They'd watched them drown in the River Avon or cut them down on its bank, tracked them into the wheat fields and gardens where they hid and into the town of Evesham itself. There the royalists pulled rebels out of churches and slaughtered them in the streets.

Besides, Ranulf would not have fled. He would have died—had died—guarding his liege. Because that's what warriors do.

I remembered the peaceful appearing field I'd visited as Magdalena Moore, remembered that ominous stillness that held back the screams of pursued and pursuer, the dying and their avengers.

Still, I had not shed a tear.

A fortnight passed without official word of Ranulf's death. I kept despair at bay with routine. Tonight, after completing supper, Father Peter drew me outside the great hall to relax upon a bench.

Tintagel's guards kept vigilant watch on the tower. I, all of us, expected King Henry's men to enact revenge. In the meantime, it was up to the woman about to drop Ranulf Navarre's heir to lead them.

I was determined to remain "tranquil," to "choose love." To remain in "a good space."

Choose to believe that there is a reason and purpose behind everything. Choose to tuck my grief away, pull it out later...someday...when I am stronger.

"He survived," Father Peter said, interrupting my roiling thoughts. I suppressed the urge to snap at him. He really must be the reincarnation of Sherralinda since he shared her inability to come up with even one accurate prediction.

The blast of a trumpet from the direction of the outer ward, warning of visitors. We both straightened in alarm. Strangers being allowed entrance after dark was a worrying turn of events. It was true that Tintagel, with its narrow isthmus, was virtually impregnable, and watchmen could successfully deny entrance to an enemy. So, the arrivals must not be King Henry's men, though assuredly, this had to do with Evesham. Had Gilbert de Clare returned Ranulf's body, deciding that he owed me, his relation, that much?

Father Peter helped me stand.

"Courage, my lady," he whispered.

We moved to where we could view the nearest portcullis, which was in the process of being raised. Those inside the great hall spilled out to join us. Lenota and Eve hurried to my side, Lenota repeating "Lord have mercy" in Latin, while Eve wept and twisted her hands in the folds of her gown.

Even as we watched, a line of torches approached, solemn as a funeral cortege.

Just like in Landlord. *Monks returning Ranulf's head. But that couldn't be so. We changed that version of our relationship.*

I clasped Father Peter's arm to steady myself. A sudden sharp contraction caused me to gasp. My fingers dug into his forearm.

The torches drew nearer, eight in all. Not monks, most likely a funeral cortege, leading a cart carrying Ranulf's body. I wanted to scream and curse. To laugh at the fool I'd been. Believing I could alter the course of our destinies when I could as easily alter the spinning of the stars.

Thomas the Steward appeared, appraising me, his expression filled with concern. From the kennels, Ranulf's dogs began an eerie howling.

I heard the striking of iron-shod hooves upon slate and guessed that the troupe had passed the stables. Closer until, in the dancing torchlight carried by a second knight, the leader emerged. Not his face but the scarlet surcoat with the hawk's head upon it.

I blinked. *No!* My vision must be playing tricks on me.

Father Peter breathed, "*Laudem Dei*. Praise God."

Eve cried out.

The leader drew rein, flung a leg over his saddle in a hurried dismount and strode toward me, spurs jingling with each step.

"Ranulf?" I whispered, disbelieving. How could this be?

Vaguely, I was aware of cries of joy, of Col and other knights easing from their horses, of those around me surging forward to greet returning loved ones, but Ranulf alone commanded my attention.

Gait impatient, eyes intent upon me, my husband approached.

When he halted, I noted the cost of these past weeks—his stained and torn surcoat; the wicked slash in the mail covering his arm; in his face which, free of its coif, was thinner and etched around his mouth with new lines. But to me, he was more than beautiful. He was *everything*.

"You're alive," I managed. "You're here." Ranulf Navarre had made one promise to me. That he would return in time for the birth of his child.

He'd kept that promise.

But how?

"Did you doubt?" Ranulf asked. "No power in heaven or earth could have stopped me." Stepping closer, so close I could smell the sweat and leather and horse and the dust and dirt of days of riding, Ranulf placed both hands on my belly. He gazed down at the material covering my mound as though he could see to the treasure beneath.

"There you are, *mon grand garçon*." His voice dipped to a whisper like worshippers inside a cathedral. Ranulf then raised his eyes to mine and in their depths, I saw such a fierceness. I knew then he spoke truth. No power could have stopped my husband from returning to Tintagel. Had he arrived as part of a ghost train, had he stood before me as revenant rather than breathing human, he would have fulfilled his oath.

I cannot say who reached out to whom, but somehow we were entwined, if awkwardly, my bulk pressed against his surcoat. The babe protested with another painful contraction.

I found myself crying, even while ordering myself to stop, fearing Ranulf would disapprove of my weakness.

"Why the tears?" he asked. "Did you not believe me?"

I could not speak, nor even manage a shake of the head. Patiently, Ranulf allowed me my breakdown, stroking my back.

"I do not understand." I finally managed. This was no time for a public demonstration, even though everyone around us was celebrating. Amid the laughter and noise, Father Peter attended to Ranulf's knights, one after the other. Each bent a knee and bowed his head for the priest's blessing and thanksgiving to God.

I drew back to search my husband's face, seeing there the suffering he—they all—had endured. "We know what happened to you...to the rebels. Everyone slaughtered. Montfort himself... And yet here you, Col, all of you are safe?"

Grooms had started leading weary mounts back toward the stables. Thomas the Steward clapped his hands and ordered food, since Tintagel's mistress was obviously remiss in her duties.

"How, Ranulf? How did you survive?"

Ranulf stepped back far enough that he could lean down to kiss the fullest swell of my stomach before once again straightening to face me.

"It's simple," he said and laughed, though it wasn't one of amusement. "Have you not yet figured it out?"

I shook my head.

"I followed Gilbert de Clare's example, Janey." Ranulf's hands once more drifted down to cocoon either side of my belly. "I switched sides."

Sixty-Five

I did not have time to question Ranulf. By the following morning, my labor had begun. Lenota and Fayette helped me maneuver the stairs to the solar, with Eve beside me, murmuring words of encouragement. I'd chosen the solar as my birthing chamber for privacy reasons. Already I'd schooled every servant, as well as Sybyl the Midwife, on the importance of cleanliness. I'd ordered everything—including the birthing stool—scrubbed and disinfected with vinegar and nixed the idea of spreading straw on the floor in order to absorb things I'd rather not think about. I'd ignored Sybyl's tsk-tsking and my maids' alarmed looks over my various peccadilloes. But nothing compared to their horror when I grabbed Ranulf's hand at the door to the chamber and said, "Stay with me."

Since men were forbidden in the birthing room, the gasps were to be expected, but I didn't care.

Against all odds, Ranulf had returned to me—to us. More than anyone he deserved to welcome our child into the world.

"Stay?" Ranulf fixed me with a curious gaze before lowering it to my belly, as though consulting our offspring for guidance.

"You cannot," Sybyl said in a tone guaranteed to cause the doughtiest of knights to quake in his boots. In another century, our midwife would have made a formidable drill sergeant. (Or dominatrix. She had that vibe.)

Thinking that was the end of our nonsense, Sybyl left us to draw recently hung curtains across the windows to curtail outside light. Custom decreed that the birthing chamber be warm and dark in order to ward off chills and protect from evil spirits, who apparently became easily confused and lost their way in the dark if physical surroundings were rearranged. Deciding that a dimly lit room might be more soothing to a newborn, I'd acquiesced.

After kissing my forehead, Ranulf groped beneath his surcoat, removed the crystal pendant I'd given him, and slipped it over my head. "Would my presence provide you solace?"

"Please."

I clasped the pendant, warm from his body heat, comforted by its return. I didn't believe it was the reason for Ranulf's survival, but who could make sense of events that made no sense? The fates might be playing some macabre joke, giving us false hope only to snatch it away when my child and I died in childbirth; I might be hooked up to some ventilator in an ICU and my dying brain had concocted this entire fantasy world.

What seemed to be true was that Ranulf Navarre was here beside me, gloriously alive, and he deserved to attend the birth of his son.

Once Ranulf had taken up watch beside me, the women worked round him as best they could. Traditionally, female friends gathered to offer marginal help, gossip, and divert the mother's attention from the business at hand. Since I had no friends and no desire to be the center of attention, I'd tried in vain to nix that particular practice. No need. One look at Ranulf's glowering presence and those few who'd dared step inside the doorway scurried away.

Pointedly ignoring Ranulf's scrutiny, Sybyl prepared a concoction containing rose oil to rub on my stomach and thighs, intermittently making a noise between her lips like that of a sputtering motorboat. Sybyl the Midwife came from a succession of midwives and had proudly informed me she'd apprenticed under a *male* doctor. She knew her business, "Never lost a bairn," and expected to be **obeyed.** She did not take kindly to Ranulf Navarre's intrusion into her domain.

Fayette and other servants went about their business ignoring the unfolding drama while Eve inspected all the herbs and potions Sybyl removed from her box (subtly so as not to poke the dragon). Lenota, however, was her usual vocal self about my breach of protocol. While she dared not directly criticize Tintagel's lord, she loudly implored Margaret, patron saint of childbirth, to return me to my senses while positioning lit candles in various strategic places. Then, after thrusting a caudle of spiced wine at me, she tried to speak her mind. "My lady, 'tis not meet to have your husband—"

"'Tis not meet that our kingdom is at civil war," I interrupted. "Or that Simon de Montfort had his head and his hands and his feet and his testicles cut off and stuffed on either side of his nose." Ignoring Lenota's horrified expression—had not Trevena's bellmen relayed those particular facts?—I wet my lips and handed the goblet back to Ranulf. "My husband will stay."

If Ranulf noticed the others' disapproval or the dramatically increased tension in the room, he ignored it. Since Sybyl was in charge, he homed in on her as if preparing for hand-to-hand combat. While she bustled about, Ranulf peppered her with questions which she answered with long-sufferings sighs and little more than grunts, accompanied by the obligatory "my lord."

After a particularly intense contraction, Ranulf ordered me to lay down on the bed, then stood guard, feet planted apart, hands clasped behind his back, ready to attack Mother Nature if she dared inconvenience me again.

"It barely hurts," I said, feeling quite brave. Eddie Rickenbacker had said, "Courage is doing what you're afraid to do." Who was I to disagree with the WWI flying ace? Giving birth in a society where one-third of women died during their childbearing years took a great deal of fortitude, didn't it? Ranulf might even be moved to grant me a new nickname, something to do with a lioness or a tiger or some fierce goddess of Cornish mythology.

After the contractions increased in intensity, I forgot about nicknames and concentrated on surviving. Holy bejesus, it hurt.

"You are sweating, Janey," Ranulf observed, his tone suggesting that was a curious reaction to being in an overly hot room on a summer's day while my guts were being torn out by Satan's pincers.

He placed washcloths upon my brow, exchanging them when he judged them too warm. After I moaned through a contraction, he snatched the jar of rose oil ointment from Sybyl and began rubbing the lotion upon my exposed belly.

Sybyl glared at him. "Should I leave ye to deliver the bairn yourself, m'lord?"

Ignoring or oblivious to the sarcasm, Ranulf responded, "That won't be necessary."

Relaxing into the touch of his fingers, I thought with amusement, *Mr. Bossy Pants.*

"What?"

I opened my eyes to a frowning Ranulf, who'd paused in his ministrations.

I'd spoken aloud? "My tongue just got tangled," I said. "Pay no attention."

"You've not caught a fever, have you?" He turned to Sybyl. "Can my wife deliver my son if she is out of her wits?"

"My lord! Everything is proceeding normally." Sybyl did not add, "No thanks to you," though she was surely thinking it.

"I oft assist in the birthing of animals, including my mares. I need not you to tell me what is normal, midwife."

Ranulf comparing me to a broodmare? That was about right.

I can't pretend that my labor wasn't painful, but it was mercifully short. Throughout, Ranulf stayed close. When I walked the length of the chamber, he allowed me to lean against him. He breathed with me during my later contractions and held my hand after Sybyl placed me on the birthing stool.

Then, more quickly than I could have hoped, our son—it would not have dared be a girl—was born. After Sybyl had cleared the infant's mouth and throat of mucous and I heard his healthy cry midst the exclamations of the surrounding women, my gaze sought Ranulf's. His expression alone made the turmoil of our past—of everything—worthwhile. Never, not even in paintings depicting the ecstasy of saints, had I witnessed such joy.

"My son," he breathed. Sybyl barely had time to cut the umbilical cord before Ranulf wrested him from her arms. Gazing down at what was assuredly a bloody mess, he said, "My Ranulf."

Lenota and Eve cooed and clucked and wept with joy; Sybyl turned her attention to me and my needs. It was not they but Ranulf who washed our babe in vinegar and placed him in swaddling bands. Gently he laid his son diagonally on a cloth—how tiny he was!—folded the corners over him and secured it all with bandages. Clumsily but carefully, all under the women's vigilant gazes.

I tried to stay awake, to share in Ranulf's joy, to luxuriate in the miracle that we'd finally, finally been granted, but I was so very tired.

I slept. And slept, save for the times when I nursed our son, a practice that was met with more tight-lipped headshaking from my maids. However, due to an omnipresent Ranulf, they dared not vocalize their disapproval of a lady breastfeeding her own child.

During those first few days of my lying in, Ranulf must have left our chamber. Bébé, as we called him to differentiate him from his father, had already been baptized, godparents appointed and festivities enjoyed afterward. Or so I was later told. I slept through most of it. (Not that I would have been allowed to participate. Until the churching, forty days hence, I was considered unclean.)

While Ranulf must have continued with manorial tasks that had been neglected since his leaving, whenever I opened my eyes, he was nearby, either standing watch beside Bébé's cradle or stretched out beside me in bed, holding our son.

"You are so tiny, *mon plaisir*," Ranulf murmured. I could hear the fear in his voice, as it is with every new parent. Imagining all the horrible things that could happen to this precious, fragile being. "But your shoulders are broad, and your grip is strong. What a warrior you will be!"

Sometimes, when Ranulf held Bébé, he stretched out his arms far enough so that I could inspect our son from a distance. However, other than when I was nursing, Ranulf guarded him, even from me.

"He is very handsome, is he not?" He stroked the top of Bébé's head, smaller than his palm. "Such a strong chin."

As if I were an expert on babies. As if all infants did not look exactly the same. Still, Bébé *was* handsome, though only his father could detect a chin, strong or otherwise.

It was during these times when we were alone, save for Lenota and Eve weaving in the far corner and Bébé's nurse sitting patiently on a stool near his crib, that I experienced a quiet happiness unlike anything I'd previously known. So much had shifted in Ranulf's and my relationship. Feeling his shoulder pressed against my own while we gazed at our son or talked of inconsequential things felt so comfortable...so normal. Easy to forget about the world beyond this chamber, certainly beyond Tintagel. Those few rebels who'd survived Evesham remained holed up inside Kenilworth Castle with Simon the Younger, who within a handful of years would die "cursed by God, a wanderer and a fugitive." While the Younger and his band remained under a siege later designated as the longest in Medieval England's history, their plight—along with the suffering of all those who'd lost lands and loved ones—seemed unreal. Here, we three. My family. Tintagel. We'd been blessed with a loyal household, a bountiful harvest, and full storage rooms. Since Simon de Montfort's ill-considered Keepers of the Peace had been disbanded, Trevena's villagers were friendlier; complaints in manorial court were few and easily settled. Everyone, at least here in Cornwall, seemed to have wearied of the recent acrimony and bloodletting and preferred to live in peace. Isolated as we were, it was easy to shrug off the machinations of kings or princes or parliaments or the lawlessness plaguing so much of the kingdom.

My world had narrowed down to *this*. Nothing else mattered.

Because I'd consigned the past to irrelevance, I made the mistake of assuming Ranulf also had.

So, I was totally unprepared when, as we readied for my churching, he suddenly turned to me and said, "Who are you, Jane of Holywelle?"

Bébé was sleeping; his nurse rocking his cradle with one foot while humming a lullaby.

I had been standing at the window frame, gazing into the courtyard, counting the days until I would once more be allowed outside. Already the ground cover was turning, while the first scents of fall wafted in on the breezes off the sea.

Uncomprehending, I turned to Ranulf. "What do you mean?"

"You return from St. Michael's Mount like a different woman, *ma hérisson piquant*. You drink poison rather than suffer me and on the heels of your pilgrimage, pretend I am your hero rather than—what did you call me?—vermin, Satan's vomit?"

I grimaced. *Poison.* The first time that particular truth had been uttered aloud. Unforgivable deed. And yet, Ranulf—all of the household—had forgiven me in their fashion. When I'd pulled them all down alongside me into my personal hell.

"What did the monks do?" Ranulf pressed. "Cast some sort of spell on you?"

"Obviously, their prayers were efficacious," I said primly. My mind had stuttered to a stop. I was unable to think of anything more.

He moved closer so that our conversation would not be overheard. "Did their prayers also give you the ability to see the future? To speak another language and sing songs no one has heard of? To crave me as a man and husband rather than quake at my touch?"

Ignoring most of his questions—for how could I answer them?—I zeroed in on the last one. "You can be a difficult man to love, Ranulf Navarre."

Something in his expression, come and gone so quickly, I might have imagined it. Ranulf arched an eyebrow. "Since when does either of us speak of love, Jane of Holywelle?"

At that I looked away, knowing what I'd seen. Pain. I'd caused that. Once, he had spoken to me of his love—openly, willingly. And I'd crushed it. No, to be fair, we'd *both* crushed it.

"If it was not love I felt, it was obsession," I said, daring to speak that particular truth. "And other things I cannot put a name to."

Ranulf studied me. "You did not answer my questions, wife."

I shrugged. He could question me forever; I had no answers to give. "Why did you switch sides?" I asked abruptly, hoping to throw him off. "Why did you not remain with the rebels?"

"Do not change the subject."

"I'll answer your question after you answer mine," I lied.

Ranulf's gaze swung to Bébé's cradle. "Weeks in the saddle gives a man time to think. Simon de Montfort was exactly as you said. He might have worn a hairshirt neath his garments and prayed incessantly and spun visions based on lofty ideals, but he was greedy. I decided I'd not gamble my future by exchanging one despot for another."

So, Ranulf *had* listened. The realization pleased me, probably more than it should. Had my warning altered his fate, perhaps both of ours? Could it have been that easy?

Ranulf faced me on the other side of the window. In the afternoon light, I admired his beauty, as I always did. *Ranulf!* It might be true that I was obsessed with him, but I also loved him. Had always loved him and only him. In all of love's complexities.

"You still did not explain how you knew that there would be a battle, that Leicester would be killed."

My hand drifted to my crystal pendant and closed around it. "The king had double the forces."

"You could not have known that. Besides, Simon had bested far larger armies. Did St. Michael's monks teach you about military tactics, Janey? "

We were treading on perilous ground. I heard a sound from the crib, alerting us of a stirring Bébé. "I have always been a student of human nature." Cruelly, unfairly, I added, "You never paid enough attention to me before to know anything about that."

His gaze narrowed. He cocked his head, considering.

I could never tell him the truth, but perhaps I could persuade him to consider other possibilities, if in a roundabout way.

"What do you know about the Cathars?" Stupid question. *Everyone* knew about them. Simon de Montfort's father, even more of a religious zealot than his son, had led much of the Albigensian Crusade, in which the sect had been brutally slaughtered.

"Heretics," Ranulf said. "What has that to do with you?"

"The Cathari believed in reincarnation, that people live many lives."

Ranulf's mouth twisted. He balled his hands in fists, as if closing them over an invisible weapon. "Do I look like I am a Dominican, that I am interested in such blatherings?"

"No, but—"

"English men and women were not Cathars. I am losing patience, wife. Why did you return from your pilgrimage a different woman? Sometimes I wondered if you were a changeling."

I tried for teasing. "That I left a mouse and returned a hedgehog?"

Ranulf frowned.

Watching him, I suddenly wondered whether he might *know*, whether this was some trick where he would have me confess what he'd already figured out.

"I am so grateful to have you here, well and safe. And with our son." I stretched out my arms in a supplicating gesture. "Let us not go borrowing trouble, please."

Ranulf opened his mouth to respond when Bébé yelped, as if startled from sleep. Soothing sounds from his nurse. My excuse to cut short the conversation. I moved to return to the bed and to nurse Bébé.

Ranulf grabbed my wrist. "Not only your changed behavior. You left Tintagel speaking one language and returned knowing another. 'Mr. Bossy Pants.'" He enunciated the words so carefully and clearly that, under other circumstances, I would have laughed. Who would have thought my husband had an ear for different languages?

"What did that mean?"

"I was confused by pain. I didn't know what I was saying."

"*Hush little baby, don't say a word—*"

Bébé let out his "I'm starving" wail. Before Ranulf strode to the nurse to retrieve his son, he tossed over his shoulder, "We are not done with this conversation."

My reprieve from Ranulf's questioning lasted until after my churching. With much of Tintagel around me, I met a smiling Father Peter and two servers in front of St. Julitta's porch. I carried a lighted candle, as did the servers. Father Peter, wearing a stole, blessed me with holy water and said prayers of thanksgiving. Afterward, I took hold of his stole in the customary fashion while he led me into the church, followed by Ranulf and the rest of Tintagel.

The churching was supposed to be a celebration welcoming my return to the sacraments. And, I did celebrate—my husband, my child, Ranulf's safely returned knights, our entire community. Following the end of mass, Ranulf pulled me aside. I'd fed Bébé and we'd left him sleeping with his nurse nearby. It would be hours before he'd have need of me.

"Talk," he said tersely. Once the crowd dispersed, Ranulf steered me toward the nearest headland. In the water below, I could see fishing boats and the heads of seals bobbing like grey rubber balls among the waves.

Knowing this was our "to be continued" conversation, I tried to divert him by going on the offensive. "Your ring can foretell the future. That's how I know things. And the crystal pendant, too. Perhaps that's the real reason you switched sides."

"Because the pendant warned me?"

"It's possible," I said defensively.

Ranulf turned so that we faced each other. He cocked his head and studied my face as if it belonged to a stranger.

"What?" I asked, unnerved by his inspection.

"Sometimes, when I look at you, I see someone else."

I felt a chill. "What do you mean?"

"Particularly when you are angry. Or that night when Bébé was conceived."

So Ranulf had figured that I'd conceived that devilish night, as well.

"I see another face. Not just in the eyes."

I turned away so that he could not see my expression. Could that be so? That somehow Magdalena Moore had leaked through the ages? I had no real mirrors to view such a transformation.

"The shape, everything," Ranulf continued. "It's you and not you. And sometimes, your body, when I close my eyes, you feel different."

I suppressed a chill and reached for indignation. "You were confusing me with your leman."

"Stop it," he commanded. "It never happened before St. Michael's Mount."

I had no idea what to say. So, Magdalena Moore, at least a younger version, had found her way to Tintagel in the flesh. Was Ranulf worried I was a witch? Witchcraft would not become a capital offense for centuries, and witches were more the stereotypical crones. But I didn't want to put ideas into his head.

"I am not a changeling," I blurted, referring to our earlier conversation. And because I could think of nothing else.

"Then what are you? You are my wife, and you are not. Even when you look like Janey you do not act like her."

I decided I would tell him as close a version to the essence of the truth as possible. "You know that saints sometimes have visions?"

He quirked an eyebrow. "You are not a saint, Jane of Holywelle."

"No, but on the way back from St Michael's, I began having dreams. Most peculiar. And so real."

"Dreams in which you speak a different language?"

"Dreams in which I live in a different place and time. Only I don't quite look like me, I'm not quite me, and...it's all so confusing. But the dreams seem real and sometimes I see things and know things."

He eyed me intently. "What sort of things?"

Could I tell him the truth without telling the truth? "About the future. About Evesham. About the deaths of kings, about the fates of nations, about things that happen hundreds of years in the future."

"And how do you fit into all of this?" he asked, his voice neutral.

"Sometimes I dream that I live in a time where Tintagel is a ruin, when London is a city of millions. When we don't ride horses to travel but machines, some of which can fly, and we've fought wars with millions of men rather than hundreds, threatening weapons that could obliterate the entire planet if we loosed them."

"Go on." His face was unreadable.

"In which I reside in a place that hasn't even been discovered yet, and where I was a woman more than twice Jane of Holywelle's age who longed so very much to have a baby that she married five times, all without success."

"Five times?" he echoed. His expression was almost amused. He didn't believe me. He thought me mad.

"Women can do that in the future. We are not treated like last week's discards, at least most of the time. At least in my dreams." I pulled myself back to Ranulf, who captured me with those mesmerizing eyes. It was very still around us, the wind had died down, and it seemed as if it were just we two. And if I'd looked down at us from a very great height, two motes of dust dancing among the stars. "They are dreams, of course. But sometimes I get confused in them. Sometimes I am not sure what is real and—"

"Am I a man dreaming I am a butterfly? Or am I a butterfly, dreaming that I am a man?" Ranulf's voice was a whisper, but it was so still around us, as if the world had hit pause.

"Precisely. The nature of reality—" I halted and stared at him. "Wait a minute. Ranulf? What are you saying? How do you know about dreams and butterflies?"

He threw back his head and laughed. His tanned neck a column, his white teeth flashing.

"What a narcissist you can be, Janey," he said in perfect English. "Did you really believe you were the only one?"

Epilogue

1267

I watch Bébé toddle to his father. He is a stocky eighteen-month-old and Ranulf's child. I see nothing of myself in him, not that I mind. He is as dark and beautiful as my husband.

Ranulf catches Bébé in his arms, and the sound of Bébé's squeals, mixed with his father's laughter, gladdens my heart.

Spring is here, but the winter has been long and like all animals, we seek the sun and the warmth. I am content to watch them.

Ranulf Navarre and Ranulf of Tintagel.

Since the day of my churching, when Ranulf momentarily lifted the veil to reveal that he knew very well his part in our *pas de deux,* he's refused to revisit it. When I bring the subject up, he looks at me as if am reciting a joke—badly.

I have so many questions. At least in the beginning, they crowded my every thought, though they've receded, just as that other life increasingly seems to have belonged to someone else. Because it did.

Still...

Explain to me, Ranulf Navarre, how, if the answer lies in reincarnation, my body changed but yours did not? Jane Holywelle looks nothing like Magdalena Moore. Yet you remain the same. Could you be some sort of time traveler, if such things might possibly exist? Why will you not give me a hint, a throwaway line, *something*? What is our connection to each other? Why did you follow me across time? Was it love? A need to right the wrongs we'd both committed, one against the other? Are you a consummate actor, or did your knowledge flicker in and out like some malfunctioning light bulb, so that sometimes you knew and sometimes you didn't?

Why won't you tell me?

Yet, it is increasingly easy to live in the moment, to accept without needing a checklist with every answer duly marked. Reminding myself nobody knows all the answers to *anything*. Such is not the human condition.

It is enough to say that I am happy here, in this century, with my husband and my son.

Could I have said that in the twenty-first? We had comforts that I miss and with every sniffle, I worry that Bébé will suffer a minor illness that will prove fatal. But with Eve's help—she is the mother of a darling girl with Col's eyes and her disposition—we've become quite skilled with natural potions, some as effective as twenty-first century pharmaceuticals, minus the side effects.

While I sometimes miss my friends and even have an occasional kind thought about my exes, I expect they remain around me in different guises. In fact, I make a game of it, matching various faces and forms to those from what is both my past and my future.

Ranulf has attended several parliaments and the country remains in turmoil. Henry III is graceless in victory and intent on squeezing all the revenue he can from the remaining rebel barons. He is a weak man, this progeny of the most despised king in England's history. Who will be followed by one of England's strongest...

"Ma-ma!" Bébé calls and gestures me to come closer, wrapped as he is in his father's arms.

Ranulf watches my approach, his gaze upon mine. Before it drops to my stomach where our second child readies to enter the world.

And smiles his secret smile.

Eternal Beloved

TRAVELS ACROSS TIME, BOOK TWO

"A word, Clarabel Lucy."

I spun around. Alaric DeLaMer, materializing out of the mist, strode toward me, crossing Trim Castle's bailey in a few powerful strides.

"What do you want?" Instinctively, my hands strayed to my girdle, which held the clutch purse containing my jewelry—and, hopefully, my ticket back to the 21st century.

Alaric faced me, long hair curling untidily from the drizzle, trademark scowl firmly in place. "Your husband's name, Clarabel Lucy."

In anticipation of this very moment, I'd concocted an entire autobiography, but I sighed dramatically to signal my annoyance. "William. William Shakespeare."

Alaric rolled the name around in his mouth, as if testing an exotic food. His dark eyes narrowed suspiciously. "Why have I not heard of him?"

"Because you're an illiterate oaf?" I wanted to respond, but he really couldn't know anything about a man who wouldn't be born for two hundred plus years. I waved a negligent hand. "Because we live at the tippy-tip-tip of Cornwall."

Alaric scanned my face. I was suddenly aware of my bedraggled appearance—limp strands of hair, mist coating my eyelashes and cheeks—totally unlike the scented mists my esthetician used to spritz on my face to add "that extra glow."

"If your holdings are in the tippy-tip-tip of Cornwall, why were you in Dublin? Because you're a spy for the Scots, as I've long suspected?"

I couldn't suppress a laugh. "You never give up, do you? You know full well—"

Alaric abruptly grabbed me by the wrist and pulled me closer. *Is this where you're going to kiss me?* I worried because he was always staring at my mouth, and that could only mean one thing. I'd outlined so many identical scenes in my novels, my brain immediately went haywire. Should I slap him? Would he gut me with the dagger at his belt? Or would he ravage me so thoroughly I'd be left breathless, barely able to stand from the delicious weakness in my limbs...

Alaric slid his free hand down my girdle to my purse and twisted open the clasp, retrieving its contents.

"Hey, what are you doing?" I tried unsuccessfully to snatch back my jewelry which was wrapped inside a cloth bundle. Alaric held it over his head, far out of my reach.

"I've been pondering your peculiar necklace, and I have further questions." My platinum necklace had been custom made in Milan, its style alien to the entire medieval period.

He slid the necklace from the cloth and inspected it so minutely that I knew he was only doing it to irritate me. "Sapphires?" Alaric arched a brow in that way he had that made me want to kick him. "Do you fear poison?"

Rather than argue about the magical property of gemstones, I said, "What I fear is you rummaging about in my personal possessions." I extended my hand and wiggled my fingers in a "give me" motion.

Alaric expanded his inspection to the rest of the bundle's contents —earrings, cuff bracelet, rings and... Oh, no! I'd forgotten about—

Alaric held out a slim tube. In a lovely pink color trimmed in gold. *"Perfect for the discreet female,"* the ad had promised.

My pepper spray!

"What is this?" His thick fingers curled naturally into its plastic indentations. "Some sort of magic stick?"

I licked my lips, my mind a blank. How could I explain an item that would not exist for centuries?

"Spin me another of your fantastical tales," Alaric taunted. "Tell me about your magic stick, Clarabel Lucy."

"Werewolves," I choked, remembering a mention of them during an earlier conversation. "I carry it in case I meet a pack of werewolves."

Alaric grunted. I remained mesmerized by the sight of his hand dwarfing the tube, his thick index finger resting on the button which would emit my "maximum strength" pepper spray. Just like the ad's description—"*comfortable grip, advanced delivery system, long-range protection up to twelve feet.*"

Minus a flip-top safety cap because I'd decided that when I was attacked by the Irish mafia, I'd be too terrified to remember to pop the cap and I'd die crying, "Wait! Wait! I've almost got it!" while they beat me senseless with their shillelaghs.

"Give me that." I kept my voice gentle, as though soothing a wild animal. Or an idiot with pepper spray.

"Another of your secrets?"

Viewing with horror the way Alaric's index finger fit so perfectly atop the trigger, the way his fingertip rested there. The way it pressed down ever so gently...

"Don't touch that!" I cried.

Just as Alaric released a stream of spray into...

Available in Paperback and eBook from Your Favorite Bookstore or Online Retailer

About the Author

I like to think of *Before I Wake* as the life I might have lived—had I been married five times, made a lot of unfortunate relationship choices, and been transported back to thirteenth century Cornwall. The kernel of my tale *is* true. As a young wife and mother, I *did* undergo a past life regression which I detail pretty much as it happened in *Before I Wake*. While I'd always been drawn to medieval England and had already started working on what would become my first historical romance, *The Lion and the Leopard*, that particular regression—whether real or simply a manifestation of my imagination—has stayed with me, lo, these several decades. I've been similarly intrigued by time travel, in the sense that a contemporary person plunked back in time would have lots of different observations and attitudes from a person born in that era. Which is a lot of fun to write about.

As it was fun to reference my real books in my real *Knights of England* six-book series, as well as my highwayman romance, *The Landlord's Black-Eyed Daughter*, which has a reincarnation theme and drives some of the narration. After throwing all the ingredients together, I hope I came up with an interesting Time Travel—sometimes lighthearted, sometimes dark, and sometimes passionate. But, hopefully, always a page turner.

One note on my hero/anti-hero, Ranulf Navarre. Initially, I wanted to portray him as I remembered him in my regression—a knight who lived for war. Very much a man of his time, including his attitude toward women. But when a good friend read an earlier version and proclaimed, "Ranulf Navarre is pretty much an a**," I knew I had to make some "adjustments." I hope those adjustments make Ranulf a sufficiently compelling protagonist.

Before I Wake is the first book in my four book *Travels Across Time* series.

www.maryellenjohnsonnauthor.com

twitter.com/mejauthor

CPSIA information can be obtained
at www.ICGtesting.com
Printed in the USA
BVHW082041160922
647226BV00015B/73